THE COPPER CASKET

DF DORAN

ABOUT THE COPPER CASKET

An eager young reporter in search of a break.

What happens when an obituary leads him down a rabbit hole of greed and corruption at the highest levels of power? Will Jim Monaghan be able to escape with his life?

It's 1963. Kennedy is president and there are mounting troubles in Vietnam.

Jim Monaghan is a young reporter stuck in the Siberia of journalism: the obituary section. But then he gets a call from a frantic widow insisting that her husband's dead body isn't where it's supposed to be.

As he starts to ask questions, Jim uncovers the truth that no one wants him to know. It goes to the highest levels of power and those people will do anything to keep their secrets safe.

WILL he escape with his life or will his first big story be his last?

PRAISE FOR DF Doran's Jim Monaghan thrillers

"A FASCINATING BOOK, which certainly kept me reading right up to the end..." - Amazon Review

"AN EMOTIONAL ROLLER COASTER..." - Amazon Review

"JIM MONAGHAN IS A VERY INTERESTING, multifaceted character with baggage..." -Amazon Review

"CRISP WRITING and accelerated page-turning as funeral home intrigue encounters investigative journalism. Romance, murder and '60s nostalgia" -Amazon Review

To my wife, Jan, without whose constant encouragement, this novel would not have been written. To our children, Danya, Shannon, Bryan, and Kevin and your beautiful families -- you are the wind beneath my wings.

ONE

SHE WANTED to say goodbye one last time.

Irene Dunn left the home she had shared with her husband for forty-two of the fifty years they were married and drove alone to Calvary Cemetery for a final goodbye.

Since her husband Patrick's death, she had been surrounded by family and friends. After the funeral that morning, people flocked to her home bearing food and memories. While her spirits were buoyed by reminiscing about her husband, Irene wanted a moment when she could be alone with her beloved Patrick one last time.

Still wearing her black dress and hat, Irene backed the sporty, red 1960 Chevy Corvair down the flower-lined narrow driveway. How Patrick had loved that car. He'd bought it only three years ago, despite Irene's objections and his failing health. She smiled at his stubborn enthusiasm and his love for the car as she drove toward the cemetery. She thought about the funeral. It was beautiful. Reverend Smallwood preached a touching eulogy and the First

Baptist Church choir sang her husband's favorite hymns. The crowd was larger than Patrick would have thought, but it didn't surprise Irene. Patrick had many friends from his thirty years teaching at Lincoln's Central High School. The glowing candlelight reflected off his stately coffin which, Irene thought, mirrored his strength and goodness. It was copper, the best according to Alex Reid, the owner of Reid Funeral Homes. It was expensive, and though Irene and Patrick had never spent money frivolously, at Reid's persistent urging she'd made the purchase.

The American Legion ceremony was dignified and stirring. Patrick was a decorated military hero in both World Wars. He was part of General Patton's Third Army march through Europe. He had never mentioned his many medals of valor, nor did he talk about his experiences. After serving in World War l, he was proud he could volunteer in World War II, despite his age. Patrick's burial with military honors was a fitting tribute to a humble man.

The afternoon sun blazed hot in the bright blue sky as Irene drove the twenty minutes to the cemetery. The Corvair's tires crunched gravel as she pulled to a stop near the gravesite. She found her way to the Dunn family plot and knew she had made the right decision to come alone. Taking a deep breath, she prepared herself to say goodbye to the man she had loved for half a century.

Near the burial plot, Irene noticed a battered black pick-up truck with a blue tarp stretched over the truck's bed. Four brawny unshaven men were perched on a mound of dirt next to the gravesite, smoking cigarettes and drinking beer. Irene wondered why the truck was parked near the gravesite, and, after all this time, why hadn't they filled in the burial plot? As she approached the grave, she realized she would be able to look down on her husband's casket. Irene slowed her steps as the men glowered at her.

"What do you want, old woman?" one man yelled. But she kept walking.

"Get the hell out of here!" another shouted as all four stumbled, trying to get up.

Irene's high heels poked in the soft grass as she approached the edge of the grave. Her shocked scream pierced the air as she peered into the hole. At the bottom of the grave, inside the burial vault, she saw a plain pine box. She looked over at the truck and saw what appeared to be a casket covered by the blue tarp.

Two of the men rushed over, grabbed her, and growled, "We told you to get the hell out of here!" They grasped her arms tightly, dragged her back to the car, and roughly threw her into the front seat.

"What have you done with my husband?" she screamed.

"You forget what you saw here, old woman, or we will bury you next to him. You understand us?" they yelled.

Irene's heart thumped wildly, and she was blinded by tears. Shakily starting her car, she left the cemetery. As she drove back toward Lincoln, her fear started to fade, and her tears turned to anger.

TWO

WITH EACH MILE, Irene's anger intensified. She decided not to go home but headed directly to the Lincoln Police Department. Determined to keep her emotions in check, she strode purposefully into the police headquarters. As she started to tell her story, the policeman at the desk motioned Captain Billy Joe Buckner over to listen in.

Buckner told Irene that she must be confused and there had to be a reasonable explanation. He suggested she go to the funeral home and visit with Alex Reid. Upset by Buckner's lack of interest and concern, Irene sped to the funeral home, screeching to a halt in the middle of the circular driveway directly in front of the one-hundred-year-old three story Victorian funeral home. She marched up the brick steps, past the massive columns, to the double oak doors.

Steve Hampton, Reid's assistant, met Irene and tried to calm her down. She shouted that someone had switched caskets, demanding to know what happened to her husband's copper casket. He told her he would get Reid immediately.

Since there were no visitations going on, Irene sat in a

viewing room in a big leather chair and waited for Reid. It took him fifteen minutes, but he finally emerged, dressed, as usual, in a black suit, white shirt, and dark blue tie. Reid hugged her and said gently, "Mrs. Dunn, what a wonderful service we had for your husband. He would have loved it. Now, Steve tells me that you are very upset. Please, tell me how I can help."

Irene's anger overwhelmed her fear and grief. Her gray eyes glared behind her bifocals and she told Reid she **was very** upset.

"I have just come from the cemetery. The grave wasn't filled in. My husband's copper casket was gone. There was nothing in the vault but a plain pine box. I demand to know how that could be. Where is my husband's casket? Where is my husband? I want an explanation!"

Reid's bland expression never changed. He pulled up a chair, sat down, and with an infuriating, condescending smile, spoke softly.

"Oh, Mrs. Dunn, you must be confused. You must have gone to the wrong gravesite. It happens, especially with some of my older clients. You have just lost your husband, your partner for almost fifty years. It is easy to get confused.

"Trust me, what you think you saw is just not possible. Your husband was buried in a copper casket just as you requested. You saw the casket at the church and you saw us bring it to the cemetery. You can rest assured your husband was laid to rest in the copper casket. You saw the casket at the burial plot, you saw us lower it into the ground. You have nothing to worry about. You just went to the wrong burial site," Reid contended.

Irene was in shock. She knew she'd gone to the right site. Yes, Calvary is a large cemetery, but she knew the way to the family plot. She and Patrick had purchased the plot many years before. Yes, she thought *I was sad and I was grieving, but I was **not** confused.*

Irene started to argue with Reid, but abruptly stopped when Reverend Smallwood walked in and pulled up another chair and sat down heavily. Clad in his trademark white suit, the buttons on his red vest ready to pop, his small brown eyes peeked out from the soft folds of his florid face. He asked why she was upset, and Irene told him of her experience at the burial plot, peering into the gravesite, and seeing a plain wooden box at the bottom, not the casket she had chosen. As Irene spoke, her lips were drawn into a firm line and there were no tears, just resolve. Smallwood told her she was probably disoriented. It would not be the first time a grieving widow was confused, he said. He suggested she go home, say her prayers, and try to get a good night's rest. Smallwood told her she would understand tomorrow that what she saw was not her husband's gravesite, but someone else's.

Irene was not about to be put off. Looking directly at Smallwood and Reid, she told them she was not confused. She knew what she'd seen. She told them if they didn't believe her they could all go to the cemetery and have their men dig up her husband's grave, and if they didn't want to do it, she would get some of her husband's friends from the American Legion to help her.

Reverend Smallwood leapt out of his chair bristling. "No, No, never, never! We simply cannot disturb the body once it is buried. That would be against everything it says in the Good Book. It might prevent your husband from coming back on Resurrection Day. Once the body is buried, it can't be disturbed. That's what it says in the Good Book, Irene. No, you can't disturb the body once it is buried."

Reverend Smallwood told Irene to go home, get some

rest, and he would stop by to see her the next day. Taking her by the arm, he escorted her to her car. As Irene was being led out, she noticed Steve Hampton standing just outside the viewing area. It was obvious he had heard every word. He looked at her sympathetically.

At her back door, Irene was met by her four grown children, asking where she had gone and what she had done. Irene gathered the children around the kitchen table, where she and Patrick had held all family meetings, and told them what had happened. As she told the story, the children exchanged glances of worry and wonder. Irene knew they did not believe her story. So, when she was finished, she announced she was exhausted and was going to bed.

As Irene laid her head on the pillow, she looked across the bed where Patrick had slept. She thought about the many times she had poked him, encouraging him to stop snoring. Tonight, she thought, *I would love to hear a snore.* Then she began to cry. She knew the kids were downstairs talking about her. *They probably think I am going nuts, but I'm not. I know what I saw and, dammit, I am going to do something about it. For my husband, for myself, I am going to do something about it.*

THREE

IRENE SLEPT LATE, finally succumbing to the exhaustion and grief of the past five days. Tying her robe around her waist, she came down the steps and into the kitchen where she found the children at the table.

"Didn't you people go home last night? You are at the same place I left you." The kids smiled and said they had gone home but came back this morning because they wanted to talk.

Irene poured herself a cup of coffee. She knew what they were going to say but decided she would just listen. They began by telling her how much they loved her and how worried they were about her living at home without their dad. They also said they were concerned about the story she'd told the past evening. It didn't make sense. They said Reid was probably correct, and since Reverend Smallwood agreed, she probably had gone to the wrong burial site. Even though Irene had raised all her children in the traditions of the First Baptist Church, none of them attended. Reverend Smallwood was the butt of their jokes, so Irene was more than a little surprised they were quoting him as an authority on her confusion. But she didn't respond.

Irene thought she would play along and asked the children if they thought she was suffering from dementia or something. No, they answered, but it wouldn't hurt to go to the doctor. In fact, they had made an appointment with one for the next day. They gave her a name, which she recognized. Dr. Michael Horst, a psychiatrist. Irene objected, telling them she didn't need a shrink. They said he is not a shrink, that he is a Medical Doctor, and did so much good for someone she'd never heard of. Since it was almost noon, Irene told them they should be off, and she would go to the doctor, if for no other reason than to satisfy them. But Irene knew she was very sane and the idea of seeing a shrink was, well, crazy.

I can only imagine what they are plotting if I don't show up at the doctor's office. Patrick would have a good laugh at their behavior, Irene thought. She sat alone at her kitchen table and reviewed the events of the previous day. She had no idea what to do next. She thought of the wooden box at the bottom of her husband's grave and the horrid men who'd treated her so callously. She didn't believe Reid or Smallwood. She thought of talking to the police again, but her sense was that they wouldn't believe her either. Captain Buckner was one of the bosses and if he didn't believe her, who would? She poured herself another cup of coffee and, as she did every morning, reached for that day's edition of the Lincoln News Tribune. She pulled out the Sports section and handed it to the empty chair next to her, then smiled sadly. Patrick began his day with the Sports section while she read the front page. A couple days ago the routine broke, and she first read Patrick's obituary. She was touched, truly, by the writing and felt the author captured what a remarkable man her Patrick was. She scanned the front page, then thumbed through the front section until she reached the editorial page. A headline read "Plush Accommodations for the County, Potholes for the Public." It was an editorial complaining that the new government buildings cost too much money when the roads were in such disrepair – and then it hit her. Maybe the newspaper people could help. She pulled out the phone book and looked up the number for the News Tribune and asked for obituaries.

"THEY SWITCHED CASKETS!" quavered the voice on the telephone.

"What did you say?" asked a startled Jim Monaghan, newly hired obituary reporter for the Lincoln News Tribune.

Jim recognized the voice as that of an older woman. He tucked his long brown hair behind his ears, pulled his headset tight, and listened intently as Irene Dunn related the incredible story of her husband's funeral, burial, and switched caskets.

Jim scribbled notes feverishly. He was immediately suspicious of the story. It sounded too farfetched. Most of Jim's work involved getting details of the burial and funeral services from funeral homes and churches. He had spoken to his share of grieving widows, but he never had a conversation like the one he had with Irene.

Jim had little experience with older people. He never knew his grandparents. His parents had died in a tragic accident when their car hit a pot hole on a country road. His dad lost control and smashed into a utility pole. They were on their way to Jim's high school graduation.

"Mrs. Dunn, my name is Jim Monaghan, and your

story, and I mean to be respectful, but it is almost unbelieve-able," Jim gently said.

"Please believe me , sir, it happened. I saw the box with my own eyes yesterday afternoon. No one believes me, sir. No one believes me," Irene sobbed.

Jim instinctively thought, if true, it could be a big story, but he needed more information and he wanted to meet Irene in person and evaluate her tale. He invited her to meet with him at the newspaper office some afternoon. He told her he would like a couple of veteran editors to sit in on the meeting since he was new.

"Would three o'clock this afternoon work for you, Mr. Monaghan?" Irene asked.

"Perfect," Jim said, "just come in the front door of the News Tribune and ask the receptionist for Jim Monaghan."

Hanging up the phone, Jim walked over to the desk of City Editor, Zack "Willy" Williams.

"Boss, either I have the story of the year or the ravings of an old woman. I think I believe her, but the story is really off the wall." Jim proceeded to tell Willy the essence of Irene's story. When Jim told him the Reid Funeral Home and Reverend Smallwood were involved, Willy leaned back in his chair, pushed his wire-rimmed glasses to his wrinkled forehead, and raised his ink-stained hand.

"You know I have been around a long time and that may be the biggest bunch of bullshit I have ever heard. Get your butt back to the obit desk and get to work. Don't bring me these pie-in-the-sky conspiracies." Willy rolled his eyes as the other reporters and editors chuckled.

"But I believe her," Jim said.

"Listen, young man. You are new around here, not even three months in the business, and you think you are some kind of investigative reporter. Well, it's not going to happen.

I am ordering you to forget this story and concentrate on your writing, which is very immature. A couple more things, the Reid Funeral Home is one of the biggest advertisers this paper has, and advertising pays your salary. Reverend Smallwood is the pastor of the biggest church in this town. You don't mess with people like that, do you understand me? And get your hair cut, you look like a hippie," Willy snarled.

As Jim walked back to his desk with the others in the newsroom either laughing at him or frowning unsympathetically, he wondered what truly great newspaper people would do in this situation.

At the prestigious Northwestern Medill School of Journalism, he was taught that the editorial side of the newspaper business was separate from the business side, so Jim wondered, *why would advertising play such an important role in whether or not a story should be investigated?*

By the time three o'clock rolled around, Jim had made up his mind. He walked downstairs to the main reception area and awaited Irene Dunn.

FOUR

STANDING NEAR THE FRONT DOOR, Jim wondered what
Irene Dunn would look like. He guessed she was very old
and probably disheveled and poorly dressed.

He noticed a mature but beautifully put together
woman stride past him. She wore a navy blue jacket with a
matching skirt and a pale blue scarf around her neck. Her
short silver hair was styled perfectly. *Well that's not her*, Jim
thought, but was stunned when the woman asked the receptionist for Jim Monaghan.

"Are you Irene Dunn?" Jim asked.

"Yes, I am. Are you Jim Monaghan? I was expecting
someone older. Where are the other reporters?"

Jim told her he was, unfortunately, the only one available and, for privacy, they needed to go down the street to
O'Toole's for their conversation. Irene looked at him with
suspicion, but since Jim was the only person who had
listened to her, she reluctantly agreed.

"It has been years since I have been in O'Toole's, but I
doubt it has changed much. I do want to thank you, Mr.
Monaghan, for talking with me."

As they walked the block and a half to the bar, Jim assured her O'Toole's was a perfect place to meet in the afternoon as there were few customers and privacy was assured. He also asked her to call him Jim. He was uncomfortable with someone her age calling him Mr. Monaghan. Irene smiled and said she would agree if Jim would call her Irene.

Irene and Jim settled into a booth at the back of the bar. Stavros, owner and bartender, anticipated Jim's order and had already poured a Bushmills on the rocks. Stavros lingered before placing it on the table. He looked quizzically at Irene then glanced at Jim, waiting for an introduction. Jim liked Stavros, but he didn't satisfy the bartender's curiosity, instead asking Irene what she wanted to drink. "Coffee with cream, please." Irene smiled at Stavros, who went back to the bar, scratching his short, black beard.

"Let's start at the beginning," Jim suggested, "and try to remember everything that happened, no matter how insignficant you may think it is."

Irene leaned back in the wooden booth, closed her eyes, and told Jim about the dreadful moment of finding her husband on the floor in the garage.

"The ambulance people tried to resuscitate him, but they told me he was already dead when they'd arrived. It was horrible. My partner for nearly fifty years, gone. We had just had lunch and everything seemed fine, and then he died."

Irene went on to tell of contacting the Reid Funeral Home and how, she joked, Patrick would roll over in his grave if he knew how much she paid for the casket. But, she explained, she was very proud and thought it was beautiful. Perfect for her loyal and wonderful husband. "Reverend Smallwood made a good point, Jim, that this was the last chance I would ever have to get my Patrick something nice. And Mr. Reid assured me, this was the best in the funeral home."

She told of the wake, the hundreds of people who came, the service at the First Baptist Church, Reverend Smallwood's stirring homily, and the beauty of the choir's hymns. She said Smallwood had objected to an open casket at the church, but since there were so many people who wanted to say goodbye, she felt it would be appropriate.

Irene's eyes sparkled with tears of pride as she recounted Patrick's legendary teaching career at Central High School.

"There were so many of his former students in attendence. And he was a war hero. He served in both World Wars," Irene said with a smile, "and he loved General Patton. 'Marched our way through Europe with old Blood and Guts,' he would say the few times he spoke about the war."

Irene told Jim there were so many people at the house after the funeral, it was just overwhelming. She just needed to get away to the cemetery for one last quiet goodbye.

"And I told you what happened at the cemetery. It was awful. But I know what I saw, and I told you on the phone this morning exactly what happened. After that horrible experience, I went to the police, and Captain Buckner implied that I was confused. So did Reid and Reverend Smallwood when I met them at the funeral home and demanded they dig up the grave and prove to me my husband was buried in the casket I purchased.

"When I went home, my kids didn't believe me either and they suggested I see a psycharitrist. I don't need a shrink. I know what I saw.

"And you, Jim, are the only person who believes me."

Jim glanced at his watch and realized Irene had been talking for over half an hour and he was so taken by her story, he had written only a few notes.

"I must tell you, Irene, my boss, the city editor, doesn't believe your story. He told me it was impossible and that Reid is a big advertiser and Reverend Smallwood's church, First Baptist, is the biggest one in Lincoln.

Jim saw the hurt in Irene's eyes. He didn't mean to be so blunt. He meant to offer a comforting word but instead he paused, lost for a minute in thought. "Irene, why was Reverend Smallwood at Reid's when you bought your husband's casket? And why was he there when you confronted Reid?"

"I don't know, Jim, you'd have to ask him," Irene answered with more frustration in her voice than she intended. More softly she said, "Jim, I don't want to cause any trouble for you, but . . .," she trailed off and then in a broken voice asked, "don't you believe me?"

"Yeah," Jim answered. "I do." Jim downed what was left of his second round of whiskey. "My boss is going to need some proof. Could you put down in writing all the things you've told me this afternoon in a diary? Also, could you get all the documents from the Reid Funeral Home? We can meet again on Monday afternoon. I intend to do some research on my own this weekend, so next week we can compare notes."

"Let me assure you, Mrs. Dunn, I believe every word you are telling me."

Irene smiled and thanked Jim. As they were walking out, she patted him on the arm. "Young man, you shouldn't drink hard liquor at three o'clock in the afternoon." That evening, Jim popped a TV dinner in the oven and sat down with a bottle of Bushmills. Pouring two fingers over ice, he thought of Irene, of Patrick and of the copper casket. He wearily wondered, '*what have I gotten myself into?*'

FIVE

THE NEXT DAY, Jim arrived at work at his usual six a.m. and was greeted by Willy who derisively asked if he had uncovered any more cockamamie stories, but before Jim could answer, the obituary desk phone rang and he went to work.

Between calls, Jim noticed in Thursday's paper the Reid Funeral Home had a burial scheduled for Saturday morning, after the funeral mass at nine a.m. at St. Patrick's. The deceased's name was Brennan. Jim remembered writing the obituary. The burial was going to be at Calvary Cemetery and since Jim didn't work Saturday morning, he thought he would go. He wasn't entirely sure why. It was where the story was, and that was enough.

As the early deadline for the day's paper passed, Willy plopped down beside Jim. "If you are going to make it in this business, you have a lot to learn. This is the real world, Jim, and I want you to see how much advertising the Reid Funeral Homes provide this paper. This is a tear sheet from Sunday's paper. It is a full-page ad. That's a shitload of money, so we have to be careful when dealing with large advertisers. That's just a fact of life.

"You can't take an old demented woman seriously, and that's not your job. You write obits. That's your job. That's it. Take the rest of the afternoon off and think seriously if this work is for you. You won't be allowed many more mistakes."

This last barrage cemented Jim's decision to not tell Willy about meeting Irene or his plans to go to the Brennan burial Saturday. As he was tidying up his desk for the weekend, Jim had a thought. *Not only is what Irene said happened despicable, I'm pretty sure it's against the law to switch caskets. I don't want to talk to the police, especially after Irene's experience. I think I will see the County District Attorney.*

SIX

THE COUNTY DISTRICT ATTORNEY's office was in the Shelby County Government building, a newly constructed glass and steel edifice, the most prominent building on Lincoln's east side.

Jim compared the building to his own office building - eighty years old, brick and mortar, single-paned windows, no air conditioning, and decorated with peeling paint and scarred woodwork. Summertime created tough working conditions, especially on Friday and Saturday nights when the windows were open and bugs felt an open invitation to swarm around the light fixtures. The News-Tribune published evening papers throughout the week, but published morning papers on the weekend, resulting in difficult working conditions on Friday and Saturday evenings during the summer time.

The DA's office was on the second floor. Climbing the circular staircase, Jim thought that the taxpayers got their money's worth on this beautiful building.

Jim's thoughts of beauty were extinguished when he entered the DA's office and saw the cluttered desks and scurrying workers toting sheaves of paper and thick books. A stern voice rang out, "Can I help you?" and Jim came face-to-face with a middle-aged woman with the demeanor of a Marine drill instructor. Ramrod straight in her prim white blouse and brown skirt, the receptionist's penetrating gaze behind horn-rimmed glasses signaled don't mess with me and keep it brief.

Hating to admit to himself he felt a little intimidated, Jim said he was from the News Tribune and needed advice on a possible criminal case he was investigating. He asked to speak with the smartest assistant district attorney. The receptionist scanned him up and down, then barked, "Take a seat and I will see if anyone has time for a news person."

After more than half an hour, Jim had almost given up hope of anyone seeing him when he noticed a tall, slim young woman with long, shiny black hair walking toward the reception desk. Her white silk blouse, black skirt, and cropped jacket emphasized her creamy pale skin and deep blue eyes. To Jim, she was drop-dead beautiful.

The DA ought to have her as the receptionist and people would feel more welcome walking in here, Jim thought.

To his pleasant surprise, the young woman approached him and asked, "How can I help you?" Jim stammered that he needed to talk to an attorney.

"My name is Mary Ryan, and I am an assistant district attorney."

Jim found her voice as beautiful as the rest of her and, for him, time stood still. Time did not stand still for Mary Ryan. "Are you surpised? You look surprised. Women can be district attorneys, too, you know," she said pointedly.

"I am sorry," Jim fumbled, feeling his cheeks redden. "My name is Jim Monaghan from the Lincoln News

Tribune. Can I speak with you privately about a matter I am investigating?"

Mary looked at him suspiciously, then nodded for Jim to follow her to her small office. She took her seat behind the desk and leaned forward with her hands clasped. Jim attempted eye contact, but he could not resist staring at her hands, notably her left ring finger. Ringless, Jim noticed, and suppressed a smile.

Jim began with small talk, complimenting the new building, asking about law school and sharing that he had thought of going to law school but couldn't afford it. He asked if it was hard being the only female lawyer at the DA's office, and Mary felt, despite herself, that he was sincere and sympathetic. The truth was, it was horrible. She lied and said it was fine. Jim told her about the small town he came from, how he wanted to be a reporter in Chicago or New York, and after a few minutes Mary realized they had moved from small talk to socializing.

"Now, what's your story, Mr. Monaghan?"

Jim smiled, softly. He liked talking to Mary, and was dissapointed to stop, but he admired her crisp professionalism. "What if a funeral home sold a casket to a family and then, after the services, substituted that casket for one of inferior quality. Would that violate any law?"

"Is that a serious question? Yes. It's fraud."

"Is it something the DA would be interested in investigating?" Jim asked.

"I worked in the Cook County DA's office as an intern, and I heard some gruesome tales and came across some terrible people. Mr. Monaghan . . ."

"Call me Jim."

"Mr. Monaghan, if someone is doing that they are the

lowest form of scum bag I have come across in my career to date."

"So, yes?"

"Yes, definitely, I'm interested. Which funeral home? Who's the victim? What proof do you have? I need more details and I'll get the police on it."

"Whoa, slow down," Jim said, "I am just speculating here."

"No one walks into the DA's office with a story out of the blue like that. It is so unbelievable. Are you some kind of fiction writer? I didn't know the News Tribune employed fiction writers for their daily paper."

Jim laughed out loud. He liked her. A lot. No, I am not a fiction writer and yes, this is a real story. Say, would you like to go out for pizza tomorrow night?"

Mary rolled her eyes. "Thank you for your time, Mr. Monaghan, I trust you can see yourself out."

"Wait, slow down again," Jim laughed, and then lied. "Did you think I was asking you out? Mary, I meant we can meet up and I can show you the evidence I collected. Not a date; strictly business."

It was Mary's turn to redden. She liked him. A little. He was handsome, despite the long stringy hair, and had the look of someone who would clean up pretty well. She liked his combination of confidence and humility. He was funny, but there was more there – she could see it in how he carried himself and how he looked at her. She wasn't sure what. Sadness, she decided. But he was not bitter, or mean. He was hurt, she believed, but hadn't gone bad. He was still sweet, and sensitive. And honest. Despite the lie about not asking her out. She had never met anyone so young from the newspaper. Most of the reporters who covered the courthouse were grizzled old veterans. Jim seemed like an idealist, at least for now. So was she, and she wanted to stay one.

"Okay, Jim. Pizza it is. I look forward to reviewing your evidence." Jim smiled, "Great, Mary, see you tomorrow." He turned and walked out, his smile dying as he recalled he had no evidence. I'll get it, he thought to himself. I have to. *I have a date with the most beautiful woman I have ever met.*

SEVEN

Jim was not comfortable in a cemetery. It brought back painful, poignant memories of his parents' fatal auto accident. That night he had plummeted from the euphoria of knowing how proud they would be to watch him receive academic and athletic awards to the shock and indescribable pain of losing them both. Though it was five years ago, Jim still deeply felt the sting of loss. It was, he told himself, why he drank.

Calvary Cemetery was much larger than the one in his home town, some thirty miles east of Lincoln. He parked his truck in a faraway corner and walked around, looking at fresh burial plots and taking down the names on the tombstones. The new plots varied in condition. Some were just fresh dirt piled on the narrow gravesite while others were covered with fresh flowers.

He reflected on his good choice to wear his old Cincinnati Reds sweatshirt and torn jeans as parts of the cemetery were overrun by weeds and there was dirt everywhere.

He found the Brennan gravesite and noticed the white chairs arranged in rows and the tent shading the six-foot hole in the ground. There, beside the mound of dirt, was the top of the vault. In the bottom of the hole was the rest of the vault. *Impossible*, he thought, *that someone could put a casket in the vault, then take it out, remove the body, put it in a box, and then bury the box.* As time for the burial service approached, Jim distanced himself. He had brought flowers and randomly picked Carol Ford, beloved wife and mother, who had died eleven years earlier. Her grave was a good distance from the ceremony. Close enough to see without being noticed. He set the flowers by her tombstone and pretended to mourn. From there, he could watch the ceremony.

Around eleven a.m., off in the distance, he watched a hearse pull up to the Brennan gravesite, followed by about thirty cars. He had written the obituary a few days earlier and he knew Mr. Brennan had died after a long bout with cancer, leaving behind his wife and three adult children. *It is so different, watching a burial as opposed to writing a quick obituary for the paper,* he thought.

When the ceremony ended, the mourners left solemnly, and Jim sat on Ms. Ford's tombstone and waited to see what would happen next. Forty minutes passed and no one from the cemetery showed up to fill the gravesite with dirt. Then a battered black pickup truck pulled up right next to the burial plot. Two men exited the cab and two more jumped out of the truck bed. Jim watched the four men hoist the casket from the vault and carefully place it on the grass. They opened the casket, and roughly pulled the body out. The men pulled the blue tarp away from a pine box, which was sitting on the back of the pickup truck. Jim hopped off the tombstone and crouched behind it. Keeping himself hidden behind the tombstone, he watched in horror as the men placed the body into the pine box, lifted the casket onto the back of the pickup and covered it with the blue tarp. Then they used the hydraulic lift to lower the box into the vault, secure the vault lid, and fill the burial site with dirt. They quickly drove off.

You have got to be shitting me, Jim thought to himself. *That's exactly what Irene Dunn said happened. Why didn't I think to bring a camera? Unbel*—Jim did not get to finish his thought. He felt cold metal on the back of his neck and heard a "click." A gun, he thought, and froze.

"I don't know who the hell you are, but you are in deep shit, boy," a malicious voice snarled. "You lay down on the ground and don't you turn around or I will make a hole in the back of your head you can drive a truck through. You hear me, boy?"

Jim, stiff with fright, did as he was told and lay prone on the ground.

"You have a watch on, kid. You look at that watch, and you don't move for one hour, you hear me? And you forget what you saw here today, or I will find you and I will put that hole in the back of your head. You understand me?"

"Yes, sir," Jim uttered. "I didn't see anything. I'm just supposed to meet a guy here to score some weed."

"Oh, so yer a druggie, huh? Well nobody would believe you anyway, punk." He laughed contemptuously.

Jim heard the man walk away but stayed face down for a full hour before he got up on his knees, looked around, saw no one, and ran to his truck.

Racing out of the cemetery, Jim drove as fast as he could toward the center of town. He pulled into a gas station and ran to the bathroom. Gagging over his experience, Jim knew he was onto a major story and crime, but he also knew he was scared to death.

Jim sped back to the News Tribune and pulled into the

parking lot. Too junior to have a parking place assigned to him, he parked there anyway and ran past the front door of the paper and straight to O'Toole's where he had Stavros pour him two straight shots of Bushmills.

Trying to calm his nerves, Jim stared into the drink clutched in his shaky, sweaty hands. He realized he had no idea what the gunman looked like, but the gunman would surely recognize him. Downing the drink in one long swallow, he told Stavros he would be back and walked across the street to the barber shop.

Jim told the barber he wanted a flat-top. "Are you sure? You've got more than year's growth there, son. Can't put it back on once its cut. And lots of young guys are wearing it that way."

"I'm sure," replied Jim. "I'm ready for a new look."

Fresh out of the barbershop, Jim walked to Oberson's Department Store where he bought a pair of khaki pants and a blue golf shirt. He looked down at his dirty boots, turned to the shoe department, and purchased a pair of brown loafers.

In the department store men's room, Jim changed into his new clothes and tossed his sweatshirt, torn jeans, and boots into the trash.

Back at O'Toole's Stavros gaped at Jim. "What the hell happened to you? I hardly recognize you."

Jim muttered, "It's been a hell of a bad day. Another shot, please."

EIGHT

Jim was scared, but angry. Every minute that passed he grew less scared and angrier. He knew he had to confront Reid and his funeral home people, but how? He decided to drive to the main Reid Funeral Home to ask some innocent questions.

Introducing himself to Steve Hampton, Jim said he'd received a couple of phone calls from people he didn't know with some wild accusations about irregularities in the funeral industry regarding caskets. Jim knew Mr. Reid ran the biggest and best funeral homes and he hoped to talk with him.

Hampton's thin, pale face grew even more ashen. He hesitated; it seemed to Jim as if he wanted to say something more than "one moment please." But that was all he said as he walked off to find Mr. Reid.

In the viewing area, Jim noticed a copper casket with a body in it. It angered him. *I wonder if that's the same copper casket that was taken out of the ground this morning?*

Jim's thoughts were interrupted by the appearance of

Alex Reid, resplendent in a perfectly tailored black suit, blue tie, white shirt with French cuffs, and highly polished wing-tipped shoes. With a smile that never reached his eyes, and a cool, perfunctory handshake, he greeted Jim, "How can I help the News Tribune today?"

Jim responded that he had received a couple of far-out phone calls and wanted to talk to someone in the business.

"I always have time for the News Tribune. Please come into my office," Reid said as he gripped Jim by the arm and ushered him into his office.

Jim had never been in such a grand office before. Reid slid onto his maroon leather high-backed chair, the glossy mahogany desktop reflecting plaques, certificates, and photos honoring his civic achievements on the wall behind.

Jim was nervous, and in trying to gather himself he let the silence build reading the certificates and plaques on Mr. Reid's wall.

"They *are* a bit vain, I suppose. In my defense, my secretary decorated and insisted – said it gave people the feeling they were being cared for by competent people.".

"Oh, not at all vain -- sir. Impressive. And that's why I am here. You are the leader in the funeral business and everyone says the Reid Funeral Homes are well-run, and considerate, and sympathetic to families. Guess that's why you have twenty-two of them throughout central Ohio," Jim opened.

"Thank you," Reid answered coolly. Jim felt the tension and thought, correctly, that the bullshit he had laid on had been seen for the bullshit that it was.

"Sir, I know how important you are to the paper – you pay my salary, really, and I don't mean any offense. I am here because I got a phone call about a month ago and it was so outrageous, I dismissed it. It was from an old woman, or at least she sounded old, but she wouldn't give me her name. Then this morning around noon, I got a call from a man, who I think was young, but he kept slurring his words and seemed kind of high, like he was on drugs.

"And the funny thing is, the two stories were pretty close. The guy this morning wouldn't tell me his name nor the name of the deceased, the day it happened, or which cemetery. But because the stories are so similar, I want to ask you if the following is possible.

"Have you ever heard of a body placed in one casket and taken to the cemetery, and then, when no one is around, taken out of the casket and put into another one? That's what this guy said he saw."

Reid kept his cool until Jim stopped talking. When Jim was done, he looked Reid in the eye. It was not the gaze of the nervous bowled-over kid who had introduced himself. His look was not accusatory, as much as knowing. It was a hard stare that said, I know what you did. Jim looked at Reid like a lion looks at a lamb, and Reid blinked. Then, he looked at Jim with disgust.

"How dare you. How dare you. You come into my place of business smelling like stale whiskey and ask me such a question? You insult my intelligence, my profession, the bereaved families I serve, and everything I represent!"

"I meant no insult, Mr. Reid," Jim retreated, trying to placate him.

"Shut your mouth, you little punk. I should call Captain Buckner and have your butt thrown out of here, but we have a service coming up, and I won't disturb the family. So, get your ass out of my office and out of my funeral home. You may be assured Bernard Hill will hear about this first thing

Monday morning. And let me assure you, you will be fired! Now get out of here!"

As Jim walked out of Reid's office, he opened the door and bumped into Hampton, who obviously was listening behind the door. Hampton looked at Jim with pleading and sympathetic eyes.

NINE

BECAUSE JIM HAD PACKED enough excitement for a lifetime into one day, he nearly forgot his date with Mary Ryan.

Her reaction when she opened the door made him wish he had cancelled the evening. Laughing uproariously, Mary faked a serious tone and asked, "So, when do you deploy, solider?"

They road to the pizza parlor in near silence. Jim's scowl had scared Mary a bit, and she didn't press him about the haircut. Still, she got in his truck and they drove for a while in awkward silence. Jim broke the silence a few minutes later. "I did not join the service, Mary."

"Ok," Mary smirked. "Young Republicans?"

"Very funny. Point of fact, I volunteered for John Kennedy and drank myself to sleep when Nixon beat him in Ohio. I celebrated when he won the presidency and drank a toast of thanks to Dick Daley and the Chicago Democratic machine," Jim said.

"That, Jim, is a lot of drinking," she answered playfully. "I know all about the Daleys and the Chicago machine. My family lives in Bridgeport, which is the 'back of the yards'

Irish enclave in Chicago. Mayor Daley lives down the street from my parents. I don't think there are any Republicans in our neighborhood and, if there are, they probably don't get their garbage picked up." She grinned.

Jim smiled, and felt that same warmth from yesterday. He was so happily charmed by Mary, and for a moment imagined himself a star at the Chicago Tribune, having dinner with Mayor Daley and Mary's parents. Then he remembered he was going to lose his job Monday and drifted back into sullen silence.

"Okay, Jim, what is your evidence," Mary asked, no longer funny. "You are the worst date I have been on in, well, ever, so how about we get down to business. Who are the funeral home bastards defrauding widows and orphans?"

The word orphan stung. Jim felt the whole day well up in him. He nearly lost his life. He lost his job. He lost his hair, for God's sake, and he lost Mary before he even came close to having her. He was an orphan the world had picked to hurt, then hurt again. He would never catch a break. He wanted her gone and to go have a drink.

"No one cares about orphans, Mary."

"What? You are making no sense. Jim, what is wrong with you? What happened to you?"

"I lost my job, Mary. There is no story, nothing to do, nothing to say. I will take you home. I am sorry, I truly am."

"Stop the car, Jim."

Jim kept driving, staring out at the road and feeling sorry for himself.

"I said stop the car."

Mary's voice turned sharp and strong, and Jim snapped out of a daze. He pulled over, put the car in park, and turned to the woman who, a lifetime ago, was the most beautiful person he had ever seen. And, to his surprise, she still was.

"Tell me what happened."

"They put a gun to my head," Jim answered. He looked away, ashamed to seem weak, and scared. "And they are going to take away my job."

"Then it's real, Mr. Monaghan. Those miscreants are really doing it. And you know what we have to do."

He looked back at her, and though he still felt scared he no longer felt weak. He stared at her from that painful place that had turned not quite mean, but close to that. Strong, dangerous, formidable. She stared back unfazed. And then he decided. "I do. And I will."

"Good," Mary answered, chipper and self-assured. "I'm starving, so let's get some food and figure out the how of this. We are going to nail those people."

Jim smiled, "Jesus, just like that? You did hear they put a gun to my head?"

"Guns are for cowards, Jim. I am not afraid of cowards. Now let's go, I'm starving."

"Christ, Mary, I think I will join the service. Less chance of getting killed."

"Well, you have the hair for it." She smiled and kissed him on the cheek.

TEN

Jim drank too much whiskey and didn't eat enough pizza. It wasn't his fault, he told himself. He had lost his job, he was sure, and nearly his life – what better time to have a drink? Still, he felt ashamed. He remembered Mary driving him home and not remembering how she got home. But he did remember she gave him her home phone number – and just like that his energy spiked, he jumped out of bed forgetting his headache, grabbed his wallet and found the napkin with Mary's number. And her name. And a heart she had drawn. He called Mary and, first things first, apologized for the night before. He thought of asking her how she got home, but decided it was a topic best buried. Instead, he asked, "Would you like to go to Reverend Smallwood's First Baptist Church for the ten thirty a.m. service?"

"You have to be kidding, Jim. I am a Catholic; I am not going to a Baptist service. My uncle would have a heart attack."

"What, is he a priest?" Jim joked.

"No. A Monsignor."

"Yikes. Mary, it's not *going* to the service, it's investigative work regarding the casket story. I want to take a measure of Reverend Smallwood."

"He's an asshole. What more do you need to know?" she asked in a bored but whimsical tone.

Jim had told Mary all about Irene. A genuine lady, he had said, but also down to earth and smart. "I just could not believe she would make something like this up," he had said.

"Smallwood convinced Irene to get the copper casket," Jim answered. "He showed up out of the blue when she confronted Reid."

"Then count me in. Pick me up or meet you there?"

"No, I will pick you up. I owe you a ride." His joke fell flat. "I'll be there at ten sharp. "As they drove to the First Baptist Church, Jim told Mary about Reverend Smallwood's involvement and his suspicions.

"Reverend Smallwood was at the funeral home when Irene was making arrangements. He encouraged her to buy the copper casket. And when Irene complained to Reid after the funeral, Smallwood again showed up. I think he has something to do with all of this. Which is why I wanted to go to this service, so I can take his measure. He is where the story is – maybe nothing happens, but I want to be where the story is."

Mary listened quietly, then turned to Jim and said, "I believe a crime has taken place, but to quote my father that and a nickel will buy you a cup of coffee."

"Cheap coffee," Jim quipped.

Mary ignored him, and pressed, "all we have is a few nameless grave robbers. You and Irene saw common criminals. Big deal. And good luck finding them. Connecting them to Reid, and now Smallwood – how do we do that?

"I should also tell you that my boss belongs to the Lincoln Country Club. I can promise you he is friends with

Reid, or at least is part of the same good old boy's network. He is going to run for Congress next year and would need deep-pocket contributors like Reid. He won't want this to be true. So, the case has to be airtight before he even sees it."

They had arrived, finding a crowded parking lot. Couples with shiny-faced children, older couples in suits and tasteful dresses, teens in button-down shirts and below-the-knee skirts swirled past them. And among them, was Irene. Jim hadn't thought it through, but of course she would be here. Not sure how to introduce Mary, Jim was relieved when Mary held out her hand and said, "Hi! I'm Mary, Jim's friend."

After exchanging pleasantries, they decided it would be best not to sit together but agreed to meet for lunch at Harlow's Cafe later.

Jim and Mary sat in the back pew with a view of the entire congregation. The red-carpeted aisle led to an elevated platform with three throne-like chairs and a podium emblazoned with a gold cross. The robed choir filed in and took their places behind the podium. Almost all the pews were full. Just as the service was about to start, Alex Reid and his wife appeared. He walked down the middle aisle like a politician at a rally, stopping to shake hands with just about everyone on the aisles. Jim noticed he paused at the tenth row where Irene was sitting alone. He gave her a warm embrace and whispered something into her ear. Irene nodded. Reid continued down the aisle to the first row, where apparently, he had a reserved seat. As he sat down, he turned to the congregation and smiled. Jim was the only one in the building not smiling. For a split second his eyes met Reid's. Reid lost composure and frowned. He quickly rebounded and greeted people in his row.

Jim pointed Reid out to Mary telling her, "That's Reid. Man is he smooth."

Reverend Smallwood's sermon was all fire and brimstone. He criticized President Kennedy and was especially critical of the civil rights movement spearheaded by Martin Luther King.

"God created man, all men, with a place where they belong. There is an order to this world, and that order keeps us safe and happy. It is what God designed. People should know their place in society," Reverend Smallwood bellowed. "We must feel sympathy for the ignorant lesser races but forcing them into white society would be cruel. They are not ready to bear those responsibilities. In time, yes – and that is the burden of the white man. To educate and uplift the negro. Without us, he would never have known our Lord Jesus. He would be worshipping false gods in Africa. His presence in our country is a blessing to him, but he is not ready to enter our society. And make no mistake. The agitators are forcing the negroes into white society before they are ready. The good negroes don't want that any more than we do."

Jim immediately thought of Edgar Johnson and his mother, Maybelle. Edgar and Jim competed on athletic fields, especially baseball. Jim was a pitcher for his high school and American Legion team. They would get to the state finals and face Edgar's team. Seemingly to Jim, when the game was on the line, Edgar would come up to bat and get a hit. Edgar's coach, Donald Hansen, a successful businessman in Lincoln, brought Edgar and Jim together and a friendship was created. Edgar had visited Jim's family farm many times and Jim had dinner with Maybelle and her family often. After Jim's parents died, Maybelle and Edgar were comforting to him.

Jim's anger over the comments about negros intensified while listening to Smallwood. He thought of his Dad. Jim was just one generation out of Northern Ireland. His father emigrated to Ohio from Northern Ireland and Jim was raised on stories of the Irish Catholics being treated as inferior to the English and Scots-Irish Protestants. When he heard Smallwood talk, he hated him. His Father had told him once that being "white" didn't count for much in Belfast if you weren't the right kind of white. Jim remembered, a few weeks before the car crash – the last serious talk he had with his Dad. "Jimmy, there's people who hate and people who don't. Those are the only two groups that matter. Your skin color won't be your guide. Just your heart. Be on the right side."

Hung over and exhausted from the day before, Jim soon tuned Smallwood out and drifted to sleep, until he felt a sharp jab in his ribs from Mary's elbow.

ELEVEN

AFTER AN HOUR, which seemed like an eternity, Reverend Smallwood walked down the center aisle and out into the sunshine to greet his flock after the service.

Jim and Mary joined the outgoing crowd and tried to avoid Smallwood, but he spied them and walked over.

Grasping Jim and Mary's hands, Smallwood greeted them, "Always delighted to see a new young couple in my congregation. Are you two new to the community and are you married?"

"No, we are just friends."

"Well, well, welcome to the First Baptist Church. We welcome young people but let me tell you we follow the example of Jesus Christ in all that we do. You two are young and there are many temptations today. Alcohol, drugs, and fornication. If come to my church and follow the word, those temptations will be tempered. Remember, young lady, keep yourself as pure as the driven snow.

"We have lots of activities for our Christian young people. Please take one of our flyers and I will see you in church next Sunday."

Jim was ready to ask Smallwood what he thought about Scripture's warnings against false prophets when Mary quickly thanked him with an earnestness Smallwood ate up but caused Jim to bite his tongue to keep from laughing. Jim and Mary extricated their hands from his grip and walked to the car. Jim was surprised when Mary held his hand as they walked to the parking lot.

"I thought I would hold your hand as we walked to the car," Mary said mischievously. "I mean, it's our second date and a minister is already talking to us about fornication." Mary laughed. Jim thought of a clever quip, but it never got past his gaping open mouth.

Pulling out of the parking lot, Jim followed a line of cars, which paused, just as Jim's car was close to the entrance to the church.

"Look, Mary! Reid is with Smallwood, and isn't that Captain Buckner of the Lincoln PD. Who is that little guy doing all the talking? Wow, he looks pissed."

"That is Captain Buckner. I know him from the court and, frankly, he gives me the creeps. He always has his hands on me – my shoulders, the small of my back – as if he is just being friendly. Nothing overt, but his touch makes my skin crawl. I don't know who the little guy is, but he sure seems to be in charge."

Jim drove on and remembered that at his meeting with Reid, the day before, Reid didn't threaten to call the police. He threatened to call Captain Buckner. *Why would he single out Captain Buckner as the one to call,* Jim wondered?

Lost in his thoughts, he heard a playful Mary say, "Earth to Jim, Earth to Jim." Jim looked at her. "Earth? That place only interests me because you're on it."

She rolled her eyes but could not hide the flush in her

cheeks nor the start of a smile she wrestled to keep from glowing.

TWELVE

At Harlow's Café, Jim was surprised to see Irene sitting in a booth being entertained by none other than Sgt. Major (Retired) Harold E. Harlow, or as he preferred, or rather insisted, Sgt. Major.

"Monaghan, how in the hell do you know Irene and are you being good to her? She is a good friend of mine. Her husband, Patrick, was a good friend and he was a hero in World Wars I and II." The Sgt. Major did a double take, just noticing Jim's hair. "Jesus, Jim, what the hell did you do to your hair? Did you join the service?" The Sgt. Major laughed out loud at his own joke.

"Hal, stop it – you don't make comments about people's appearance," Irene said sternly and, turning to Jim said sweetly, "your hair looks very fine, young man."

" I see you know the Sgt. Major, Jim – he and Patrick were very close. He was on General MacArthur's staff. And, Hal, if you are talking about heroes you had better not forget yourself – Patrick told me all your war stories, you know." Irene was one of the very few people who could call the Sgt. Major "Hal," instead of Sgt. Major. But that was only when she was addressing him. To anyone else, she was more insistent than Hal that he would be addressed as Sgt. Major. "Jim, I am so pleased you chose Harlow's for us to meet. Patrick and the Sgt. Major were great friends. They spent hours trading war stories. Patrick in Europe and the Sgt. Major in the Pacific and then Korea," Irene said with the warmest smile at the Sgt. Major, "Two wars are enough."

"One is enough. Unless a lady like you is at the end of it, Irene, in which case a man would fight in a dozen." Hal smiled warmly, but Irene feigned offense and asked, "Only a dozen? My goodness, what it a woman worth?"

Hal laughed loud and long. "An average woman, who knows? You, Irene, are priceless!" Hal kept on laughing and said, "You guys need some privacy, so I am moving you to the back booth. I will make sure no one sits close to you. And today, Irene, lunch is on the house, so order up." Harlow beamed.

Coffee was served, and Jim began the conversation. He told Irene that Mary was more than just a friend. She was an assistant district attorney and she prosecuted crimes. Irene smiled at Mary.

"You are way too young, and so pretty, to be an attorney." Mary blushed. She enjoyed the compliment but resented the sexism. Her boss had said the same thing in her interview. Jim explained he had told Mary what had happened, but it would be best if Irene told her story from the beginning.

"You know, Jim and Mary, I am a retired teacher and Jim gave me an assignment on Friday. When I was a teacher and gave an assignment, I expected my students to complete it. I went home Friday and immediately set to it. It was good therapy. I wrote, then remembered more and rewrote. I have it here in my purse, plus all the documents from the Reid Funeral Home. Everything they gave me when I bought Patrick's casket."

Irene handed the documents to Mary. Reading them, Mary paused to look at Irene, saying, "I am so sorry. I am so sorry. This is just awful."

When she looked at the Reid Funeral Home documents, Mary exclaimed, "What? Four thousand dollars for a copper casket! Christ, does it bring people back from the dead?" She looked up at Irene, aghast, and Jim, cringing. "I am so sorry – that was terrible. I – I am so sorry."

"It's okay, dear," Irene answered. "Are you saying I was overcharged?"

"Yeah," Mary answered. "Just a bit."

"The problem is," Jim added, "we have no proof that your husband's body – "

"Patrick's body," Irene interjected.

"Patrick's body," Jim allowed, "was actually taken out of a copper casket and placed in a pine box. We just know what you saw and the reaction of the four men at the grave. Their behavior would seem to indicate they were doing something nefarious. But what?"

Mary studied Jim. He had not mentioned what he saw, the body clearly moved, the gun to his head – he made eye contact and she understood. He was managing expectations and keeping options open. Irene may need to just walk away, and if she knew everything she never would.

She followed along. "And that isn't evidence. It isn't hard proof."

"The evidence is in the ground, then. Patrick is in a pine box. I know he is. So, what do we do next?" Irene asked.

"Short of exhuming the coffin, I don't know," Mary

answered.

"Then exhume it," Irene answered resolutely. "It will break my heart, but not as much as letting these people get away with what I know they did."

Mary decided she liked Irene. She was a fighter. "I will research the law and find out how and if we can dig up the grave and inspect the vault and the casket. If we can do that, I can get a judge to issue an order. I am sorry, I don't know grave digging law off the top of my head. I didn't take the grave digging class at law school." Again, her joke fell flat. She laughed all the same and said "Look, I have a light day on Monday and I will do the research, but I will do it privately. When we have all the information, we can go to my boss because I would need his authority to go to a judge," Mary concluded.

"Then, we have a plan," Jim said. "We will wait for Mary's research and then decide what to do next.

Mary turned to Irene and took her hand. "Irene, I am sorry for your loss, truly. And I admire your fighting spirit. But I want you to have your eyes wide open going into this. There is a good chance that we can't prove anything – that Reid will say he had nothing to do with any of this and it was just a random robbery. And he will walk. It happens all the time. Are you going to be able to handle that?"

Irene smiled at Mary and then at Jim. "The truth leaves marks. You two will find them. I promise."

Before either could respond, the Sgt. Major came back to the table. "Irene, I'm so sorry about Patrick. If you need anything, and I mean anything, you can count on me and the guys down at the Legion. We will do anything you ask."

Irene thanked the Sgt. Major and the three walked toward the door. Jim thought to himself, I wonder if that includes digging up a coffin.

THIRTEEN

Jim asked Mary what plans she had for the afternoon. She told him she had none and why didn't they go to Hamilton University and walk around the quad.

"I think the place is beautiful. The Dogwoods are in full bloom. It is a perfect day for a walk"

Under the canopy of the nearly sixty-foot American Elms, Mary held Jim's hand as they walked. "So, Jim, tell me about the truck. I am not sure I have ever been in a truck quite so old. Actually, I am not sure I have ever been in a truck before. What is a hot shot newspaperman doing in a farmer's old truck?"

"The truck is the first vehicle I ever had. It is twelve years old and we used it on our family farm. I grew up on a farm about thirty miles east of here near a small town called Dale, population one hundred fifty. It's not really on the map. Everyone there was Irish and Catholic except one guy, who owned the Grain Elevator. I have one brother Hugh, who still lives and works the farm."

"He must be the favorite," Mary teased. "The good son who stayed home, and you're the prodigal son in the big city. You must be such a disappointment to your parents." She smiled, but from Jim's face she knew she touched a nerve and retreated, "I am kidding – I am describing myself, my parents have never forgiven me for leaving Chicago . . . "

"My parents were killed in an auto accident on their way to my high school graduation."

"Oh, Jim." Mary started to tear up. "I am so sorry." She tightened her grip on his hand. "I – Jim, I don't know what to say. I can't imagine --."

"It's okay, Mary. It's life and you have to deal with it. I had work to do and crying about it didn't get the work done. I poured myself into my studies at college.

Mary looked at him tenderly, but incredulously. "Jim, you lost your parents. You were just a boy. Trying not to feel it does not work. You need to feel it."

"I don't want to feel it. It doesn't matter if I feel it. I'm not saying it wasn't hard. I was the valedictorian of my class. I was giving a speech and had a special moment in it for my mom and dad, and they never got to hear it. I hadn't told my parents I was getting the Athlete of the Year award. It was a surprise. Look, Mary, I don't want to talk about it. The truck is from a farm, I am from a farm, that's my story."

Mary knew better than to press so she changed the subject. "Athlete of the year – impressive. What did you play?" she asked.

"Baseball. I was a pitcher. We were a small school, but in high school and American Legion, we always got to the finals. We went up against Lincoln Academy, ironically, both my junior and senior years, for the title."

"Did you beat them?" Mary asked.

"No. We came close. Lincoln had this kid, Edgar Johnson, who always seemed to get a hit at the right time. We were a better team all around, I think at least. But he was the best baseball player we ever went up against."

"My hopes for a major league career ended with Edgar Johnson at bat."

"Did Edgar go on to the majors?" Masked.

"No. He's from the Simpson Housing projects at Fourth and Bradley. Kids don't tend to get out of there. Funny thing, his mom and my mom knew each other. Edgar was the only black kid on Lincoln's team. His mom, when Lincoln travelled to our town to play, sat next to her. Just the two of them. The other moms didn't want to sit next to a black woman, but my mom said she is a guest in our town and will be treated as one. No one argued with my mom, but no one would sit with her or Edgar's mom, Maybelle.

"One day, Edgar's coach, Mr. Donald Hansen, a Lincoln businessman, showed up at the farm with Edgar. He said we should know one another. It started a friendship, which exists today. Edgar has been at the farm for dinner and I, often, show up at his place in the projects for dinner. His mother is great. She and Edgar came to the funeral. I'll never forget that. I still remember Edgar kicking my butt in baseball, but he and his mom will always have a special place in my heart for honoring my parents. It was a long drive into an unfriendly town for blacks. But they did it."

"So how did you end up in Lincoln?" Mary asked.

"Well, I got an academic scholarship to Northwestern, and I knew early on I wanted to be a reporter, so I when I got accepted into the Medill School I was thrilled. Then, last summer, I interned at the Columbus Post-Dispatch. They didn't have any openings, but the editor called the News Tribune and I got a job here. Right now, I mostly write obituaries, but I have hopes for some general assignment work soon."

"Maybe investigative journalism, Jim – uncover a seedy story of fraud and corruption?" Mary smirked, but more gently than usual. She was stung, and sad, by Jim's story. Jim smiled earnestly, and aware that he had been talking about himself for too long switched gears. "What about you, Mary? Why are you in Lincoln?"

"Because it isn't Chicago. I grew up in an Irish Catholic family on the south side of Chicago, like I told you on Saturday. The Daleys and a lot of politicians live in the neighborhood and just about everyone I know is Catholic. And a Democrat. I don't think there are very many Republicans in our part of town. And everyone knew me. I wanted to leave.

"You and I have something in common: I was valedictorian of my class too. I got a scholarship to the University of Chicago. My dad is a police captain on the Chicago Police Force and he, if you can believe it, encouraged me to be an attorney. I had offers from many law schools but chose Hamilton because of Dean McCallister. He is a retired federal judge. I was one of the lucky ones he would invite to dinner at his house. His wife would tell him, "These kids have more to do on Friday night than listen to your old war stories about your time on the bench." But we were enthralled by his wisdom and often we would be there until midnight.

"His wife was a lovely lady, but she passed away last year. My God, I wonder if the judge used the Reid Funeral Home? That would be awful."

For the next few hours, they walked and talked. They admired the marble columns of the library and the ornate cornices at the tops of many buildings. They reminisced about their college experiences as they watched students hurry about or relax in the sun on a blanket on the grass.

After dinner at a local hamburger joint, Jim walked Mary to the door of her condo. They embraced for a sustained period, telling one another what a wonderful day they'd had together. Jim pulled back from the embrace, looked at Mary's smiling eyes, closed his, and kissed her.

As he drove away, he thought it was the best kiss he'd ever had, then laughed that he hadn't had many. Still, what kiss could be better than that one? Smiling, he drove home, but memories of a gun in the back of his head and the confrontation with Reid were intruding on his joy. Monday was tomorrow, and he would have to answer for his visit to Reid Funeral home.

FOURTEEN

Jim picked up his headset and readied himself for another boring day writing obits. That part of the day, for the first time since he started the job, was what he was looking forward to. Willy looked over and yelled, "Hope you got your head screwed on right over the weekend. And hey, nice haircut. About damn time."

Jim gave a tepid smile and gave him the thumbs up sign. He wondered if Reid would follow up on his threat to call and complain. If so, Jim knew he could lose his job.

Jim was convinced Irene was telling the truth, and, if Mary could get the research and they could open the grave and find Irene's husband in a pine box, then Jim would have the story of the year and there was nothing Willy could do about it. Jim could take the story to the Columbus Post-Dispatch or maybe to the Chicago Tribune or the New York Times.

The phone rang, and the reality of an obituary writer took over. *It seems a lot of people die on the weekends,* Jim thought. Monday was usually busy, but this Monday was almost overwhelming.

At eleven twenty a.m., ten minutes before the deadline, Paula, his partner on the obit desk said, "This is someone from the Reid Funeral Home asking to talk to you."

With a heavy weight in the pit of his stomach, Jim punched in to take the call. He feared it was Reid, calling to gloat.

"Mr. Monaghan, this is Steve Hampton at the Reid Funeral Home. We met on Saturday and I don't have much time, but I want to give you an obituary, then I need to talk to you."

Excited to hear from Hampton, Jim replied, "Let's do the obit quick. I can write it up and then maybe we can meet for lunch."

Hampton proceeded to give the details of a pending service and burial, and as he was talking, Jim overheard someone in the background. All Jim could decipher was Hampton saying, "Yes, sir, yes, sir."

Jim said, "Ok, I have all the information I need. Now, when can we meet?" Hampton replied, "Forget it. I can't. I'm sorry." And he hung up the phone.

Jim finished the obituary, sent it to the city desk, leaned back in his chair and thought about Hampton. *He is scared, but he wants to talk. How do I get him to talk? I wonder how Mary is doing on her research.* Jim averaged about three thoughts before returning to thinking of Mary.

Looking over at the city desk rim where two or three editors read copy for content and corrections, Jim saw Willy on the phone glaring at him. *Shit,* Jim thought.

Willy hung up the phone and screamed, "Monaghan, get your ass over here now." Jim didn't move, but rearranged papers on his desk, trying to collect himself.

"I said Now." Willy yelled.

Everyone in the newsroom heard Willy's command, and all eyes were on Jim as he approached his city editor.

"You are in deep shit, young man, and I mean deep shit. I told you, no, I ordered you to let that crazy casket story alone. I didn't want you to do shit with it. But you disobeyed a direct order from me, didn't you? Didn't you?"

Willy rose to his full five-foot-seven height, face mottled red with anger and frustration. "You're done. You'll never work in journalism again. Go back to work, you're still on the clock until I go see our publisher and get your ass canned."

Jim walked back to his desk and thought about calling Willy a sell-out, a phony, an asshole . . . he thought about making a grand speech about integrity and truth, and then walking out. Instead, he sat down at his desk and thought about Mary, Hampton, and Irene. He thought about how Willy had intimidated him from day one, but after the worst ripping the guy had given him in all the time he worked for him – he wasn't remotely intimidated. *I had a gun to my head, and I pressed on with my story. Screw that guy. He won't stop me either.*

That guy was, a minute later, standing at his desk. "You have a meeting in the publisher's office at one thirty p.m. and you best get your ass there on time, because Hill is pissed, and he is pissed at you. Actually, show up late. Piss him off some more, you little shit. In fact, you might as well go have lunch now, because after I fire you, you will be out of a job with no money for lunch. Get the hell out of my sight but be in the publisher's office at one thirty sharp. Do you understand me?"

Jim stood up. Willy was inches from Jim's chair when he delivered his speech, so when Jim stood up there were only inches between them. Jim towered over Willy and stared at him. He didn't move, he just stared, like he stared at Reid. Willy, like Reid, blinked. He backed away, then from a distance recovered and said, "You better god damn be there." Jim just stared, and Willy walked away.

The newsroom was deathly quiet. The news wire machines clicked ominously. Most of the staffers stared at their desks. Some of the veterans smirked, others scowled.

As Jim slumped out, the sports editor said quietly, "You must be doing something right or they wouldn't be that mad at you. Willy threatens to fire me all the time. Go have lunch. Have Stavros get you a double shot and then see the old man at one thirty. Bernard is tough, but he is fair."

FIFTEEN

JIM PERCHED on a hard chair outside the publisher's office at exactly one twenty-five p.m. He had seen Willy walk into the publisher's office, but he knew he should sit and wait to be called in.

During lunch, which he drank, and the walk back to the office, he had reviewed everything he had done. The romance of being fired and taking his story to the big city papers had faded, replaced by fear that he really would have to wash dishes to get by. He knew the only thing he had done wrong was everything. Willy had told him to drop it, but he went ahead and investigated. He felt in his heart that Irene Dunn had told him the truth. He also knew what he had seen at the cemetery. And he thought Reid was lying to him and overreacting. He also thought it was strange that Smallwood, Reid, Buckner, and that little man were so engaged after a church service. Jim knew he was right, but it is one thing to glamorize idealist battles, and another to accept the crushing consequences of fighting that battle. Idealists lose. He felt anguished and uncertain.

This is my first real job as a newspaper man and I am

blowing it. How could I go from being editor of the school paper at Northwestern, graduating with honors, interning at the Post-Dispatch, to sitting outside the publisher's office about to be fired? How the devil did this happen?

Absorbed in his thoughts, Jim didn't notice the person standing in front of him.

"You look like you just lost your best friend, or your girlfriend just dumped you. Which is it?"

Jim had no idea who she was but was taken aback by how attractive she was. He guessed she was a secretary in the publisher's suite of offices. Jim had never been in this part of the newspaper building and he knew no one there.

Jim was struck by her deep blue eyes. Her long hair was pulled into a neat bun, and she was dressed in a tailored gray suit with matching shoes. *They must pay the secretaries well down here,* he thought. He thought of Mary, and how what she said at pizza. "I am lawyer, but if you don't know that and see me in the office you'd think I am a secretary. It isn't fair, Jim." It wasn't, and Jim felt bad for his guess and his quip, then grateful he had kept it to himself. He finally blurted out, "I think I am about to be fired after only two months on the job."

"You're Monaghan, aren't you? The young man from Northwestern, who interned at the Post-Dispatch?"

Now, how the hell did she know that, Jim thought and was about to ask her who she was when Willy stuck his head out of the publisher's door and yelled, "Monaghan, get your butt in here."

SIXTEEN

JIM EXPECTED a posh office with wood-paneled walls, fancy desk, and an imposing chair like Alex Reid's. The room was spartan. No leather sofas or comfortable chairs. Hill's desk was plain and cluttered with newspapers and other stacks of papers. There were two things impressive in the office. One was the walls lined with plaques and certificates memorializing all the newspaper awards the Lincoln News Tribune had won. His eyes were drawn to the biggest plaque on the wall, awarded two years ago by the Associated Press for Investigative Reporting.

The other was Bernard Hill.

Jim knew Hill was the owner of the Hill Family Enterprises, which included a chain of weekly newspapers throughout Ohio along with ten radio stations and two television stations. The Lincoln News Tribune was the flagship, the first purchase Hill had made years ago, and according to rumor, his pride and joy.

Hill sat perfectly still behind his desk, but his eyes were locked on Jim as he took the seat Willy pointed to. Hill was trim in a blue suit with a crisp white shirt and striped tie.

His silver hair was parted on the left. His tan and slightly weathered face displayed no emotion.

As Jim sat down, he feared his fate and he was scared to death. He didn't want to wash dishes, but the truth is he wouldn't even get that job. Stavros had a dishwasher. He would go back to work on the farm with his brother and be a laughing stock at the farm and in the town. He knew he would not get another newspaper job after being fired after two months at the News Tribune.

Hill, erect in his chair, looked at Jim and asked, "Tell me, young man, why you want to bankrupt this newspaper by thoroughly pissing off one of our biggest advertisers?"

As Jim started to answer, the woman from outside the office pulled up a chair right beside him.

Jim started to answer again, but Willy interrupted him, "This is cut and dried, Bernard. He came over last Thursday with this cock and bull story about switching caskets. He said some old lady called him and said she had purchased a copper casket and when she went to the cemetery, she looked in the hole, she found a pine box. Biggest bunch of crap I have ever heard, and I have heard some big ones.

"I ordered him to let the story die, to do nothing, but he didn't. He ended up at Alex Reid's office and, well, you know the rest."

All through Willy's tirade, Bernard's expression didn't change.

"Willy, I asked this young man to tell his story. I know your side of it. I want to hear his," Hill said.

Literally shaking, Jim cleared his throat and began,

"Everything Mr. Williams has said is true. I received a call on Thursday morning after the deadline from a woman who made the claims. I talked to Mr. Williams and he told me it was a BS story and I should ignore it. He was very direct. He told me to do nothing. To forget it.

"But I had told the lady I had doubts about her story and needed to meet her in person. She had agreed to come in at three that afternoon. I couldn't get a hold of her, so at 3 p.m., I went downstairs to meet her and tell her we were not interested in the story, but, to be honest, when I saw her she seemed, well, credible. She was well dressed, carried herself well – she wasn't at all what I expected. I was intrigued. I had a gut feeling.

"When I talked to her, I knew she was not a raving idiot. She is a very classy lady. I took her to O'Toole's and she told me her story from start to finish, and it is an incredible story. I asked her to produce a diary and all the bills and documents from the funeral home.

"The next day, Mr. Williams reminded me of his directive and chided me about the story. But I believed this lady and I noticed Reid was having a funeral service at Calvary on Saturday morning, so I planned to go and observe. I did this on my own time – I didn't take time off the obit desk to pursue this.

"I also wondered if a law was broken, so I went to the County District Attorney's office where I talked to an assistant DA about the general facts of the case without mentioning any names and asked if any laws were broken."

"You what? You went to the district attorney? Bernard, this guy needs to be fired now! He is totally irresponsible!" Willy exclaimed.

Hill, with his eyes directly on Jim, said, "Hush, Willy, I want to hear his story."

"I went to the cemetery on Saturday morning and I observed the Brennan funeral. He was buried in a copper casket, too, just like Irene's husband. After everyone left the burial site, four guys showed up in a truck. They took the casket out of the vault and the body out of the copper casket. They put the body in a pine box, put the pine box in the vault, took the copper casket, and put it in the back of the truck. I was too far away to see the faces of the men, but I saw them switch caskets.

"As I was getting ready to leave, I felt a gun on the back of my neck and the meanest sounding guy I ever heard – no offense Willy" –

"Screw you, Jim," said Willy.

"He said he would blow a hole in the back of my head if I moved and told me to lie there for an hour, which I did."

Jim paused. The memory scared him. And he took the chance to look at the room and see how his audience took that bombshell. Hill was impossible to read; he had no reaction. Willy looked stunned.

"I was scared because I knew he would recognize me, so I cut my hair and threw away my old clothes.

"I wanted to talk to Reid, so I went to his office and, Mr. Hill, I was very respectful to him. I never accused him of anything. I told him I went to him because he was the best, a leader in the industry, and I wondered if something like this could happen. I never told him the funerals were his -- ones he had provided the services for."

"He became outraged and threatened to call the police and have me thrown out of his office. Let me correct that. He said he would call Captain Buckner, and that's significant because we went to Reverend Smallwood's service on Sunday and after the service, Reid, Smallwood, Buckner, and a short man were engrossed in an intense conversation.

"What is the significance of Reverend Smallwood?" Hill asked.

"Oh – right. Smallwood was with Reid when they

convinced Irene to buy the most expensive copper casket. And, when she told Reid the story, Smallwood showed up again."

Jim studied Hill for a reaction; Hill looked back at Jim betraying not even a hint of a reaction. Jim pressed on.

"Back to Buckner -- when Irene went to the police, Buckner was the cop who told her she was confused."

"Wait a minute," Willy interrupted again, "you went to the Baptist service on Sunday? Aren't you Catholic? And who is 'we'?"

"Yes, I am Catholic and the 'we', is Mary Ryan from the district attorney's office. She is the lawyer I talked to. She is pretty damn interested in this story and is investigating, too."

"Formally?" Hill asked.

"Sir?" Jim asked back.

"Does George Rogers know?"

"I'm sorry who is that, sir?" Jim answered.

"Jesus," Willy muttered.

"He is the District Attorney, Jim," said the woman from the hallway, who had been listening so quietly Jim forgot she was there. "He is the one who will fire Ms. Ryan for chasing a defamatory false story accusing his two good friends of wrong doing. Unless you're right and can prove it. And being right doesn't count. Just proving it."

I don't know if he knows," Jim answered honestly. "That's my story, Mr. Hill. I think Reid is switching caskets and Smallwood is involved, as is Captain Buckner. But I can't prove any of it. Not yet."

SEVENTEEN

"Well, Jim, some problems with your story," Willy began. "You had a gun to your head. Why didn't you go to the police?"

"And tell them what, Willy? I couldn't identify the guy with the gun, nor could I identify the people working the casket switch. I didn't have enough information to go to the police. And I couldn't go to you.

"Why the hell not?" Willy asked.

" Irene who?" Hill asked.

"Sir?" Jim asked, and became conscious that, despite himself, he stumbled when talking to Bernard Hill. The man had an aura of authority. He was graceful, dignified, but overwhelming.

"Your source, dumbass," answered Willy. "The Irene you droned on about – the one you risked your career for."

Risked, thought Jim. That isn't fired.

"Irene Dunn," Jim replied.

"Irene Dunn, the teacher?" asked the woman from the hallway.

"Yeah," answered Jim. "Her husband Patrick died – he was a war hero, and a teacher too."

The woman stared off. "Irene Dunn was my sixth-grade teacher. "Jim felt hope and pressed on. "She called and asked for me because I wrote the obituary for her husband. I believe her, and everything that has happened since I talked to her tells me she is telling the truth."

"Your belief is, literally, worthless. The only fact we have is one of our biggest advertisers called the publisher because one of our rookies failed to follow my direct orders. We have a business to run. We run factual stories, not part-fact, part-fiction. We have, best case, evidence of rogue criminals – but even then, it's flimsy and too outrageous to be believed. And what are we reporting? Two people saw something crazy, and one of them is an ambitious kid who wants a big story to make his name. The other is an old woman whose husband just died, and my first thought is she's gone nuts from grief and old age. Readers will think the same thing. If we don't fire Monaghan, he must be suspended. And the story dies. That's my recommendation, Bernard"

There was silence in the room. Jim stared at his shoes. Even a suspension would be devastating. He lived paycheck-to-paycheck and he couldn't afford a suspension, no matter how long or short.

Jim looked at the woman next to him and noticed she was staring at Bernard.

He wondered who she was, and as if she could read his mind she turned and said, "I never properly introduced myself. I am Audrey Hill, Bernard's daughter and the assistant publisher of the News Tribune. And, Jim Monaghan, I believe your story.

"Now, before we go any further, who in your world of

sources knows what portion of the story? I have the feeling you are the only one who knows everything, is that right?"

"Irene knows her part, I haven't shared anything else with her. I've told Mary pretty much everything."

"I'll bet you have," Willy smirked. "I know who Mary Ryan is – she prosecuted the Newsome case. Pretty girl, wouldn't you say, Jim?"

Jim flushed, but answered, "She is competent, and she believed Irene. Being pretty is irrelevant."

Audrey smiled at Jim appreciatively; Willy laughed and said, "Yeah, right!"

Jim ignored him and continued, "One more thing, this morning as I was finishing up an obit, Paula, my partner, said someone from the Reid Funeral Home was on hold and they wanted to talk to me. I picked up the line and it was Steve Hampton. He is one of Reid's assistants and was the guy I met when I walked in their door. I know he was listening to my conversation because I bumped into him as I walked out of Reid's office.

"He told me he had an obit and needed to talk to me. Because we were on a deadline, I took the obit, but I heard someone in the background and Hampton saying, 'Yes, sir, yes, sir.' I finished the obit and asked him when we could meet. Hampton then said, 'Forget I said that,' and hung up the phone. I think he knows something and he wants to talk, but he sounded scared."

Audrey looked at her father and said, "Ok, Pops, what do we do next?"

Bernard said, "I will call Reid and tell him I have personally disciplined Jim. You do feel disciplined, don't you, Jim?"

"Yes, sir," Jim replied.

"I know Reid from the club. I don't like him. He is kind of sleazy with his tailor-made suits from Chicago and his new Mercedes every year. I hear he cheats on his wife, and I can't respect any man who does. None of that makes him a criminal, though.

"But Jim's story takes this to a different level. Willy, you're right, all we have now are two witnesses who saw unidentified common criminals. We don't know if the gravediggers work for Reid or not. Doesn't make any difference because we don't know who they are or anything about them.

"I think my call will keep Reid satisfied. Willy, make sure Jim is on the obit desk taking calls. This is a small town no matter how big it gets, and I am sure Reid will keep tabs on Jim. No one can know anything about any of this except the four of us."

Willy objected, "Why not suspend him for a week? I am the leader in the newsroom and everyone knows he directly disobeyed my order. If he is not suspended, my authority is going to be questioned. Second, it keeps Reid happy."

Jim nearly sprained his neck, turning to look at Willy. *What did he say?*

"How does a suspension play if the story breaks?" Audrey cut in. "We look deceptive. And I could care less about satisfying Reid. Where else is he going to advertise his funerals? We are the only newspaper in town."

"Jim stays on the obit desk," Bernard declared. "We still run a newspaper and we need his help. And, we need to stay in touch with him about this story. Jim, I am not sure I believe your story completely, but you have not given me any reason not to. We are going to be careful going forward.

When your assistant DA obtains her research about digging up graves, we should have another meeting.

Audrey, please set up the meeting. Jim, please bring Mrs. Dunn and Mary Ryan to join Willy and Audrey. In fact, I might sit in on the meeting and bring a friend of my own. And, Willy, have Art Wilks come and see me."

"Why do you want to see Art? He's got an assignment taking pictures at the city council meeting tonight, so I let him go home early. Why would you want to see him?" Willy asked. Bernard didn't answer but looked sternly at Willy.

"Ok, I will call Art and have him come back in and see you."

Bernard continued, "Audrey, set the meeting up at the Hill Family Offices and use the conference room in the back where we can have privacy. And, again people, let's keep this meeting and this story among us. No one else is to be involved. Understood?"

EIGHTEEN

Jim walked upstairs to the newsroom, catching inquisitive glances from his colleagues, which he ignored. Sitting at his desk, he thought what a turn of events. Not only was he not being fired or suspended, he was on a first name basis with Bernard and Audrey Hill. He was still at the obit desk and he had to watch his p's and q's, but he felt things had turned a positive corner. He knew Willy was going to watch him like a hawk, but he was okay with that. He would be careful, and felt he had allies in the executive offices.

He hoped the time would pass quickly; he couldn't wait to see Mary. He hoped her research would give them the authority to dig up the grave. What an experience that would be. He thought about who he would bring to the dig and immediately thought of Sgt. Major Harlow. Harlow was one of the first friends Jim made after going to work at the News Tribune. He loved talking to Harlow. He was a war hero, over six feet tall and strong as a bull. But he was kind and gentle.

Jim sat at his desk and picked up a copy of the Columbus Post-Dispatch to catch up on his beloved Cincinnati Reds. Frank Robinson was his favorites, but Rookie Pete Rose was quickly climbing the ladder. As the clock ticked toward the end of the day, Jim made plans in his head for his meeting with Mary. Just as he was about to leave, the mail boy dropped an envelope on his typewriter. Only his name was scrawled across the top. Believing it was just interoffice mail and unimportant, he left to pick up Mary at the DA's office but stuffed the envelope into his back pocket.

Before he started his truck, though, curiosity got the best of him. He opened the envelope and quickly read the letter. He knew his life had changed and it had nothing to do with his meeting with Mary Ryan. Or did it?

"MR. MONAGHAN, your life is in danger if you continue to probe into the Reid Funeral Home.

You need to contact Steve Hampton, but you can't talk to him at the funeral home. You must meet him privately.

Mr. Reid is a very powerful man and he has powerful friends. You don't want to cross him, but what is happening at this funeral home is wrong."

THE LETTER WAS NOT SIGNED. He believed it and was deeply troubled. Not knowing what to do, he sat in his truck, his heart pounding. He drove from his offsite parking spot back to the News Tribune and parked in a reserved spot. *I need a parking place here,* Jim thought as he jumped out of his truck and ran into the executive office area, where he found Bernard and Audrey in the publisher's office.

"Did you forget something, Jim?" Audrey asked with a smile.

"No, but you guys need to see this," and he handed over the letter.

Bernard read the letter first and didn't react or comment. Audrey, after reading it, said, "Dad, this could get out of hand."

"I know it is going to be hard, Jim, but you have to try to relax. This is a threat, yes, but it might be just that, a threat. But, Audrey, let's get that meeting set up for tomorrow afternoon."

Shaken, but confident the threatening letter confirmed the story was true, Jim sped over to the DA's office and waited for Mary to come out from work. Seeing her walk out of the office, Jim's heart thumped.

Jim walked briskly, almost running, to Mary, gave her a big embrace, and told her he had wonderful news. Mary was eager to hear it.

Driving to a coffee shop next to the Bail Bonds office, Jim relayed the essence of his meeting with the Hills and Willy. "I was certain I was going to be fired or at least suspended, but now I am on a first-name basis with the Hills and they want to have a meeting tomorrow and you are invited." Jim grinned. He did not tell her about the threatening letter.

At the coffee shop, Mary told Jim how happy and proud of him she was, and she had great news. "I know just the judge who would issue the order, to exhume the bodies, but I have to get my boss to sign off on it, and, as I told you, he belongs to the country club with Reid, and he has political ambitions. Reid would be at the top of the list of potential contributors."

Jim told her they would make the decision after the meeting on Tuesday.

The balance of the evening was spent at an intimate dinner with lots of smiles and hand holding.

The only negative part of the evening occurred when the bill came, and Mary grabbed it. "Jim, I am a little older than you and I make good money in the DA's office. I know brand new reporters don't make that much and I am happy to pay for dinner."

"Absolutely not. You are not paying for dinner," Jim responded, taking the check. They smiled, holding hands, and drove to Mary's condo where another warm embrace ended the evening.

NINETEEN

JIM AND MARY entered the Hill Family Enterprises office building through the back door and were met by Audrey, who shepherded them into the conference room. She left her trusted assistant to wait for Irene Dunn.

As they entered the room, Bernard directed Jim to sit at his right and introduced him to a tall, lean, white-haired gentleman with half-moon glasses perched half- way down his nose. "This is Judge Douglas McCallister, Dean of the Hamilton School of Law and retired Federal Judge."

Jim told the judge he had heard many good things about him. Mary was ecstatic. "Judge, it is so good to see you! I so enjoyed your seminar and dinners at your house were always great. I am so sorry about your wife's passing."

"Mary, I am not surprised you are knee-deep in this story Bernard has told me about. You were one of my brightest students and I know your legal advice will be top notch. And one more thing, I may have some insight into this story when it is appropriate for me to comment. But for now, I am just a listener."

When Irene Dunn walked into the room, Audrey jumped up and embraced her.

"Folks, this is Irene Dunn, my sixth-grade teacher at Washington Elementary. She was one of my very favorite teachers."

"And you, Audrey, were one of my best students ever. Though you had a mischievous streak, to be sure. You were a joy to have in my class. I was looking forward to seeing you today. It brought a smile to my face thinking about some of the stunts you and your friends pulled. I have so enjoyed following your career here at the newspaper and your charity work at Mercy Hospital."

Bernard called the meeting to order and reminded everyone the meeting was confidential.

"Since Jim has been at the center of this story from the beginning, I will ask him to give us a summary of everything that has happened since Irene called him last week."

Before Jim spoke, he turned to Irene and said, "Irene, you are going to hear some things that I have never told you. I am sorry I didn't, but I just didn't feel comfortable because I did not want to scare you."

Irene answered, "It's ok. But I don't scare easily."

Jim began with Irene's phone call on Thursday. He spoke of his doubts about her story which were mitigated when he met her in person. He told of going to the cemetery and his experience that ended with a gun at the back of his neck.

When he finished the cemetery story, a shocked Irene stared at him with tears in her eyes. "Jim, I am so sorry I brought you into this," she said.

Bernard interrupted, "Jim, please continue."

Jim told of his fright and concern about being recognized and deciding to change his appearance. He told about meeting with Reid and his reaction. He told about going to Smallwood's Sunday service and the impromptu meeting among Smallwood, Reid, Buckner, and the unidentified man.

At the conclusion, he provided all the participants a copy of Irene's diary, along with his own, detailing everything that had happened since Irene's phone call Thursday morning. Everything, that is, except his interactions with Willy. He ended by telling of the strange telephone call he had with Steve Hampton Monday and showed everyone the unsigned letter.

He then asked Mary to brief the group on the legal process to open the graves, which she did. When she concluded, she passed out the legal arguments and process. She suggested the two graves to be opened would be Dunn's and Brennan's, as both graves were the basis for the probable cause argument.

There was silence in the room as everyone read Mary's legal arguments, Irene's diary, and Jim's notes.

The first person to speak was Judge McCallister.

"Let me begin by complimenting you, Jim. Your notes are detailed, clear, and descriptive. Excellent research. Mary, I am so proud of you. Obviously, you paid attention in your law classes. This is first-rate research and any judge would issue the order immediately.

"Now, in reading Irene's diary, I was taken back almost a year to when my wife died."

The judge closed his eyes, twisted the gold wedding ring on his left hand, and paused. "My wife and I were members of Smallwood's church. She was more active than I, but I attended occasionally. I found Smallwood to be a bit pompous, and I could only take his sermons in small bits.

My wife loved singing in the choir, so we remained members. But I digress. When I was in the casket room at the funeral home, Reid pulled all the same crap. Then Smallwood came in, too. I found the whole experience distasteful. Reid told me I should make up for what I had failed to do in life by burying her in the best casket. Then Smallwood sermonized about honoring our beloved in the best possible way, as the Lord honors the faithful. It was disgusting. I had decided to get the copper casket before I even came in the funeral home. My wife had been dying for some time, and we made plans. I almost didn't get it. But I got it all the same and left as soon as I could. It was all repulsive.

"Mary, add my name to the list of those gravesites that should be uncovered. Like Irene, I want to know."

There was hushed silence after the distinguished jurist spoke, finally broken by Irene.

She told of her experience with Steve Hampton in the funeral home and his look of sympathy after she had confronted Reid and Smallwood. "I think it is important and significant that he insisted on talking to Jim yesterday, asking for a meeting and then saying to forget about it. It is not a coincidence that shortly after his call, Jim got an unsigned letter.

"I have an idea. I will go to the funeral home and visit with Steve Hampton and invite him to dinner to thank him for all he did for me with Patrick's funeral. I will tell him there will be others at the dinner, including someone who got an unsigned letter. I will do it privately, so no one will know anything except him and me. Of course, Mary and Jim will be at the dinner. What do you all think about that plan?"

A flurry of conversation was peppered with questions of

legality, appropriateness, and danger. Finally, Bernard spoke. "You are quite the courageous one, aren't you, Irene?"

"No, I am the angry one," Irene declared.

All agreed to wait to see if Irene was successful in wooing Hampton to dinner. Judge McCallister urged Mary to hold off on seeking a warrant and telling her boss anything. "It might be premature. Let's see what this dinner brings before we take another step. It would be a public step, and once there, you can't put the genie back in the bottle."

TWENTY

JIM AND MARY spent the balance of the afternoon and evening at her condo talking about the fascinating series of events of the afternoon, interspersed with less important and lighter topics. "They call him Charlie Hustle – sort of a joke because he was walked but sprinted to first base!" Jim relayed.

"How can he run and walk at the same time?" Mary asked, looking genuinely confused.

"No, he *was* walked. The pitcher threw 4 balls."

Mary just looked at him confused.

"So, a pitcher throws a ball and it has to be in the strike zone . . ."

Mary burst out laughing. "Jim, you need to work on your investigative journalism skills. I know what a strike is, and a ball, and a walk. Never heard of Pete Rose. I'm a Cubs fan."

Jim laughed, "then this is over. No Cubs fans are allowed in my life. They're bad people, Mary."

"This?" Mary smiled. "What is 'this,' Jim?"

Jim leaned in to kiss her, and then a blaring telephone

interrupted the moment. "Don't answer that!" Jim pleaded. Mary answered the phone and her eyes widened and her mouth dropped open. "It's for you, Jim. It's Irene Dunn."

"How did you know I would be here, Irene?" Jim asked.

"I might be old, Jim, but I am not an old fool. Of course, you would be there. If you weren't, you wouldn't be as smart as I think you are." Irene laughed.

Irene recounted her visit to the Reid Funeral Home after supper. She told of going to a wake, thankful Reid didn't appear. The deceased, whom she had known vaguely, was interred in a copper casket. She described her conversation with Steve Hampton. She reported he seemed nervous and kept looking around as if to see if anyone was watching.

She told Hampton she wanted him to come to her home for dinner, so she could show her appreciation. Hampton had asked her in a whisper if she was sure she wanted him to come to dinner. She told Hampton, yes, she was sure, and in fact there were a couple of people whom she wanted him to meet. She told Hampton one of them was someone who had received an unsigned letter on Monday.

"Hampton looked me in the eye and very quietly said 'six o'clock tomorrow night and tell Monaghan to be careful.'"

"Tomorrow night, I'm preparing my famous meat loaf. Can you and Mary be there just a little early, so we can make our plans?"

"We'll be there at five thirty."

After briefing Mary on the call, Jim called Audrey and provided her with the details. Audrey suggested perhaps a deputy ought to be there, but Jim talked her out of it, saying Mary's presence would be intimidating enough and he felt the meeting would be safe. Audrey reluctantly agreed.

TWENTY-ONE

AT IRENE'S HOUSE, Jim noticed a faded red pickup truck parked at the corner and a slouching man behind the wheel. Jim slowed down for a closer look, but the man, who had his baseball cap pulled down low, looked away. The emblem on the truck door caught Jim's eye. It was an Eagle clutching on a rifle with a scope, *like a sniper's gun*, Jim thought. *Man, there are some strange people in this world.*

Irene's home was a modest two-story frame house with a wide, welcoming, front porch. The yard was well-tended, filled with plants Jim couldn't name. Stepping carefully along the mossy flagstone path, lined by flowers, Jim and Mary knocked on the door. As Jim entered, he looked back for the red truck, but it was gone.

Mary showed Irene the tape recorder she had obtained from one of the investigators in her office. Mary's plan was to tell Hampton about recording the conversation since it was better to have a recording than just Jim taking notes, especially if this turned into a criminal investigation. But, if Hampton was uncomfortable with it, she would turn it off.

As the clock ticked closer to six twenty, the trio started

to doubt Hampton would show up. At six thirty, the doorbell rang.

Hampton hugged Irene and told her how sorry he was for what she had gone through. As Jim closed the door, he noticed a dark green pickup truck parked across the street. The driver had a straw hat pulled low and held something in his hands, but Jim couldn't see what it was. Again, on the driver's side door was the strange eagle emblem. *Quite a coincidence,* he thought, and guessed the two trucks belonged to the same house. As he entered the living room he saw, through Irene's picture window, the truck drive away.

Hampton cautiously shook hands with Jim and Mary. The palm of his right hand was wet, and his breathing was fast and shallow. His neatly combed red hair highlighted his frowning, freckled face. He was nattily attired in creased khaki pants and a long sleeve dress shirt, buttoned to his neck. It seemed to Jim Hampton could either bolt or vomit at any minute. When Hampton asked Irene if he could trust Jim and Mary, she assured him he could.

Jim introduced Mary as his girlfriend, but said she was also an assistant district attorney. He said he suspected illegal activity at Reid's Funeral Home. If so, Mary would know what could be done about it. Hampton said he had no objection to a tape recording. He finally wanted to make amends for his part in the deception of so many grieving families. His thin shoulders shook as he broke down and cried.

Staring at the floor, Hampton began in a soft, almost inaudible voice, lamenting his role and how grateful he was to talk about how difficult life had been for him. He said he thought about going to St. Vincent's, but the priest knew his family. His Aunt had gone to him for help to keep her nephew from "sinning" with other men. The priest would be no help. And he couldn't go to the First Baptist Church because of Reverend Smallwood. Quietly sobbing, he admitted being ashamed of his role at the funeral home and what it had done to him. Hampton looked up and stared forlornly. His eyes lingered on Mary, and he said he knew the practices at the funeral home were wrong and against the law.

"Let me tell you what has been going on, but be warned, when you know all the repulsive stuff that happens there, all of you will be in danger. Reid is an evil man, and he has evil friends."

Hampton said he wanted to start at the beginning when he went to work for Reid ten years ago. "You both are new to town. I was born and raised here, and it is no secret that I am gay. It's not easy for someone like me to get a job and I thought Reid was fair, progressive – a great man doing the right thing. I am not ashamed of being gay, but I hide it as best I can. Reid didn't seem to care. Looking back, Reid hired me because I was gay. He knew I had to have this job and that he could bully me. And, technically, I can be thrown in jail for what I do in the privacy of my bedroom. Reid would ultimately threaten me with that,"

Hampton said he started out as a maintenance man, cleaning up and doing whatever Reid asked him to do, but then Reid noticed he was good with grieving families. "I am a very compassionate man," Hampton said. "My parents died when I was young, so I know how death affects people."

Hampton explained that he was promoted to be Reid's assistant, helping with casket purchases, assisting at wakes, driving the hearse, and bringing the caskets into the churches. A little over a year ago, a family purchased a copper casket and he noticed there was a small dent on the side. He told Reid about it as the funeral home had a warranty from the casket company, but Reid said not to worry about it.

Two weeks later, another family picked out a copper casket and, as Hampton was preparing the body to go in, he noticed a dent in the casket in the exact same place. Hampton wanted to tell Reid about it, but at the last minute, he changed his mind. He polished the casket and tried to make the dent less visible.

Two more weeks passed, and another family purchased a copper casket, and there was the same dent in the same place. Then, he said, he knew something was askew, so he confronted Reid.

"I told him it looked like the same casket had been used three times, and Reid told me I was a smart kid. And would I like to make some money." Hampton looked away and paused. "He said he needed a bookkeeper. That I would get triple what he paid me. I told him no. He said, 'You're at a crossroads, faggot. Make more money with me than you'll make anywhere else or turn me down, lose this job, and next Saturday night you and your boyfriend get arrested for sodomy.' It was what he said next that sealed the deal. He said, 'And don't try to be a hero and go telling people about this. I can get you arrested, sure. But that's not the half of it. A faggot dead in a ditch – a lot of people around here would say that's just a sinner getting his due.'"

Hampton unbuttoned his long-sleeved striped shirt and extracted a manila file folder filled with pages of names and dates. Included in the list were the names Dunn, McAllister, and Brennan.

"I took the job. But I made a file for the day I found the courage to finally do the right thing. It's yours"

Mary and Jim knew immediately they had the mother-lode of evidence for indictments and one hell of a great story, but they did not react.

Hampton started to sob. Trying to catch his breath, he morosely spoke of how upset his mother and father would be if they knew what he was a part of, how embarrassed he was, and how he wanted to make everything right. Irene hugged him, told him he was doing the right thing, and that she was proud of him. Finally, controlling his emotions, he asked Mary if he was going to go to jail.

"I don't know that you've done anything wrong. He threatened your life. You were under duress. Reid, on the other hand, could be in serious trouble. But we still don't have concrete evidence," Mary told him.

Hampton's teary green eyes sought Irene's and he clasped her hand. He said sadly, "If you dig up the graves of these people, you will find the bodies buried in a plain wooden box inside the vaults. I am so sorry, Irene." Irene shook her head as tears streamed down her cheeks.

"There is more, Mary. What I gave you is a copy of what you will find in Reid's desk." Hampton told them Reid kept a duplicate ledger in the bottom right hand drawer of his desk where he tracked each funeral in which caskets were switched. He noted Reid usually kept his office locked, but one afternoon when he was gone, Hampton needed to get some keys from the office. It was unlocked and so he went in. He got the keys from the top drawer of the desk and sat in Reid's big maroon leather chair. "I always wanted to know what it would feel like to sit in such a chair. I noticed the bottom drawer partially open. I shouldn't have done it, but I opened it and saw the ledger book.

"I looked through it and recognized some names from the list I was keeping. I didn't want to take the chance of making a copy of his ledger, but I have a good memory and when I went back to my office in the basement, I wrote as many of them down as I could remember. They corresponded with the list I had been keeping, so I am confident they were all switched. I knew I had to do something, but I didn't know what to do. I didn't know who I could talk to. Mrs. Dunn, your husband's name was in Reid's ledger book."

Hampton went on to say he was relieved when Jim came in on Saturday. He knew he had to get Jim in with Reid, and he listened outside the door. Hampton told Jim he had heard everything, and Reid's reaction was typical.

"He is an evil man, a mean man, and you were threatening his empire. I wanted to talk to you, so I called in the obit on Monday, but Reid came up to me and saw that I was giving you the information on the funeral and told me to keep it short and come see him. I went to see him, and he said he forgot what he wanted. Lying bastard. He then asked if I had plans with my boyfriend that night and smirked at me. 'If you do,' he said, 'watch out for the cops.' Pretty thinly veiled threat.

"So, on my lunch hour, I typed up the note, put it in an envelope, and dropped it off at the newspaper. I had to warn you because I knew Reid was suspicious.

"I feel so much better now that I have this off my chest. Oh, and one more thing. Reverend Smallwood of the First Baptist Church is in on it, too. I don't know how, but he is always in on the purchase of the caskets, even if the people are not members of his congregation. And he always has money and flashes it around town.

Jim thanked Hampton for coming forward and for sending the note. As an afterthought, he asked if Captain

Buckner from the Lincoln Police Department could be part of it.

"I don't know, but Buckner is around a lot and he meets with Reid, Smallwood, and some little guy I don't know. But what does that mean? I can't tell you for sure."

After a somber, but pleasant dinner, Hampton gave everyone, including Jim, a hug and left. Jim and Mary got into Jim's truck and drove away, unaware they were being followed by a pickup truck.

At Mary's condo, Jim called Audrey and gave her all the details of the meeting with Hampton. Audrey said they would meet at the Hill Family offices at three o'clock the next day and to tell no one about the Hampton meeting.

A smiling Jim, his arm around Mary, told Audrey, "We got him, Audrey, we got the son of a bitch."

TWENTY-TWO

A PENSIVE GROUP gathered around the conference table at the Hill Family offices: Jim, Mary, Bernard, Audrey, Irene, Judge McCallister and, inexplicably to Jim, Art Wilks, chief photographer for the Lincoln News Tribune. Conspicuous by his absence was Willy.

"I will update Willy when this meeting is over," Bernard said and asked Jim to summarize the meeting with Hampton.

Jim did and provided everyone copies of his detailed diary of the meeting. Attached was Hampton's list of presumed switched caskets. Jim included everything in his diary except the coincidence of the two pickup trucks which, he would later lament, he had thought so insignificant he had forgotten about.

The room was silent as everyone read Jim's diary and Hampton's list. The judge's chin quivered, and his eyes moistened when he found his wife's name on the list. He looked at Jim and said, "Thank you, young man." His voice wavered, and Irene put her hand on his shoulder and said, "I am so sorry, Judge."

Bernard asked Mary and Irene if they had anything to add. Mary said she did and played the tape.

Jim beamed. "We have him, Mr. Hill. Mary thinks there is enough information in Hampton's taped testimony for an indictment."

"Not so fast, Jim," the judge said, "Mary, you now have solid probable cause to open the graves. You don't have solid facts. Further, we don't know who the burial crew is or who they work for. Reid's ledger book might be the missing link, but until we either open the graves or have the ledger book, we just have probable cause."

"Oh, we have a little more," Bernard said. "Art, show these folks what you have."

Wilks, a veteran photographer, smiled and as he opened a manila envelope, said,

"When the boss told me about this assignment, I thought, I have heard some strange ones, but this may be the strangest."

Wilks explained that he and Bernard kept an eye on current obituaries. They settled on a prominent family's patriarch, who was buried that morning.

"I got out my old Ranger camouflage and my longest lens and scouted out Calvary Cemetery. I found a spot where I would blend in, but still get good shots of the gravesite. I had my assistant with me, and we both had hand-held radios. He was about one hundred yards back and kept sweeping the area to make sure no one was going to creep up behind me.

"Just as Jim has said, after the family left, a pickup truck pulled up and let me show you what I shot."

Wilks opened the envelope and brought out pictures showing the pickup truck arriving, the casket being pulled out of the vault, the body being removed and placed in a plain wooden box, and the original casket placed in the bed of the pickup truck and covered with a blue tarp.

Shocked gasps echoed in the room as the photos were passed around. None of the pictures clearly showed the faces of the men and when Jim complained about still not knowing who they were, he noticed Bernard and Art were smiling.

"No, we don't know who they were," Wilks said, and then handed out his last picture which showed the pickup truck with the license plate clearly visible.

"We don't know who they were, but we sure know the license number of the truck," Wilks chortled.

Conversation buzzed about what to do next. Mary, Jim, and Audrey were discussing options when they noticed Irene and the judge looking at each picture morosely. Finally, Audrey spoke, "Judge, Irene, we are so sorry. We are treating this as a story, but this is such a tragedy for the two of you."

Judge McCallister cleared his throat. "We need to get this information to the DA right away. I will call and ask him and his chief investigator to come to my office at the law school. We will have privacy there. I want Jim, Mary, and Irene to come with me. If we all show up at the DA's office, the whole town will know about it before supper."

The judge left the room and was back in less than ten minutes. "The meeting is all set. They will meet us at my office in half an hour. Let's go." As he was about to exit the room, he turned to Audrey and said, "On second thought, Audrey, why don't you go with us? Right now, your newspaper has a story that you will probably win another award for, but premature publication could hurt the DA's efforts.

Let me suggest you work with his office so no mistakes are made."

Audrey, with a nod from her father, quickly agreed.

TWENTY-THREE

DISTRICT ATTORNEY GEORGE ROGERS and his chief investigator walked into Dean McCallister's wood-paneled conference room and stopped abruptly when he saw Mary Ryan sitting next to the judge.

"Mary, what are you doing here?"

"Sit down, George," Judge McCallister said. "I will explain everything. I hope you have your legal pad with you because you and your investigator are going to want to take notes. I think you know Audrey Hill, and this is Jim Monaghan, a News Tribune reporter. And this is Mrs. Irene Dunn. We have a case here that's tight, but it involves one of the most prominent people in town."

"I have lots of questions already," Rogers said. "Why is my newest assistant here without my knowing anything? And why are the newspaper people here?"

"Relax, George. Hold your questions until we are done. Now, since Jim has been involved in this case from the beginning, I am asking him to lead the briefing."

Rogers and his investigator were spellbound listening to Jim and Irene. Mary told of her research and played the tape of Hampton's testimony. Jim provided copies of his diary and of Wilks's photographs. Rogers and his assistant looked around at the gathered group in stunned amazement.

"Who else knows about this?" Rogers asked. Judge McCallister assured him the only people who knew the entire story were in the room. Audrey added that her father also knew, but no one else at the newspaper knew everything. "The judge cautioned us about printing anything until we briefed you, George, and we are not going to print anything until we know what is going to happen. We all have some ideas what should happen next, but we want to cooperate with you and your team. At the same time, if there is going to be an arrest, we want to be tipped off, so we can get a jump on the story and have photographs of anything newsworthy."

The DA ordered his assistant to call the office and tell his top prosecutors they would be staying late, adding it might be best for their top paralegal to do so, too. He went on to say there was enough probable cause for an arrest, but they needed a search warrant to get into Reid's office and obtain the ledger book, as well as other records.

"We need to act quickly; I want to go before the judge tomorrow for an arrest warrant and a search warrant."

He told Mary he wanted her to work with his top assistants, but she was a material witness to Hampton's testimony, so he and she would be very careful what she was assigned.

"People, there is going to be a lot of heat on this one. Alex Reid is one of the most prominent people in town. He owns, what, twenty some funeral homes? I know he is a friend of the mayor. They frequently have lunch together.

"Hell, before now, I would tell you he was a friend of

mine. He contributes to my campaign and I know he is on the board at the First Baptist Church. I will give this a lot of thought, but I may have to recuse myself from this case. I will talk to the judge in chambers before we ask for the warrants."

DA Rogers said, "Mary, I want you to go back with me and start to work. Jim, if you could come with us, I would appreciate it, as you know so much about the case. Audrey, I appreciate you and your father cooperating with us on this and, before we do anything, I will personally let you know. Irene, we will call you later for your testimony and potential trial preparation."

TWENTY-FOUR

MARY BUBBLED with excitement on the drive to the court-house. She bounced in her seat and said she was so excited to tell her father about her role in bringing down Reid and his organization. "I can't wait to tell them all about this! I won't tell my dad yet, but I am going to tell mom about us." Jim felt a jolt of excitement when Mary mentioned "us."

At the DA's office, the team started work on the case. The senior prosecutor, after looking through all the evidence, pointed to Mary and declared, "George, we told you she was going to be great, and she sure has proved it on this case. Most of our work has been done. It won't take us long to get enough information to take to the judge. I expect we can get the warrants for tomorrow afternoon."

Mary flushed with embarrassment, and Jim beamed with pride.

The team worked until three a.m. when they concluded their case was tight and their pleadings to the judge were perfect.

They thought they could present their case to the judge Friday afternoon and obtain the arrest and search warrants.

"We could hit Reid's Funeral Home and his home around five p.m. By seven, we could have all the records and if we work all weekend, we could indict him by Monday afternoon," the top assistant suggested.

Jim remembered that there were services scheduled for Friday evening at the funeral home. "Two things: one, there are two visitations scheduled Friday night and they go until around nine. There is no sense disturbing those families. Why don't you wait until the visitations are over and then make your entry? One other thing. If you go in at five, then the television stations will have the story. If you go in later, we can lead with it on our Saturday morning edition. I know the Hills would really appreciate it. And I don't know how this works, but will Captain Buckner be advised, or will you just use the sheriff's deputies for the raid?"

The DA asked Jim why he was concerned with Buckner and Jim diffused the question by stating, "I think Buckner and Reid are close friends."

The DA assured Jim it would be a county operation and anticipated Jim's next question, telling him they didn't have enough probable cause to get a judge to consent to a warrant against Smallwood. He told Jim, once Reid was arrested and they had access to his files, they may find out more about Smallwood.

TWENTY-FIVE

JIM WOKE up Friday morning after just a few hours' sleep, went directly to work, and walked into Audrey Hill's office. He updated her on the events of the night and early morning and she advised him to try and behave normally. After the morning news deadline had passed, she and her father wanted to visit with him about the planned coverage in Saturday morning's paper.

Trying to act normal was difficult. He called Mary every hour. At three, she told him the team was having a private meeting with the judge to finalize their evidence and recommendations. She promised to keep him informed and promised the DA would not raid the funeral home until after the visitations. She also asked that Jim and Audrey keep the DA's office informed of how they could be reached as final decisions were made about the raid.

At five o'clock, Jim, Bernard, Audrey, and Willy were visiting in Bernard's office when Mary walked in. "We have both warrants, an arrest for Reid and search warrants for both his house and his main funeral home. We will get warrants for his other places of business, but we feel most of the information is in the main office. DA Rogers told me, Jim, that you can go along on the raid, but you must stay far back of the officers. We presume you want a photographer to go, too, but he must stay in the background. We can't have any newspaper people barging in the front door when our officers do."

Willy squirmed in his chair but didn't ask any questions or raise objections.

Bernard turned to Jim and said he knew Jim would be disappointed, but he wanted his top police reporter to go along with the deputies and then write the story of the raid. "You can go, too, but before you do, I want your story detailing this whole sordid affair. We will lead with your story under the banner on page one. Art will get some pictures and we will place them on the front page along with the story on the raid. If Art gets enough, we can include more pictures and jump your story and the raid story to page three. Not sure when we will use Art's pictures of the casket exchange from the cemetery. Pretty invasive for the family so, I will have to give that a lot of thought.

"Mary has all the warrant information, so you can start writing it now. I want to see every word before it gets published. Write it tight. No opinion, just straight facts. If you have it written, and it is acceptable, I will let you go to the raid, but not until then. Understood?"

Excited beyond belief to write a page-one banner story, Jim said, "Yes, sir!"

At eight o'clock, Bernard and Audrey poured over Jim's draft, and with only a few changes for grammar and punctuation, they gave it their seal of approval.

Willy wrote the headline and sent the copy to the back

shop for it to be turned into type. Half an hour later, he brought a tear sheet to Bernard's office.

Casket Switching Scandal

By Jim Monaghan
News Tribune Staff Writer

A telephone call to the News Tribune Thursday, June 13, 1963, ignited a lightning-fast, week-long investigation by this newspaper and the Shelby County District Attorney's office resulting in the arrest of Alex Reid, owner and operator of the Reid Funeral Homes chain, Friday evening.

Reid was arrested late Friday at his home following a raid on his main funeral home, located at 101 Clover Crest Drive, and his home at County Club Estates.

The facts of the case are as follows. At eleven forty-five a.m., Thursday, June 13, Irene Dunn, former teacher at Washington Elementary School, called this reporter claiming her husband's casket had been switched prior to burial at the Calvary Cemetery.

Jim went on detailing his accounting of the week-long story.

Reading the tear sheet, Jim beamed, but then became noticeably sad. Bernard put his hand on Jim's shoulder and asked, "What's wrong? You wrote a great story?" Jim answered that he wished his parents could see the story. Mary embraced him, and the Hills comforted him, telling him his parents would be proud. Meanwhile, personally led by District Attorney George Rogers, the Shelby County deputies staged their raid at the Reid Funeral Homes and Reid's private residence.

The reporters who had been on the scene rushed into Bernard's office with their notes. "Steve Hampton let them in the door at the funeral home and led them into Reid's office. They had to break into Reid's desk and were successful in finding his ledger book. They also confiscated all the paperwork in his desk and locked file cabinets," the reporters noted and continued.

"But Reid was not so receptive at his residence. Reid opened his door and immediately yelled at the deputies. He threatened he would get them fired. He kept repeating how important he was, that he belonged to the country club, and that he was friends with the mayor and the district attorney.

"The officers ignored his rants. They told him he was under arrest for fraud and grand larceny. The officers searched throughout Reid's house. On a comical note, as they walked Reid to the patrol car, his wife asked him what time he would be home, reminding him they had a brunch at the club on Saturday."

After the reporters completed their briefing, Bernard told them to write their stories, and he personally supervised the editing and layout of pages one and three. When completed, he pulled Jim and Mary aside.

"When the paper comes out tomorrow, Jim, Reid and everyone will know of your involvement, and I have some concerns. I think it was a good decision to keep Mary's name out of the paper. But you and Irene are all over the front page. I think, perhaps, we should take some precautions."

Jim thanked Bernard for his concern but dismissed it. "Reid is a funeral home director, not the head of a criminal mob. I am not worried, but thanks for your concern."

"One week ago, Jim, you were in the cemetery and there was a gun on the back of your neck. That is a serious situation. But, ok, let's sleep on it and see how Reid responds and how the community reacts."

TWENTY-SIX

MARY AND JIM stopped by the Shelby County Jail to check with the deputies to see how Reid reacted to being incarcerated following his arrest.

The front desk was teeming with attorneys. Reid's attorney had brought in a team of high-profile defense attorneys from Columbus, who kept harassing the deputy officer about an arraignment, so their client could be released on bond. But the deputy said the courthouse was closed for the weekend and the earliest an arraignment could be held was on Monday. The attorneys kept up the pressure, implying they could get an emergency hearing in Columbus. The deputy quipped, "We're in Lincoln, not Columbus."

After a few hours of chaos, Rogers's chief prosecutor walked in and told the attorneys to quit bothering the deputy. He told them the arraignment was set for ten a.m. on Monday and nothing was going to change that. They could visit with their client as much as they wanted, but the arraignment was not going to change.

An officer who worked the night shift at the jail, and knew Mary, walked over grinning. "Your prisoner was quite a problem last night. He came in kicking and screaming, and the first thing he wanted was to make a phone call. He called his attorney and then called someone who he called Mr. Chairman or something like that. Funny thing, when he was talking to the attorneys, he was yelling and screaming, but when he was talking to this chairman, he was soft spoken. He kept saying he was sorry. He also kept saying, I don't know, to apparent questions he was getting.

"One thing for sure, Monaghan, he doesn't think much of you. He mentioned your name to this chairman fellow many times. Not sure what it meant, but I thought you would want to know."

Jim asked, "I thought they only get one phone call?"

"That's the normal procedure," replied the officer, "but the Sheriff said to cut him some slack. I'm guessing because he has so many friends and there'll be a lot of eyes on this case."

Mary reached for Jim's hand. At lunch, they avoided discussing the deputy's comments, although both were bothered by the implications. Rather, they chose to talk about planning a trip to Chicago to meet Mary's parents.

TWENTY-SEVEN

JIM ARRIVED at the courthouse early Monday morning, briefly had a cup of coffee with Mary, embraced her, and wished her luck.

"It's only an arraignment, Jim. Nothing exciting is going to happen."

Saving a seat for Irene, Jim sat behind the DA's team. Courtroom A-1 was packed. *Not surprising,* Jim thought, *that there is standing room only for the arraignment of one of Lincoln's most prominent citizens.*

Irene joined Jim and the crowd hushed when Reid, hands handcuffed behind his back, was escorted into the courtroom between two sheriff's deputies, who were tightly grasping his arms. Jim tried to make eye contact with Reid, but Reid stared straight ahead. *No fancy suit, this time,* Jim smirked at the ill-fitting, jail-issue denim Reid wore.

The packed courtroom stilled when the judge gaveled the arraignment to order. The silence of the crowd was pierced by the shout of an elderly man. "Hey, Reid, where is my wife's casket, Asshole!" The yell broke the ice, and the room reverberated with cat calls and ugly accusations.

Reid's posture stiffened, but he did not turn around. The judge again gaveled the crowd to silence and said he would brook no more outbursts in his courtroom.

Reid's five attorneys were a perfect tableau of confident, expensively-dressed successful professionals. They listened intently and took notes as the judge read the charges.

Asked how he pled, Reid murmured, "Not guilty." The judge asked him again and Reid, scowling, spoke loudly, "Not guilty."

Citing the fact that this was Reid's first offense, the judge ordered him released if he posted a ten-thousand-dollar bond. The DA leapt to his feet, objecting, saying the seriousness of the crime demanded a higher bail. The judge asked if the DA considered Reid a flight risk. "Probably not," he had to admit. The judge overruled the DA's objection.

Jim and a horde of reporters, including TV reporters from Columbus, waited outside the courtroom for Reid. But he never walked out. Mary stopped by and told Jim that Reid was taken back to the county jail and he would post bail there, complete some paperwork, and then be released. She estimated it would take about an hour and a half. After waiting for half an hour, most of the media contingent went on to other assignments.

Jim found the perfect spot to observe the parking lot and planned to interrupt Reid's walk to his car. After almost two hours, Jim noticed a group of deputies escorting Reid to his car where his attorneys were waiting in the parking lot east of the county jail. Reid shook hands with his departing attorneys and stood alone by his car. Jim decided to make his move to interview him but stopped when he saw a Lincoln City police car pull into the parking lot. It came to a stop right beside Reid and it was followed by a pickup truck.

Captain Buckner exited the police car and shook hands with Reid. Buckner put his hands-on Reid's shoulders as if he were comforting him. The truck stopped behind Buckner's squad car and Reverend Smallwood got out of the passenger side. The same small man Jim had seen after church on Sunday got out on the driver's side. The four men engaged in what appeared to be a vigorous discussion.

Buckner looked up and over toward Jim, who ducked behind a tree before Buckner could make eye contact. Unsure if Buckner saw him, Jim turned to slip away, but his eye was drawn to a decal on the truck.

That's the same emblem on those pickups that were near Irene Dunn's home, Jim thought, and remembered Bernard Hill's advice. *This isn't just a corrupt funeral director.*

Jim went back to the courthouse for the next phase, the order by the judge to open the graves. It was a short hearing, as the judge had read the pleadings in advance in chambers and knew what the DA wanted. With the order in hand, the DA said he would assemble the professionals he needed and would meet everyone at ten a.m. Tuesday at Calvary Cemetery. He also said he would personally call the families.

TWENTY-EIGHT

IT WAS a somber group that met at the gravesite of Patrick Dunn. Irene was joined by Sgt. Major Harlow and a contingent from the American Legion. Judge McCallister and the Brennan Family were also in attendance, as was the family whose burial was photographed by Wilks.

Jim, Wilks, and Audrey were the only media members at the site. The DA urged the families to stay away from the gravesite as the result of the dig could be very disturbing. He pleaded with Irene to stay back.

"Irene, yours is the first grave. I beg you not to watch."

"I have the Sgt. Major with me. I will be all right. I want to see everything."

Initially, a mechanical hoe pulled the dirt away and then two men shoveled out the hole until they reached the top of the vault. Carefully sweeping dirt from the top of the vault, they called for the hydraulic lift cables to be dropped into the grave. Attaching them to the top of the vault, they slowly lifted the top above the burial site.

As the vault top ascended, Jim and the DA were the first to peer in. Before they could stop her, Irene was at the precipice and looked down. Without emotion, she said, "That's exactly what I saw on the day Patrick was buried." And, clinging tightly on the arm of the Sgt. Major, she walked away.

After taking Irene to her car, Harlow walked back to Monaghan and the DA. "You don't have to worry about spending the taxpayers' money to prosecute Reid. The boys from the Legion and I will take care of him."

"No, you won't, Sgt. Major. You leave this to us because, I swear to God, if one hair on Reid's hair is mussed, I am coming after you," the DA warned. Jim told his friend the best thing he and his fellow legionnaires could do was to comfort and take care of Irene.

The professionals lowered the vault top back into the grave and prepared to move on to the Brennan gravesite.

The Brenan's, Judge McAllister, and the other family met with the DA and told him they'd decided to wait near their cars and he could tell them all together what he'd found.

Led by the judge, the families discussed what they could do. The judge told them he was certain a lawsuit was in order and he would get the best plaintiff's attorney in Ohio to help them.

After an hour, Jim and the DA came to the families and told them all their loved ones were buried in pine boxes. The DA told them he was going directly to Reid's Funeral Home and demand the bodies be placed in proper caskets and reburied.

Art Wilks shot pictures of the pine boxes in the vaults. Wilks took other pictures, too, as he thought Bernard might not publish the pine boxes.

He was wrong.

TWENTY-NINE

Caskets Swapped for Pine Boxes

By Jim Monaghan
News Tribune Staff Writer

WITH GRIEVING FAMILIES WATCHING, **four graves were dug up and the bodies exhumed at Calvary Cemetery by the Shelby County District Attorney's office Tuesday morning.**

Much to their horror, the families found their loved ones, who were to have been buried in expensive copper caskets were, in fact, buried in pine coffins. This ghastly operation is part of the ongoing investigation into the Alex Reid Funeral Home scandal, which resulted in Reid's arrest late Friday evening.

Reid pled not guilty Monday morning and was released on bail. When confronted by the Shelby County DA, he said he didn't know

anything about what the authorities found in the cemetery. "It must have been the grave diggers," he told the DA. "But out of public service, I will replace the pine boxes with the appropriate caskets."

The DA told the News Tribune he would station a deputy at the gravesites and at Reid's Funeral Home to make sure all the bodies will be reburied by sundown Tuesday evening. The DA reported all were.

"Two PAGE-ONE BANNER stories in one week," Jim told Mary. "Now, I know what it's like to be a big-time reporter, but Willy still has me working on the obituary desk.".

After a leisurely dinner, Jim and Mary found themselves driving by the Lincoln Country Club. On a hunch, Jim decided to drive past Reid's house, which backed onto the twelfth hole at the country club. Jim turned onto Reid's street, but hit the brakes when he saw a Lincoln City Police car parked in front of Reid's house. Right behind the police car was a pickup truck with an emblem on the driver's side of an Eagle clutching a rifle.

Jim slammed the truck into reverse. "We've got to find out who owns that pickup. I think there is more to this story than just Reid. I hope your team is really investigating Reid's records. A big-time reporter from the New York Times once told our investigative journalism class that, in white collar crimes, follow the money. After your team looks at those books, I want to look at them, too."

THIRTY

FOR ALMOST TWO MONTHS, Reid's defense team and the DA's office worked feverishly, preparing for the trial of the decade in Shelby County.

Jim and Mary's time together was limited as she worked tirelessly on the case. Jim's work on the obit desk continued with occasional staff writing assignments.

The top assistant prosecutor prepped Jim on his testimony since he was going to be called as one of the early witnesses. Jim was unpleasantly surprised when Mary told him Reid's defense attorney wanted to interview him prior to trial. This was not routine, Mary said, and someone, not her, from the DA's office would accompany him to the interview with Reid's attorney. "My boss is making an exception because of Reid's prominence. You are the only witness they asked to interview and the DA gave his approval. All of us disagree, but he is the boss."

"This is bullshit, I don't want to talk to Reid's attorneys. Screw them," Jim said. Mary laughed. "You don't have a choice. We must give Reid's attorneys all our work, including statements and the tape from Hampton. All the statements we have will go out to them in the morning. They know you are going to be a witness, and they have asked for you. You should expect a call from them in the next few days."

"We need to get Hampton out of there," Jim urged. "Have you talked to your boss about him? Once Reid knows Steve was one of our primary sources, he will go after him. I worry about his safety. Please talk to your boss tomorrow morning."

Mary said, "Of course! I'm embarrassed I hadn't thought of Steve's plight still working for Reid."

Just as Mary said, Jim was called by Reid's defense team and was told he was to be at their office at nine a.m. two days hence. Jim objected, saying he was part of putting a paper out in the morning and he would be available in the afternoon. The snarly attorney told him he didn't care. Jim was to be in their office at nine.

Jim was surprised, when he walked into the attorney's conference room, that he was going to be interviewed not by one, but by three defense attorneys. Sitting in the middle of the trio was, Wilber T. Waters, the most prominent defense attorney in Ohio. He had represented high profile clients throughout the Midwest and boasted none of his clients had ever gone to jail, or at least not spent much time in jail.

As Jim sat down, the lead attorney smiled confidently and asked Jim if he planned to submit his newspaper articles to the Pulitzer committee for award-winning newspaper reporting. Shaken by the question, Jim answered that decision was above his pay-grade.

The interview began with the attorneys questioning Jim about his relationship with Mary Ryan. They asked if he was sleeping with her and how many times they were intimate. The Assistant DA objected repeatedly, and Jim's anger intensified with each question. Then, without explanation, they switched to questions about his time in the cemetery and how did he know it was a gun at the back of his neck? Had he ever had a gun at the back of his head? How would he know if it was a gun or not?

Jim realized they were beginning to tie him in knots. He had to admit he never knew for certain, had a gun at the back of his head but he had assumed that it was a gun.

"So, everything you told the DA about your time in the cemetery is just an assumption, and not based on fact, correct?"

"No! I know what I saw, and when we dug up the grave, there was a pine box in the vault. I didn't assume anything other than that I thought it was a gun at the back of my head. It felt like what I thought a gun would feel like and the guy threatened to blow a hole in my head."

After the interview, Jim stopped at O'Toole's, talked to Stavros, drank a couple of Bushmills, and headed over to Mary's.

Since that fateful Friday in June, when Jim and Mary had first met, they had begun to steal every possible moment to be together. When they were not working professionally on the Reid case, they would sit at the quadrangle at Hamilton University and hold hands, or they would go to a concert, a movie, or a play at the University. Most often, they met at Harlow's Café, drank coffee, and talked.

Soon, it became almost daily meetings, if just for a cup of coffee or a glass of wine for Mary and Bushmills for Jim.

Their physical relationship began to evolve and while they never talked about it, they both knew the direction they were heading.

Jim picked Mary up and they went to the nicest restaurant in town. There Jim told Mary about the interview and how uncomfortable he was. He told her he admitted he didn't know for sure about the gun at the back of his head but was certain on his other testimony. Mary suggested one of the deputies could put a gun to the back of his head and he could compare the feelings. Jim told her he didn't want to talk any more about the trial. He had something more important he wanted to tell her.

Mary knew what he was going to say. Sitting on the loveseat in her modest condo, Jim told her he was in love with her. Mary wrapped her arms around him and said she loved him as well.

After giving it more thought than she'd imagined, she invited Jim over for dinner on Sunday, August 11th, Jim's birthday. Mary wanted the evening to be perfect because she knew the road she and Jim were going down was very serious.

Mary was unusual in 1963 for a twenty-four-year-old young woman. She was a virgin. She had heard stories about the first time, but she, for sure, wasn't going to talk to her mother about it, and the women at work would be of no help. She was not embarrassed about being a virgin. She had never loved anyone before and, in fact, had never dated anyone seriously.

But she knew she loved Jim Monaghan, and he loved her, and Sunday night was going to be the night. And it was.

Jim and Mary woke up early Monday, hugged, told one another they loved each other, and left for work feeling happy knowing their future was truly bright. Jim promised that when the trial was over, they would go to Chicago and meet her parents.

THIRTY-ONE

As THE TRIAL DATE APPROACHED, Jim found himself spending more time at the DA's office than at the newspaper. Just about every afternoon, he was there being put through his testimony again and again. He took the opportunity to study the Reid financials, but he was never good with numbers and, after an hour or so, his eyes glazed over.

Someone who knows what they are doing needs to do this, he thought.

At lunch, Jim asked Mary and the DA where they had hidden Hampton. The DA smiled and said, "If an investigative reporter can't find him, then I feel he is secure. We got him out of Reid's Funeral Home and out of his apartment just in time.

"I am beginning to pick up chatter from the deputies in the jail that Reid is more than just a funeral director; he is a dangerous man. Jim, I am going to urge you to be careful."

"You know, Bernard said that earlier, but I just can't take it seriously. For goodness sake, he is a funeral director, not a crime lord."

Neither the DA nor Mary responded. Mary finally said, "Jim and I will be careful, boss."

Having a rare free afternoon, Jim drove over to check up on Irene. His head snapped when he saw Steve Hampton coming out of the kitchen. "Want a piece of pie, Jim? It's fresh out of the oven." Jim laughed. "Well, hiding in plain sight. Who would have thought you would be hiding here?"

"Steve and I are getting along famously. We sneak him out at night sometimes, but mostly we watch the soaps and cook. It's been great for both of us. Steve is an excellent cook and has some recipes that are just sensational. When that nasty Reid is put behind bars, I am going to talk to the Sgt. Major about hiring Steve as a cook and sprucing up that menu at Harlow's Café."

Jim just smiled at the turn of events. "Steve, I have a question for you. There is a short thin guy, I see around Reid, Buckner, and Smallwood. He drives a pickup truck with an emblem of an eagle grasping on a rifle. Do you know him?"

Steve's face darkened. "He is a very dangerous man, but I don't know his name. I do know Reid is terrified of him. Don't mess with him, Jim."

"He can't be that dangerous, Steve, c'mon. This is Shelby County, Ohio, not some crime capital. Are you sure you don't know him?"

"No, I don't, Jim, and please don't try to find out who he is!"

Jim changed the subject. "Mary told me Reid's attorneys offered, in exchange for a deal, that Reid would testify that Smallwood was the force behind selling the copper caskets. The DA interviewed Smallwood, who told them he got a commission on the caskets but didn't know anything about the switching of them. The DA is going to indict him as a co-conspirator anyway. It's going to be fun watching the rats turn on one another."

THIRTY-TWO

THE WEEK BEFORE THE TRIAL, Jim became apprehensive when Willy told him the Hills wanted him in their office in an hour. Mary was scheduled to pick him up at the office at four o'clock because his truck was on the fritz again so, prior to the meeting, he asked the receptionist to direct Mary to the Hills' office.

Bernard told Willy and Jim that he didn't want Jim covering any more of the Reid trial, because Jim was a major witness. He advised them that he wanted the regular court-house reporters to cover the trial. Perhaps Jim could write a column about what it was like being a witness in a high-profile case, but he wanted to think about it and asked Willy and Jim to do the same.

For the next hour, they discussed the ins and outs of the case and were finishing up when Mary walked into the meeting. She gave the group the latest from the DA's office, saying that Smallwood shook every time they interviewed him. "We are certain he is going to plead to a lesser charge and we hope we can turn him against Reid, but that's still in progress, so let's keep it amongst ourselves, ok?"

Art Wilks entered and said, "You all better sit down. I have shocking news. The Lincoln Police Department received a call from a jogger in Crystal Park. They found Steve Hampton's body about two hours ago near the lake. He had a gunshot wound to the head and a gun in his hand. Looks like he'd been dead ten to twelve hours. And get this, he left a suicide note, and I have a copy of it.

Art passed it around for all to see.

I AM SO SORRY. I am in such pain. I have lied to people about Mr. Reid and his wonderful funeral home. I am so sorry. I am a loser and I am miserable. I am taking the path that will ease my pain. Again, Mr. Reid please accept my apologies if I have caused you any problems. I am sorry. I can't live this way any longer. Please cremate me. Don't bury me in the cruel earth.

Steve Hampton

THE FIRST TO SPEAK WAS MARY. "THAT's not his signature. I have been working with his notes and ledgers, and I can tell you that's not his handwriting."

"It's impossible," Jim said, "I visited with him the other day. He was fine. His spirits were great. We talked about his cooking, and Irene was going to help him get a job at Harlow's Café when the trial is over. He didn't commit suicide. Someone murdered him. We need to check on Irene right away."

Audrey offered to call her and left the room. Mary told

the group she had to call her boss and report Steve's death. "I won't call it a suicide."

Audrey came back five minutes later, saying Irene was fine but she was worried about Steve. "We'll have to tell her," Audrey said, "before she hears it from someone else."

Mary returned, red-faced, and reported the DA wanted Jim and Irene to have security until the trial. Then, crying, she embraced Jim.

Finally, Bernard spoke, "I agree with DA Rogers. Jim, you need to stay out of sight. Maybe the Ramada Inn at the edge of town. I will make your reservation, and the newspaper will take care of the charges. I will call George and ask for a deputy to check in on you during the night. Then tomorrow we will all meet again and plan something more permanent. Why don't you two," looking at Jim and Mary, who were holding hands, "go get some dinner?"

THIRTY-THREE

At DINNER, to keep from thinking about Hampton or the DA's concern, Jim and Mary talked about themselves and their future. They made plans for Jim to meet Mary's parents.

"Mom will love you, and Dad will probably pull the Chicago Police Captain attitude on you, but he really is a teddy bear."

Startled, Jim looked up to see a smiling Willy approaching their table. "Hey, your garage delivered your truck and parked it in the sports editor's spot. Good thing he wasn't there because he really gets ticked when people park in his spot. Anyway, thought you would want to know. I knew you needed your truck to get to the Ramada. Hey, you kids have a great dinner."

That's the last thing I expected from Willy, Jim thought. *He is never thoughtful or polite, and I can't remember him smiling, at least not at me.*

As they walked toward the newspaper parking lot, Mary looked up at Jim and said, "You know I am not going to let you go to the hotel alone, don't you? Why don't we take my car? We can go together, and you can take me to work in the morning."

"No, I have to move my truck out of the sports editor's spot and your car is secure where it is parked. Besides, you tell me you love riding in my truck," Jim joked.

They drove to the Ramada Inn. Mary was sitting as close to Jim as she could. She told him she loved him, and they would have a great life together. Jim replied that he loved her, and he was the happiest he could ever remember.

Entering a darkened intersection, Jim noticed a pickup truck barreling down from his left. He had time only to yell to Mary to hold on. The truck smashed into the driver's side door, propelling Jim's truck into a utility pole which snapped in two from the force. As if from a far distance, he heard tires squeal and race away.

Jim tried to move but was pinned beneath the steering wheel. Before he lost consciousness, he looked for Mary, who had been sitting close to him. All he saw was a jagged, gaping hole in the windshield. He cried, "No! No!" before he slipped into the darkness.

Police cars, fire trucks, and an ambulance raced to the scene. Using the jaws-of- life-tool, firefighters cut the crumpled door to get Jim out of the truck and rushed him, by ambulance, to Mercy Hospital. His truck was practically wrapped around the remnants of the pole. A fireman, inspecting the outer perimeter of the accident, yelled out for a gurney when he found Mary's nearly lifeless, broken body.

By the time the ambulance got Jim to Mercy, he had regained consciousness and the triage unit in the emergency room quickly treated him for trauma, lacerations of the face, and significant bruising around the torso. After a series of xrays of his head and chest and other examinations, they classified him as not seriously injured.

The second ambulance bringing Mary brought an altogether different reaction.

Mary's mangled body brought the entire triage team together and they rushed her to the emergency operating room where a team of surgeons immediately went to work on her injuries.

Jim was conscious and asking about Mary while being treated and observed by the nurses for the typical concussion protocol. He was getting frustrated because no one would tell him anything.

Sister Mary Mark, Mercy's Administrator, completed her evening walk through the hospital, ending at the emergency room, usually a hot bed of activity on a Saturday night.

The head nurse reported it was relatively calm other than a very bad accident. One of the victims was in surgery with multiple injuries while the other was in the emergency room creating a disturbance. She said a sheriff's deputy told her one of the victims was a deputy district attorney and the other was a reporter for the Lincoln News Tribune. Sister walked into the emergency room and quickly observed Jim, who was trying to get off his gurney, but was being restrained by the orderlies.

"I want to know where Mary Ryan is. I want to know how she is doing!" Jim yelled as he was being restrained. One of the ER doctors told Sister he was giving Jim a mild sedative to calm him down as he needed to rest and be observed. The ER staff briefed Sister on Mary's condition.

Audrey Hill was a hospital board member, so Sister immediately called her. She told Audrey about Jim Monaghan's condition and that of Mary Ryan. Audrey asked Sister Mary Mark to tell the sheriff's deputy to call the DA, and she and her father raced to the hospital.

Dr. Andrew Cunningham, Mercy's Chief of Surgery, who, with a team of top surgeons, had been frantically working in the Emergency Room and the surgery unit, briefed Bernard, Audrey, and the DA. "Monaghan will be ok. He has suffered some trauma, but he doesn't have any broken bones, nor does he appear to have a concussion. From what we hear about the accident, Monaghan was very lucky.

"Mary Ryan, though, is in extremely critical condition.

"She went through the windshield and her face was severely lacerated. She has lost one eye, but her head trauma has us most concerned. Plus, most of her ribs were fractured and she sustained massive internal injuries. She is out of surgery, but we have her on life support."

After hearing the morbid news, the DA went to Sister Mary Mark's office, called Mary's family in Chicago, and broke the news. They told the DA they would be there as fast as they could.

In the waiting room, a suspicious Audrey suggested the DA send a deputy or Lincoln police officer to Irene Dunn's home to check on her. Bernard suggested the police take Irene to a hotel room for her own safety. The DA agreed. He called the Lincoln Police Department and was told that they would be sure Irene was ok. An hour later, Captain Buckner called the DA. He said his officers had to force their way into Dunn's home and found her at the bottom of the stairs where she had obviously fallen. The ambulance crew and firemen said she had a broken neck.

THIRTY-FOUR

AT MERCY HOSPITAL, doctors and nurses closely monitored Mary, as friends kept a tearful vigil. Jim was released and was pacing the floor.

Mary's family made the six-hour drive from the south side of Chicago to Lincoln in record time. The hospital receptionist had been alerted to look out for Mary's family and she immediately escorted them to the intensive care waiting room. Audrey, who had been at the hospital all night, greeted them and dispatched Sister Mary Mark to summon Dr. Cunningham.

Cunningham told them Mary was in the intensive care unit on a ventilator and other life support. He told them that Mary had suffered cerebral hypoxia, a shortage of oxygen to the brain, and she undoubtedly suffered significant brain damage. He told the family that Mary was put on life support upon her arrival at the hospital and while she was in surgery for several hours, with the best surgeons available working on her, her broken body just could not be repaired. Without life support, Cunningham said, the consensus of the medical staff was they did not expect her to survive. Mary's father was stoic. His lips were drawn in a straight line, but the clenching and unclenching of his fists betrayed his emotions. Mary's mother collapsed into the arms of her son and Mary's sisters' sobs echoed loudly.

"We need a priest, and we want to see our daughter," her father said, blinking back tears.

As Mary's family waited for the priest, her mother noticed a tall young man standing in front of the gathered group of friends who had greeted them when they arrived at the hospital. She had not seen the young man before, but seeing his face, contorted with grief, lacerations on his face, wearing a blood-stained shirt, tears streaming down his face, she knew who it was.

"You must be Jim Monaghan," she said as she walked toward him, arms outstretched. Jim walked tentatively toward her, took her in his arms, and sobbed, telling her that he loved Mary and he was so sorry.

That evening, Jim joined the family that surrounded Mary and said the prayers of the last rites with the hospital chaplain.

The next day the doctors removed the life support equipment. With her mother and father holding one of her hands, Jim holding the other, her brother and sisters tearfully praying, Mary Ryan slipped from life into death.

THIRTY-FIVE

By ANY STANDARDS, even Chicago's, Mary Ryan's funeral was huge. All three Chicago newspapers ran stories about the young attorney from Chicago and University of Chicago graduate who had spearheaded an investigation into a corrupt funeral home operation that switched caskets. The stories made her an instant heroine.

The Cardinal of the Chicago Archdiocese insisted he preside over the funeral, and the Chicago Police Department, out of respect for her father, lined the streets. Jim, Judge McCallister, Bernard, his wife, Audrey, and DA Rogers were present. The Donnellan Funeral Home oversaw the arrangements, and Mary was buried in a simple casket. Mary's parents insisted Jim walk with the family at the funeral, but he declined. He sat with the Hills in the back of the church, but his sobs were heard throughout the service.

Jim and the Lincoln contingent stayed at St. Joseph's Cemetery after Mary's family left. Jim watched Mary's casket being lowered into the ground.

The burial crew were hesitant to fill the site up as they

watched Jim shake with grief while peering down into the grave.

Judge McCallister stepped up and stood beside Jim.

"Jim, the Jewish religion has a tradition which I really like. Once the casket is placed in the ground, those that loved the deceased take a handful of dirt and toss it on the casket. It is part of their tradition called levaya, a final act of kindness. If you don't mind, I am going to do that."

Jim nodded his assent and the judge walked over to the mound of dirt and tossed a handful into the site. He was followed by Bernard, his wife, the DA, and Audrey.

Jim walked unsteadily to the mound, peered down at the casket, and tossed his handful of dirt in. He then collapsed into Audrey's arms.

Bowing to Jim's wishes, the group did not go to the Ryan family home but drove back to Lincoln. Before they left, Audrey called Mary's mother explaining that Jim just couldn't go.

THIRTY-SIX

OVER THE FIERCEST objections of Reid's attorneys, the DA had convinced the judge to postpone the trial due to the deaths of Mary Ryan, Steve Hampton and Irene Dunn. Reid's attorneys said they were ready for trial and the DA should be, too. But the judge disagreed, and on Tuesday morning, at nine a.m., a packed courtroom prepared for the most important trial in years in Lincoln.

After opening arguments, Jim took the stand. His blue sport coat hung on his now slight frame. His face was gaunt and pale. Despite efforts of the Hills and Harlow to get him to eat, he had no appetite. Often, he opted to drink his lunch. Gazing down at his glass at O'Toole's, Jim usually met Stavros's attempts to communicate with a vacant, mournful stare.

The DA slowly and meticulously took Jim through the series of events from the first phone call from Irene Dunn earlier in June. During his testimony, Jim broke down numerous times.

Despite interruptions and vociferous objections from

Reid's attorney, Jim completed his halting, painful testimony.

He told of his experience in the cemetery and while Reid's attorney objected, the judge silenced him, telling him his objection was overruled and he, the judge, wanted to hear the testimony.

After the DA finished his three hours of questions, the judge called a recess for lunch. As Jim walked off the stand, he looked at the jury, many of whom had tears in their eyes.

When court reconvened, Reid's attorney challenged all of Jim's testimony. He strode back and forth in front of the jury and at one point, slammed his hand on the bannister in front of where Jim was sitting and yelled, "It is all hearsay. There are no facts here."

Jim's composure stayed intact during the afternoon session, until the end, when Reid's attorney preened. "I have just one more question for you, Mr. Newspaper Man. Isn't most of this story simply an attempt by you to get banner headlines for your newspaper, win Pulitzer prizes, and impress a woman you were dating?"

Jim sprang from the witness chair, but before he could reach the attorney, the bailiffs restrained him.

"No more questions, your honor," the attorney said as he walked back and sat beside a smiling Alex Reid.

THIRTY-SEVEN

By mid-September the closing arguments of the trial of the year concluded at noon, and the jury retired to consider a verdict in the case of the State of Ohio versus Alex Reid.

Jim was visiting with the Hills, Mary's family, and Judge McCallister when another assistant DA came up and told them Reverend Smallwood had pled down to theft and had been sentenced to four years. Smallwood had also met with the head trustee of First Baptist and had been fired.

By four thirty, the jury signaled the judge that they had a verdict and the crowd gathered again with standing room only in the courtroom. Jim sat with McCallister, the Hills, and Mary's family as the judge read the verdict. Jim was sitting directly behind the district attorney. His location placed him within twenty feet of Reid, who looked over and scowled.

As the judge began to read the verdict, Jim thought of Mary and how it had to be Reid and his people who'd smashed into his truck. But there was no evidence. No one could find the truck that hit him. He was also certain that

Irene had not fallen down the stairs and that Hampton had not killed himself.

The judge intoned guilty on all counts and sentenced Reid to seven years in the state penitentiary. Reid loudly protested, and his attorneys shouted they would appeal.

Incensed over the short sentence and thoughts of Mary, Jim vaulted over the barrier that divided the courtroom and leapt toward Reid. Just as he was about to pounce on Reid, he felt stronger arms grab him from behind. It was Mary's father who told him, "That scum isn't worth it."

After a tearful goodbye to Mary's family, Jim went to O'Toole's and drank all night. In fact, he slept in the back booth.

THIRTY-EIGHT

Almost a month later, Jim was back at work doing general reporting, but he wasn't the same.

His story on Reid and the casket scandal was a finalist in the AP Investigative News Award, but he didn't care. His straggly hair had not been cut for weeks and it appeared it had not been washed either. His overall appearance deteriorated with each passing week. He wore the same Cincinnati Reds sweatshirt and his blue jeans appeared to be so dirty, they could stand on their own. His friends and colleagues were worried about him. They knew he was fragile and yet they were reluctant to say anything to him. They all handled him with kid gloves. He never smiled and never made small talk.

Jim was bored with his stories. One was about a retired teacher who fixed clocks, and another was about the opening of a new fishing equipment store. But what nearly pushed him over the edge was a story about the owner of one of the downtown stores who built a parking garage that had three levels. He knew he was wasting his time. Immediately after work, and often at lunch he went to O'Toole's.

Stavros, the bartender, tried to engage Jim but he never talked, just sat on a barstool and stared at his drink. As October moved on, Jim finally felt the need to drive to Chicago. He drove directly to Mary's grave. On his knees, crying, he felt a gentle hand on his shoulder.

"How are you doing, Jim?" a soft voice inquired. Jim turned to Mary's mother.

They embraced and wept together. Mary's mother invited him to her home for dinner where the entire family welcomed him. He called the paper the next day and told them he would not be in for a few days. No one minded.

Jim spent almost a week with Mary's family, visiting her neighborhood, and meeting with friends she'd grown up with. He cried himself to sleep every night, dreaming what could have been.

On the fifth day, Mary's father took Jim for a walk.

"Listen to me, young man," her father said, his Irish brogue almost too thick to understand. "I know you loved my daughter and she loved you. Now what do you think she would think of you moping around here? She would tell you to get off your ass and go back to work. Life goes on. Sometimes it's hard, and this is hard. We all miss Mary and we always will, but you must go on, Jim."

Jim hugged Mary's father, and with tears in his eyes, said, "I know you are right. She would kick me in the butt if she were here."

THIRTY-NINE

EARLY FRIDAY MORNING, Jim noticed he'd been getting to work earlier and that he felt better after having his hair cut the day before. He hoped his story assignments would be more challenging than his recent ones but was floored when Willy told him they were short on the obit desk and asked if he could help.

Jim moved to the obit desk and put on his head set. He put on a good face but knew his time at the News Tribune was limited. *Maybe at the end of the year I will quit and join the Marines*, he mused. It was a slow day on the obit desk, located next to the AP and UPI wire machines. Jim heard the AP wire bell ring, meaning an important story was coming. He checked the AP tape and to his immense surprise, he read "The Associated Press Editorial Board has named Jim Monaghan of the Lincoln News Tribune the winner of the AP Investigative News Award." Jim tore off the sheet of copy and strutted back into the newsroom. He shouted, "Hey, everybody!"

Everyone fell silent, aware of how fragile Jim had been. But he smiled for the first time since Mary had died and announced, "I just won the AP Award." The entire news-room broke into applause and staffers hugged and congratu-lated him. Bernard and Audrey showed up with bottles of champagne, much to Willy's chagrin, who kept yelling, "We have a newspaper to get out. Back to work!"

Audrey, having grown to view Jim as the brother she'd never had, gave him an extra hug and told him Mary would be so proud of him. Blinking back tears, Jim nodded. Then the obit phone rang, and it was back to reality.

After the first edition was put to bed, Jim gave the other obit writer time off and said he would cover the desk for the next edition. This gave him a chance to read the stories on Pete Rose and the Reds.

Engrossed in the paper, Jim was jarred by the incessant ringing of the AP and UPI wire machines. Willy shouted, "Hey, Monaghan, see what the hell the wires are saying. Maybe you won another prize."

Jim looked at the UPI tape and gasped in shock and anguish.

Dallas, TX UPI 12:34 CST
President Kennedy Shot

FORTY

SATURDAY MORNING, the newsroom was chaotic. People scurried around helping one another as the JFK assassination story affected everything in the newsroom. Audrey tapped Jim on the shoulder and said her father needed to talk to him.

Jim walked into Bernard's office and was surprised to see the publisher counting out hundred-dollar bills on his desk. "Sit down, Jim. I have decided we need a reporter at the Kennedy funeral, and I have decided it is going to be you. I have talked to the UPI office and they will host you in downtown DC and get you press credentials. You will stay at the Hay Adams hotel close to the White House. Here is some money for food. Your hotel is paid for. Stay for a few days after the funeral and write human interest stories. Talk to people and get their impressions of what it was like to be at the funeral. Interview our congressional delegation and get their reactions. Then just file the stories from the UPI office. They will take care of you. Now, go home and pack. There is a flight for DC leaving Columbus at four thirty p.m. and here is your ticket.

"Do us proud, young man."

For the first time, in a long time, Jim thought about the days ahead, not the days past.

FORTY-ONE

Christmas, 1963

Jim Monaghan stared at the barrel of a 22-caliber Browning pistol.

It had been his father's.

He placed his wet, clammy hand on the engraved walnut grip, held the gun under his chin, and tilted it upwards. Putting his thumb on the trigger, he believed he was ready. Ready to end his life and join his beloved Mary and his parents in death. He started to cry, and the gun shook from side to side.

He thought of his parents, who died in an auto accident five-years ago. He thought of Mary Ryan, the love of his life, who died, only four months previously. They were riding in Jim's truck after a romantic dinner where they planned their future together.

He could see them all in his mind, but was troubled, because they were not smiling. *I am coming to be with you,* Jim said out loud. But they never smiled.

Jim's hand shook, and he placed the gun on his lap. He

thought he would find courage if he prayed, but his heart was so heavy, he couldn't. He turned to the side table and looked at the bottle of Bushmills. There was enough left for one good swallow. He drank it and flung the bottle against the wall where it shattered, spraying glass in all directions.

He thought of the past few days.

Everything was a blur since the previous Friday. It was his last day of work before his vacation. He wasn't sure he wanted to go back to be a general assignment reporter and obituary writer for the Lincoln News Tribune, a medium size newspaper in Lincoln, Ohio. Lincoln, a city of 100,000, was located 30 miles north of Columbus.

The distraction of covering the John F. Kennedy funeral in November began to evaporate about a week after he got back. More than a distraction, he enjoyed it despite his grief. He loved filing stories from the nation's capital, rubbing elbows with storied journalists like Merriman Smith, and even meeting Pierre Salinger, JFK's press secretary in a bar late one evening. Interviewing the two Ohio Senators and the Ohio Congressional delegation in the House of Representatives went smoothly. The UPI Washington Bureau chief even had a brief discussion with Jim about his possible interest in relocating to the DC office.

Back in Lincoln, Jim ended every evening drinking at O'Toole's, a local bar, and with every drink his depression deepened. He talked only to Stavros, the owner and bartender.

As the days had ticked towards Christmas, Jim's depression seeped out of his skin. He wore it on his face. He could not fake small talk and stopped caring about his appearance and then, his job. Arriving later and later to work, he began to draw the ire of Zack "Willy" Williams, the longtime city editor of the News Tribune. Jim took Willy's criticism without saying a word in return. His stringy hair was never combed and had not been washed in days. He wore the same dirty shirt and pants every day.

Willy pulled Jim into the small conference room, adjacent to the city room, and told him his days were numbered at the paper.

"I know you have a special relationship with the publisher and his daughter, but this shit of you coming in late and writing sloppy stories has to stop. When is the last time you took a shower? People don't want to be around you, because you stink. And we are all getting tired of these conspiracy theories you keep spouting about some criminal organization being responsible for that old woman's death. Irene Dunn fell down the stairs, that's what the police said, and that's what happened.

"And the truth is, Monaghan, you are responsible for Mary Ryan's death. You were so intent on getting into her panties, you weren't watching where you were going when that truck hit you. You are always talking about pickup trucks and all that crap, but truth is you just weren't watching where you were going. You are responsible for that woman getting killed. She was in your truck and you were driving.

"And that Hampton guy. Well, he was just one of them queers, and who knows what goes through their minds. And the police said it was a suicide. So, what you must finally admit, the only person responsible for anyone being dead is you.

"Now when you get back from vacation, I expect you to be clean-shaven, have decent clothes on, comb your hair and be ready to work on time, or don't bother coming back. Am I clear?"

All through Willy's diatribe, Jim just stared at him and

when Willy was finished, Jim shuffled out of the conference room and down the stairs.

Bernard Hill, publisher of the News Tribune and owner of a media empire, which included a chain of weekly newspapers, ten radio stations and two television stations, was aware of Jim's deterioration, as was his daughter and assistant publisher, Audrey.

They weren't sure what to do. But when Audrey saw Jim slowly making his way down the stairs, unshaven, hair askew, and wearing ratty clothes, she pulled him into her office.

The Hills had become close to Jim during the copper casket investigation, initiated by a call from Irene Dunn, an elderly widow, who said her late husband's casket had been switched to a cheaper model. Irene was found dead in her home, and Steve Hampton, who worked for the funeral home, was also found dead on the same day. Later that evening, Jim's truck was rammed into a utility pole and Mary Ryan was ejected through the windshield. She died 24-hours later.

Jim's investigation had forged a working relationship that became deeply personal with Mary Ryan, an Assistant District Attorney. Mary died in a horrific accident for which Jim wanted answers.

The investigation concluded with Alex Reid, owner and operator of a string of funeral homes, being sentenced to the Ohio State Reformatory in Mansfield for seven years for defrauding people by switching and reselling caskets.

The Hills were with Jim the night Mary died. They consoled him during Mary's funeral and the days after. It was Bernard's idea to send Jim to Washington, DC to cover Kennedy's funeral.

Closing the door to her office, Audrey, her long brown

hair pulled into a neat bun and dressed in a tailored navy-blue suit with matching shoes, said "Jim, you look like hell."

"You're not taking care of yourself at all. What can my father or I do to help you?" Jim smiled ruefully at Audrey's honesty.

"Nothing," Jim mumbled slouching in his chair, folding his six-foot frame into the nearest chair.

"For Christ sake, Jim, sit up and get that poor puppy dog look off your face. Look, we know you loved Mary. We all did. We know you are hurting. We all are. But what did Mary's father tell you to do? He told you Mary would kick your butt and tell you to get your act together. You did a great job in DC on the Kennedy stuff, but for the past couple of weeks, you have gone downhill. I know you think Willy has it in for you, but he is right, you can't keep showing up late for work. We all have jobs to do and your job begins by being here on time. Do you understand me, Jim? Do you?"

"I don't think the accident *was* an accident," Jim countered. "I think some of Reid's people intentionally rammed my truck. And I don't think Irene Dunn fell down the stairs or Steve Hampton committed suicide," Jim said, looking at Audrey directly. His cold blue eyes reflected someone who lives for nothing more than revenge. "And Willy just told me my beliefs are conspiracy bull and the only person responsible for anyone dying is me. I was driving and wasn't paying attention and that's why Mary died.

"Is that what you believe, Audrey? Do you believe I am responsible for Mary's death?"

"No, Jim, I don't." Audrey placed her hand over Jim's clenched fist. "I think it was a truly unfortunate accident, and I don't understand how the police have never found the truck that hit you. It doesn't take a genius to see the damage to your truck.   Of course, you were hit. That was an awful thing Willy said, and I will speak to him. He is just insensitive sometimes, but even he can't really believe you were responsible for Mary's death."

Jim abruptly pulled his hand back. "Then who is, Audrey? Why didn't the truck stop? Why can't anyone find the truck? Some son-of-a-bitch rammed me into that utility pole and Mary died, and he is out there right now.   And I am just supposed to walk through life like nothing happened? Don't tell me it was just random. It wasn't an accidental hit and run – he did it on purpose. And Irene Dunn fell down the stairs? Christ, she has been walking down those stairs for almost 50 years, and she trips on the same day Mary dies. And Steve Hampton decides to kill himself, also on the same day. And, oh yeah, every one of them was a part of the Reid case. That just defies reason," Jim said angrily. "I don't believe they were all accidents for even a split second. I believe – no, I know -- Reid's people were responsible for it all. It all happened one week before the trial. Anyone who doesn't see that is insane. Come on, Audrey."

Audrey was clearly taken aback. The deferential young reporter she had known, just months ago, seemed to have died the night Mary, Irene, and Steve Hampton died. But, she knew, he wasn't wrong. "Jim, I am sorry," she said cautiously and softly. "I know how hurt you are and how frustrated. But there is nothing you can do. The police investigated and found no wrongdoing. Irene tripped, Steve committed suicide, and you were hit by a random, probably drunk driver, who fled the scene. That is the end of it. It doesn't have to be true, but that is still the end of it. You have to let it go and move on."

"Screw the police, Audrey. And screw moving on."

Frightened at Jim's dramatic weight loss, Audrey urged,

"Damnit Jim, cut it out. Get your act together. You must move on with the rest of your life. You need to go home, get some rest and some decent food. We are going to have Christmas dinner at my dad's house and he wants you to come. Judge McCallister will be there, too. I know you enjoy the judge, so let's celebrate Christmas at my dad's."

"The hell with Christmas," Jim said getting up to leave.

"Yes, the hell with Christmas," Audrey said and laughed. "But be there at two o'clock." Jim did not share the joke, so Audrey said sincerely, "Please, Jim. Please come. You won't disappoint me and my dad, will you Jim?"

Jim stood by the door and, for a moment, did not know what to say. He decided to lie. "I will be there, Audrey."

FORTY-TWO

Jim woke to a gloomy Christmas day. Overcast and cold, the weather mimicked his mood. Even though he was invited to the Hill's home to be with people he liked and admired, he didn't want to go. Nor did he want to join his brother Hugh and family at the family farm.

He was also invited to have dinner with the Johnsons. Jim and Edgar Johnson had been competitors in high school and American Legion baseball. It was an unusual relationship. Jim was from, Dale, small farming community thirty miles east of Lincoln, and Edgar lived at Simpson Village, a public housing project in northeast Lincoln, comprised of mostly Blacks, some Hispanics, and a few poor whites.

Indeed, it was a unique relationship. Edgar was a star athlete, invited to attend Lincoln Academy, a private school for the wealthy families of Lincoln. He was given a scholarship, and the rumblings of parents offended by racial integration were silenced when, as a freshman, Edgar led the school to a conference championship in football and a state championship in baseball. Edgar and his mom knew the school only let him in to play ball, but it was better than

Lincoln Central High with its outdated school books, violence, and run-down buildings.

He was the only black kid at Lincoln Academy, and when he played Jim Monaghan's Dale Bulldogs, he was the only black kid on either team. He had few friends, even at his school. The kids from Dale would have nothing to do with him and often hurled racial slurs at him.

The one exception was Jim. Jim's father was born in Ireland and, as a Catholic, had experienced discrimination and bigotry, as had his father and his father's father. He taught Jim that a man is a man, and his skin color made no difference. His character did. Jim was in awe of Edgar's extraordinary skill, and though he had every reason to show-boat and brag, Edgar was humble and soft spoken.

Jim shook Edgar's hand after a game, and the next game talked to him for a while, and then for an hour as Edgar's mom and Jim's mom chatted in the stands. Edgar's coach, Donald Hansen, a successful Lincoln businessman, recognizing the talent both young men possessed, brought them together. Jim's mom invited them to dinner and the families became friends. It cost Mrs. Monaghan some friends in Dale and earned her some whispers and glares when she went into town, which she ignored.

Edgar and his mom came to Jim's parents' funeral. Jim never forgot that. But he was not going to Christmas dinner at Edgar and his mom's house. He would have Christmas alone, drinking, and feeling sorry for himself which, he felt, he was more than entitled to be.

Jim really wanted to have Christmas dinner with Mary and her family in Chicago. He had planned on buying a diamond ring and asking her to marry him. They talked about it, and he wanted it to all happen at Christmas, at Mary's house, after he asked her father for her hand. He fantasized about it, even now, though Mary had been dead for months.

She died, and Jim felt certain that that bastard Alex Reid had something to do with it.

Jim looked down at the gun on his lap. His hand had stopped shaking. It was time. He imagined Mary and his parents and seeing them soon, and the image was crystal clear in his mind.

They were not smiling

I thought you would want me to come to you, Jim said out loud.

His mind went blank and he stared at the barrel of the gun. *Now,* he said to himself. *Now is the time.*

As his finger put pressure on the trigger, Jim closed his eyes and waited for the shot that would put him out of his misery, out of the depths of depression he was immersed in.

A loud banging stirred Jim out of his stupor and he took his finger off the trigger. He realized the noise was someone banging on his door.

"Jim! Jim! Jim!" the voice from outside the door yelled.

Staring at the door, as the knocking grew louder, Jim remained in his chair, gun in his hand, paralyzed.

"Jim, come to the door! Open this door or I am going to break it down!"

The voice sounded familiar, but Jim couldn't place it. Holding the gun at his side, he opened the door.

Edgar and Maybelle Johnson stood at the door. Edgar saw the gun and grabbed Jim's hand, his face twisted with fear, shock, and anguish. Jim surrendered the gun to Edgar, sat back in his chair, placed his head in hands and began to sob.

Maybelle was the first to reach him. Dressed in her Sunday best, her black hair streaked with gray, she effortlessly lifted Jim from the chair and embraced him, hugging him tight. Edgar, holding the Browning 22, put the safety on, emptied the cartridges, put them in his pocket, and placed the gun in his back pocket.

Maybelle brought Jim over to the sofa and sat him down.

"Oh, Jimmy, Jimmy, it's okay. We here now, and we are gonna take care of you. We never should have left you alone today. We know how sad you are and how much you miss your Mary and your mom and dad. But this is not the answer, Jimmy. This is not the answer.

"What you gonna do with that gun, Jimmy? What you going do? That's not the answer, Jimmy. That's never the answer."

Jim's sobs became uncontrollable and he shook with grief in Maybelle's sturdy arms.

Edgar noted the empty Bushmills bottles, broken glass on the floor, dirty dishes piled in the kitchen sink, and trash strewn all over the room. He went into Jim's bedroom and found newspapers scattered, more trash, and dirty clothes everywhere. He told his mom, "We have to get him out of here."

"We gotta clean him up first, Edgar. You get him in the shower and let him sit under the water until he sobers up. I'm gonna make some strong coffee and put these dirty clothes in the washer. I'm not going to take him home looking like he does. We going to clean him up and clean this place up."

Edgar, sad but determined, looked down at Jim and said, "We are a long way from the baseball diamond, bro."

Jim looked up at his friend but couldn't speak. He just nodded and put his head in his hands. Jim's mind drifted to the ball field. It was the bottom of the ninth inning of the

Ohio state championship and Dale was ahead by one run. But Lincoln Academy had runners on second and third, and when Jim hung a curve, Edgar hit it over the outfield fence for a game-winning home run. Jim's friends on the team hated Edgar for it. Jim figured if someone had to beat him, he was glad it was his friend Edgar.

FORTY-THREE

As EDGAR, Maybelle, and Jim, newly showered and dressed, were getting ready to leave the apartment, the phone rang. Jim told his friends, "Don't answer it."

"That's not nice, Jimmy. If someone calls you on Christmas day, you answer it."

Jim and Maybelle stared at one another before she picked up the phone and announced, "Jimmy Monaghan's residence. How can I help you?"

"You can help me by telling me just where Jim Monaghan is. This is Audrey Hill and we were expecting him at my parent's house for dinner a couple of hours ago, and he hasn't shown up. Is he there? And who are you?"

"My name is Maybelle Johnson, and, yes, he is here. Who did you say you are, again?"

"This is Audrey Hill. I am a friend of Jim's."

Maybelle put her hand on the phone to block the noise and turned to Jim. "Audrey Hill, Jimmy – is she ok?"

Jim nodded. "She's my boss. She's ok."

Maybelle, eyebrows raised and stunned, whispered

"THE Audrey Hill?" She didn't wait for Jim to answer. "Oh dear," she said and put the phone back to her ear.

"I am so sorry, Miss Hill. I know you and your father from the good things you do at my community center. You good people. Jimmy's in bad shape. We found him in a mess over here. And Miss Hill, he had a gun in his hand when we found him. We gonna take him to our home and get him back to health. He won't be makin' it to dinner. I'm very sorry."

"My God, are you kidding, a gun? Jim had a gun?"

"Yes, Miss Hill, he did, but he didn't use it, and my son Edgar has it now. So, he be safe."

"Can you bring him over here? We have plenty of food and Dr. Ross lives next door. I can have him come over and examine Jim."

"No, Miss Hill, we can take him home. We can take care of him."

"Mrs. Johnson, I can't thank you enough for being there for Jim, but I feel responsible for him. He had a very hard day on Friday and I was one of the people who was tough on him. We have plenty of food and I would like Dr. Ross to give him a good exam to see if he needs to go to the hospital. We would like you to join us for dinner."

"Well, Miss Hill, we can bring him over to see the doctor and for some supper, but then we gonna take him home for a while. That okay with you?"

Audrey quickly agreed, hung up the phone and told her parents, her husband, and the judge, they were having some unexpected guests for a late supper.

FORTY-FOUR

On the way to Bernard Hill's home, Jim kept insisting to Maybelle and Edgar he just had too much to drink, and that he was fine.

Maybelle retorted, "Fine, that's what you tellin' me. Fine? Mm-hmm. Fine don't have a gun in his hand, drinking like whiskey is water. Mm-hmm, no sir. You a long way from fine. You ain't shaved in days; your apartment is a pig sty. Those pigs on your family farm live cleaner than your apartment. And how much weight have you lost? You as thin as a page from one of those newspapers you write on. No, Jimmy, you not fine. And you coming home with me and that's final. But first we gonna stop at the Hills for supper. I haven't eaten yet, and you so skinny you look like you haven't eaten in a month of Sundays. But then you're comin' home with us, and I am gonna to take care of you, so no lip from you, young man, and that's final," Maybelle said sternly.

"I wouldn't argue with her, Jim," Edgar shrugged his broad shoulders and grinned.

Edgar pulled his light blue 1954 Chevy Bel Air into the circular driveway of the Hill estate, on the edge of the Lincoln Country Club. Festive green and red Christmas lights highlighted the eaves of the two-story white frame home, and a tall flocked Christmas tree sparkled in one of the front windows.

Maybelle and Edgar each grabbed one of Jim's arms as they helped him to the door, which was opened by Bernard Hill. "Welcome folks. I am Bernard Hill. Come in and let's get some supper," Bernard said graciously.

As Edgar and Maybelle walked Jim towards the sofa in the living room, Jim's legs gave out and he slumped, passed out, to the floor. Audrey's mother rushed to him with a cold towel.

Dr. Ross, whom Audrey had summoned from next door, knelt beside him and suggested they lay him on the sofa. Jim recovered enough to answer Dr. Ross's questions.

After the exam, Dr. Ross reported, "He has a severe headache and difficulty staying awake. His skin is clammy, and his mouth is dry. When he tried to stand, he became dizzy. In my medical opinion, he is drunk off his ass."

No one laughed, and Dr. Ross continued, "He is dehydrated and obviously, he has consumed way too much alcohol and not enough food. We could admit him, give him an IV of saline solution, or we could have him drink a lot of water. But you need to get some food in him and soon."

The white carpeted room was quiet as everyone listened to Dr. Ross and looked at Jim who was lying asleep on the gold damask sofa, an embroidered pillow under his head, when Jasper, Audrey's husband, stumbled into the room.

Slurring his words, he mumbled, "What the hell is this? You guys taking in bums off the street now? That guy looks like shit." Staring at Maybelle and Edgar, he said, "Whoa, Bernard, do you know you got niggers in the house?"

Maybelle cast her eyes downward while Edgar glared at Jasper and said with controlled, cold rage, "My mama's no nigger." Jasper, eyes wide and mouth agape, took a step backward, almost upending a crystal lamp.

Audrey, eyes blazing, took her inebriated husband by the arm and told him, "Shut up, Jasper. Go back to the den and watch the football game." Bernard looked angrier than Edgar. His wife, Jane, humiliated, turned to Edgar and Maybelle and said, "I am so sorry. I can't believe him. I am so sorry."

Bernard slammed his fist on the table so loudly his wife and Maybelle flinched. "Enough! That son of a bitch. He doesn't deserve to spend another minute in this house."

"Mr. Hill, that's not necessary," answered Maybelle. "We're quite used to it, and we'd spend our whole lives bothered if we let those words hurt us. Thank you, but don't think twice about it." She smiled sadly.

"Young man," Judge McCallister turned to Edgar, "that combination of strength and restraint will take you far."

"I am sorry, Maybelle, Edgar, no guest of mine should be treated like that," Bernard offered. "And please, Maybelle, call me Bernard."

"And, you can call my husband asshole." Audrey had entered the room without being noticed. "I am humiliated."

"You have no reason to be," Edgar answered. "You treated us with respect and kindness."

Maybelle nodded, and smiled at Audrey. "Let's talk about Jimmy." With that introduction, Maybelle held the floor for some time. Audrey was stunned at the sight of her parents, Dr. Ross, and Judge McCallister, all paying rapt attention to Maybelle, who stood to deliver her proclamation. She paced the room telling them what was going to happen next.

"We'll make sure he gets plenty to drink and plenty to eat. I 'm not sure when he can to go back to work, but we'll get him all fixed up and healthy. Y'all know about Rev. Jeremiah Jefferson from our church. He and Jimmy are close. I'll make sure the good Reverend spends a lot of time with Jimmy and maybe we can get him out of the funk he is in."

Dr. Ross suggested a therapist might help, and Jim might consider Alcoholic Anonymous if his drinking cannot be controlled. Judge McCallister suggested he would be in touch with a couple of psychologists at Hamilton University who could be helpful. "He has suffered a lot of grief for a young man and talking about it with professionals might help," the judge offered.

Maybelle said they should all trust her and Rev. Jackson. "We'll take care of Jimmy. But we'll keep your suggestions in mind." And that was that. Maybelle was poor, black, and a woman – in the house of the wealthiest man in town, who sat beside a retired federal judge and the city's most prominent doctor. But in her mind, this was about her Jimmy, and hers was the final word.

Audrey mused, *there is so much more to Jim Monaghan than I thought. He is comfortable with Judge McCallister, the UPI office in Washington, me and my dad, and at the same time, he inspires fierce loyalty in Maybelle and Edgar, who live in the projects. And yet he must feel so alone. His parents are dead and so is Mary. He is a good person, and life has not been fair to him. But there is so much hope for him. He is an excellent reporter and writer. He can't throw it away drinking and being depressed. Looking over her shoulder at the den and thinking of the newspaper, she concluded, I must help him. It will be difficult, but I can handle it. I have to.*

FORTY-FIVE

As EDGAR DROVE NORTH, approaching the intersection of Fourth and Bradley, Jim could see the two-story units stretching two long city blocks that made up Simpson Village. There were three rows of buildings separated by narrow dirt roads. The rows of units were broken up by small entry roads. There were no garages. Parking was behind the units on unpaved ground. The Johnsons lived at Number Eight, which was close to the intersection of Fourth and Bradley and catty corner from Rev. Jefferson's church, The Fellowship of the Disciples of Christ, or simply The Fellowship.

The Johnson's unit, one of four in the building, had a faded red brick façade on the first floor and once-white aluminum siding on the second level. Inside, there were three bedrooms and a bathroom upstairs, and a kitchen, dining room, and living room on the first floor. The rooms were small as were the few windows. In contrast to the neighborhood around it, the Johnson residence was spotless. Maybelle made sure her children completed their chores.

Jim had stayed overnight many times when he was in

high school and on breaks from college, and he always slept on the sofa in the living room. He couldn't count how many times he had dinner in Maybelle's homey dining room, with its mismatched chairs and framed prints of JFK and Dr. Martin Luther King.

The front door faced Bradley avenue. Separating Simpson Village from Bradley Avenue was a six-foot high black wrought-iron fence.

Jim remained silent on the five-mile drive from the Hill's estate, but as Edgar parked the car near the back door he said, "Maybelle, I am sorry. I appreciate you taking me in."

"You're family, Jim," Edgar answered.

"That's right, Jimmy." Maybelle echoed. "You is ours, and you ain't gettin' rid of us, if you try."

Edgar's 18-year-old sister Haley met them at the door. In her senior year at Lincoln Central, Haley was slender, but wiry. Unlike Edgar, whose skin was a deep mahogany, Haley's was lighter with a sprinkling of freckles across her nose. Her hair was short with tight curls. She was an excellent student and had hopes of going to college, but like so many in her community, Haley had no idea where the money would come from.

To Haley, Jim Monaghan was a mystery man who often showed up for dinner and slept on the sofa. Jim knew Haley had little interaction with white people. There were none, or nearly none, in her neighborhood and even fewer at her school. She felt awkward around him, and not entirely because he was white. Jim went out of his way to make her comfortable with him but, truth be told, Haley had a crush on him.

Haley's hand flew to her mouth when she saw Jim struggling up the two steps to the back door. Her mother and brother had him by each arm. Jim looked emaciated, so different from his former athletic build. The Jim Monaghan Haley knew was a strapping six-foot, 185 pounds of chiseled athletic muscle. He always had his brown hair neat, except for last summer, when he wore a flattop, for reasons Haley never knew. Tonight, Haley was shocked to see his hair long and stringy and a month-long beard on his Irish face.

Maybelle and Edgar brought Jim in and Edgar offered his bed to Jim, but Maybelle said he had to be on the sofa where she could make sure he got plenty of water to drink during the night.

True to her word, Maybelle woke Jim every two hours and made him drink a big glass of water.

FORTY-SIX

Morning came too soon for Jim, and as he rolled off the sofa, he looked over at the dining room table and was surprised to see Maybelle and Rev. Jefferson drinking coffee.

"Did you sleep at all, Maybelle?" Jim asked. "What time is it anyway?"

"It's 8 a.m., and it's time to start your rehabilitation. Me and the Reverend are in charge, in case you were wondering. Now let's get some coffee into you, but first a glass of water."

"Maybelle, if I drink any more water, I am going to float away. By the way, where is everyone?"

"Edgar is at work and Haley is at school. I called in to work and told them I was going to be late. Those toilets over at Mercy Hospital can wait to get cleaned. I wanted to get you breakfast and get you and the Reverend talking before I left."

Maybelle proceeded to fry up bacon and eggs, toasted some bread, and stood over Jim as he ate every scrap.

"So, Jimmy, you listen to what the good Reverend has to say to you. And I don't want you to leave. I expect you to be right here when I get home."

"Don't want to disappoint Maybelle, do you Jim," Reverend Jefferson said.

"No, I don't," Jim shrugged.

After getting his coffee and saying goodbye to Maybelle, Jim and the Reverend sat down to talk.

"Jim, why are you feeling so sorry for yourself? Don't think I don't understand. I know you are grieving for Mary and your parents but drinking yourself to death and planning suicide just isn't right. If you had killed yourself, what would Mary and your parents think about that? They would be so disappointed.

"For goodness sake, Jim, you are a young white man with a college education, working a fine job for fine people. Everyone has good and bad in their lives. Yes, you have had some very tough times, but Jim, those problems can be handled. And you have so many blessings."

Jim just stared at Reverend Jefferson, stunned at how bluntly the conversation started.

"You don't understand, Reverend. It's not just missing Mary. Do you know how she died?" Jim didn't wait for an answer. "She was murdered. We were investigating the Reid funeral home."

"I know Jim. I read the stories you wrote, and Maybelle told me everything that didn't make it into the paper."

"I am convinced Reid and his people are responsible for the accident that killed Mary. And I don't think Irene fell down the steps, and I am certain Steve did not kill himself. But no one believes me."

"And how does drinking yourself into a stupor and

contemplating suicide help you solve the problem of those poor people dying? How does it help? You can't accomplish anything drunk and certainly not anything if you are dead. The only way you can find out the truth is if you are in good shape, physically and mentally. You've been sad long enough. God gives us strength if we trust in him. You understand me, son?

"God gave you many gifts. You won that big award from the Associated Press. You did a great job in Washington D.C. writing all those stories about our president's funeral. You talked with our Senators and Congress people. How many people can say they have done that? Then you come home, get drunk every night, don't keep yourself clean, and live in squalor.

"You know some people live that way and they can't help it. You can; you don't have to live that way.

Jim looked away, annoyed, but the Reverend seemed to read his mind and said, "Look at the scars on my cheek. That happened in April in Birmingham, Alabama. Bull Connor had his dogs and fire hoses turned on us. I was beaten with a policeman's nightstick. I was thrown in jail, and I was beaten up by the guards. And all for the grave sin of wanting to eat at a restaurant.

"Jim, you can eat anywhere you want. My brothers and sisters can't. In some areas, we will be beaten and arrested if we try to go into certain places. And it's not just in Alabama or Florida or the South. It's right here in Lincoln, Ohio. We are always afraid. What if we don't say, 'Yes sir,' in the right way to our boss. What if the police stop our car at night.

"You don't have to live like that, Jim, and it is a blessing. Yes, bad things happened to you. I can take you through this neighborhood and you can meet scores of folks who lost loved ones. And a lot of them lost them to murder. You say what Reid's people did was unfair, and I get that. We live in unfair, here in Lincoln. Be a man and do something about it."

Jim was stunned. Looking at Reverend Jefferson, dressed in his black suit, white shirt, and striped tie, his gray hair neatly combed, and his short beard trimmed, Jim saw him in a new light. The diminutive man exuded strength. His eyes reflected intensity, sincerity, and conviction. Jim had been disgusted when he had seen the television news showing Bull Connor and the Birmingham police unleashing German shepherds and using fire hoses on the peaceful demonstrators and beating defenseless people with their batons. He never knew of Reverend Jackson's story from Birmingham. He never knew any of it, and he thought he was close to the Johnsons and the Reverend. *And why wasn't his story in the News Tribune?* he wondered.

As their conversation continued until almost noon, Jim's stomach started growling.

"I don't want to take your entire day, Reverend, but I am enjoying our talk. It's almost lunch time. Are you hungry?

Reverend Jefferson smiled and said his wife was preparing lunch for them, and he had told Maybelle they would be walking across the street, and she was okay with that.

As they got up to leave, the phone rang. It was Audrey, who had asked for Maybelle's number, checking in. Reverend Jefferson answered. Audrey and her family were the largest donors at the Simpson Village Community Center, and she and the Reverend were well acquainted. He told her Jim had a good night's sleep, plenty of water, had eaten a good breakfast, and was headed for lunch. Audrey expressed her gratitude. She said Jim was on vacation until Thursday, January 2, and hopefully he would be able to go back to work then. Audrey asked Rev. Jefferson if he thought a week would be enough for Jim to be recover?"

Rev. Jefferson assured Audrey Jim would be ready by the middle of the next week.

FORTY-SEVEN

AFTER A WEEK of Maybelle's food and Reverend Jefferson's counseling, Jim was feeling better. He had drunk no alcohol and had put on some of the weight he had lost. He was grooming his hair, and wore clean clothes, and he decided to grow a beard. But he was still gaunt and was having trouble sleeping at night. Reverend Jefferson had insisted Jim attend a meeting of Alcoholic Anonymous. Jim initially said no.

"Jim, you want to get better; you want to be physically and mentally alert if you are going to pursue your conspiracy theory. You can't investigate if you are drunk and depressed. You stopped, and that's great. AA keeps you from starting back up again. Besides, what harm can come to you if you attend an AA meeting? You have nothing to lose."

"What if someone recognizes me there? My reputation would be ruined."

"First of all, what reputation? The reputation of someone sitting in a chair with a gun, drunk out of your mind? The person who shows up late for work every day, unshaven and looking like crap. Is that the reputation you are trying to protect? Second, there's no shame in AA. There's shame in not doing all you can to keep from drinking again."

Unable to counter the Reverend's arguments, but giving it a lot of thought, Jim went to his first AA meeting in the basement of the First Baptist Church. *Never thought I would come back to this place,* Jim thought, remembering when he and Mary attended a service at First Baptist to take the measure of Rev. Smallwood. Jim believed, correctly, he was in cahoots with Alex Reid in the casket switching scandal. Smallwood pled to a lesser charge and was serving four years in the Ohio State Reformatory in Mansfield.

In the church basement, Jim entered a spartan room. About thirty men, most of them smoking and drinking coffee, sat at simple tables and chairs. The Twelve Steps of the AA program were on the wall and most of the men were engaged in quiet conversations.

I thought everyone here would be drunk, Jim thought, before taking a seat in the back row. As the meeting started, each man introduced himself as an alcoholic. When it came to Jim's turn, he said he was just interested and didn't give his name.

"If you are 'just interested' you are probably an alcoholic," the older man next to him quietly said. Jim didn't respond.

Listening to others talk during the meeting, Jim found some similarities in his situation, but the topics were mostly about problems the older men were facing, and Jim found nothing in common with them. He knew he wasn't an alcoholic because he could stop any time he wanted. After all, he hadn't had a drink in a week.

As the meeting ended, the man next to Jim pulled him

aside. "Young man be thankful you are here at your age. It took me 35 years before I walked into these rooms, and it was the best day of my life. Except for every day after, because every day since that day has been better. If you come back and just listen, I guarantee you, your life will get better and you won't have to waste the years I did drinking."

Jim looked coldly at the man, surprised that he was clean shaven and dressed in a business suit. His graying hair was neatly trimmed and his whole demeanor was in sharp contrast to Jim's perception of an alcoholic. But since Jim was sure he himself wasn't an alcoholic, he dismissed the man, saying "Thanks," and he walked away.

On New Year's Day, Jim and Edgar listened to the football games on the radio and talked about old times. Jim was feeling good, especially proud of himself for not having a drink on New Year's Eve. *First time since high school*, he thought.

Sitting around the kitchen table, of Number Eight with Edgar, Maybelle, and Haley, Jim said casually, "I went to an AA meeting the other day as Reverend Jefferson wanted me to. It is not for me. Mostly old men, who really have problems. And besides, I can stop any time I want to. I haven't had a drink in over a week. And, thanks to you guys, I think I am ready to go back to work. Maybelle, thanks for cleaning up my apartment and washing all my clothes. I called Audrey and left a message that I will be at work early in the morning. So, on the first evening of the new year, I am going to sleep in my own bed. By the way, Edgar, do you have my pistol?"

"Don't even think about that pistol, Jim. Don't even think about it. I took it to your brother Hugh out at your family farm. He said he would take care of it."

At that moment, four pickup trucks came flying through

the intersection of Fourth and Bradley, not even slowing down at the stop sign. The first pickup screeched to a halt in front of Number Eight. Jim, Haley, Maybelle, and Edgar raced out the front door and saw two burly men, clutching beer cans, cigars dangling from their mouths, and dressed in Oshkosh strapped overalls. They sneered at Jim and said, "Hey, white boy, you know you're with a bunch of Blackies?"

Jim ran towards the wrought iron fence separating the truck from the residence, but before he could get far, Edgar grabbed him from behind and pulled him back to the porch.

"They're not worth it, Jim. If you go over the fence, they will just beat the shit out of you. Screw them."

"But it's not right, Edgar; it's not right. This isn't the deep South, for God's sake, this is Lincoln, Ohio."

"You don't know crap, Jim. You don't know what it's like here. You just come and visit. You don't live here."

Jim was more than slightly bewildered, but he walked back to the porch. The men in the truck laughed. "Check this out, Clyde," one yelled out. "The black guy smarter than the darkie-lover." He laughed out loud until the other man hit him on the arm. "Don't use my name, dumb ass."

"Oh, what the hell is he gonna do?" The men got back into their truck and sped off.

Disgusted and angry, Jim walked with Edgar back into the Johnson's home. He started to comment but was interrupted by a phone call from Audrey.

"Audrey, I am fine. I feel good, and I haven't had a drink in over a week. Thanks for your concern and help. I will be in the office in the morning. Thanks for calling." Edgar hearing only Jim's end of the conversation, look suspiciously at Jim and said, "She sure checks up on you a lot."

FORTY-EIGHT

Dressed in pressed khaki pants, ironed shirt with a collar, month-long, but trimmed beard, hair combed, Jim showed up at work at 7 a.m. and went directly to the u-shaped desk and looked at Willy.

"Willy, you probably heard I was sick, while I was on vacation, but I am better, and I am ready to go back to work doing whatever you assign me to do."

Looking at Jim suspiciously, Willy ran his hand through his thinning white hair, peered over his wire-rimmed glasses and said, "Obit Desk. We will talk after the last deadline, but plan on the Obit Desk for a while."

Delighted Willy didn't yell at him or ask any questions in front of the other reporters and editors seated around the desk, Jim walked to the Obit Desk, put on his headset and waited for the phone to ring.

After the last deadline of the day, Willy called Jim to the conference room where he closed the door. "You look ok today, but I want you to know you are on a short leash. Your behavior the weeks before Christmas was not acceptable. We all know you and the publisher, and especially his daughter, have, what shall I call it, oh yes, a special relation-ship. But that will take you only so far. Bernard has told me to treat you no differently than anyone else. So, short leash, understand?"

"I understand." Jim's fleeting gratitude that Willy had not publicly shamed him evaporated, and, once more, he resented his boss. Restrained, Jim continued, "I think there is a story out there that's worth a look. I have been staying at Simpson Village."

"What the hell for?" Willy interjected, dumbfounded. "Were you in such a bad way – Jesus, Jim, don't you know what kind of people live there?"

"Yeah," Jim answered, "my friends and good people. And they are being harassed. When I was there, guys in pickup trucks drove by and shouted obscenities at me and my friends. And it happens a lot – sometimes they throw trash over the fence. I haven't seen anything in the paper about it. The people there have tolerated it for a long time, but that is changing and fast. Dr. King is inspiring action right here in Lincoln. Looks to me like something serious might happen and we need to be on it."

"For Christ sake, kid, will you ever understand your role in this newspaper? You are an obit writer, and sometimes, repeat, sometimes general assignments. You're the lowest position in the newsroom. You think you are Jimmy Breslin or some other high-profile columnist. And what is your fantasy with pickup trucks? You saw them at Irene Dunn's house; you saw them in the cemetery; and a pickup rammed your truck.

"But the police investigate and find nothing. We have police reporters who cover the crime in this town, and you are not one of them. If there is something going on over at the projects, our police reporters will pick it up. It's their job, not yours. And they haven't found shit. Let's see if you can do a good job writing obituaries and remember, young man, you are on a short leash," Willy concluded.

Chagrined at being told again, to ignore stories he thought were important, Jim decided, *normally, I would go to O'Toole's and drink my lunch, but not today. I think I will go down to Harlow's and have a cheeseburger and a coke.*

On his way downstairs from the newsroom, he spotted Bernard and Audrey talking outside their offices. "I just wanted to thank both of you again for all your help during my little walk through the valley," Jim told them, half joking.

"We are glad you are back at work, Jim," Bernard said. "I just talked with Judge McCallister and he asked you to stop by his office at two p.m. today. Make sure you are there on time. I will tell Willy you won't be in the rest of the afternoon. I think the Judge has scheduled at least an hour with you."

"What does he want, Bernard?"

"Just be there at two p.m., Jim, and that's a directive from your publisher," Bernard said sternly while Audrey just smiled.

FORTY-NINE

Now, what could that be about? Jim wondered as he walked briskly to Harlow's, his breath visible in the icy cold air.

As soon as Sgt. Major Harold Harlow, decorated veteran of World War II and Korea, and Jim's friend, saw him walk into his café he grabbed him by the shoulders and pulled him into his kitchen. "What's this shit I hear about you sitting in dirty clothes, half-drunk out of your mind, and holding a loaded gun?"

"Jesus, Sgt. Major, how did you know?"

Everyone, with rare exception, called Harlow "Sgt. Major," his retired rank from the Army. He had, folks felt, earned it. His physical size commanded respect. Six -foot two and an athletic 220 pounds, his thinning brown hair was almost always cut military style. Light complexion, Harlow's brown eyes penetrated through his horn-rimmed glasses.

"Look, I was having a bad day, but it's behind me. I am okay now."

"Sounds like more than a bad day. A man doesn't recover with the snap of his fingers -- what the hell do you mean you are ok? Why didn't you call me? You think you are the only one who is hurting over Mary and Irene. For Christ sake, Jim, I am your friend. Friends help people when they are hurting. Now let's gets some lunch into you. You look like you have lost 20 pounds."

For the next hour, Jim was lectured by Harlow on friendship, grief, and acting normally.

"I simply can't eat any more, Sgt. Major," Jim complained after consuming two cheeseburgers and two baskets of fries. "Besides, I have to see Judge McCallister in a few minutes. I have to go, but I promise we will stay in touch."

"You better, or I will kick your ass, you hear me, Jim?" The Sgt. Major said, only half in jest.

FIFTY

Jɪᴍ ᴀʟᴡᴀʏs ꜰᴇʟᴛ comfortable with Judge Douglas McCallister. He met the judge during the copper casket investigation, where McCallister began as an advisor, and through Jim and Mary's detective work, discovered he was a victim, too. He thought he had buried his wife in an expensive copper casket, but before she was interred her body was removed, put in a pine box, and the casket was sold to another victim. The judge was grateful to Jim and took an interest in him. He was often with Jim immediately after Mary's death. The judge accompanied Jim to the funeral and burial. Their bond was tight.

"Why is your desk so messy?" Jim joked as he walked into the judge's office. Three walls of his office were lined with bookshelves to the ceiling, and his desk was piled with stacks of papers.

Standing tall, the judge, in a gray suit, white shirt, and dark green tie, was the epitome of a gentleman. His full head of white hair was perfectly cut and parted on the left side. Looking at Jim over his half-moon glasses, perched in the middle of his nose, he quipped, "If a messy desk indicates a scattered mind, what does an empty desk say of a man?"

Jim laughed. The judge continued, "There is someone I want you to meet."

They entered the judge's private conference room, and Jim noted a woman, who he guessed was in her mid-forties, in a tailored black suit with a string of pearls around her neck. Her black hair was cut short and was tucked neatly behind her ears.

Jim stopped in his tracks, but the judge pulled him over to where the mystery woman was standing.

"Jim, I want you to meet Dr. Donna Nance. She is the chair of the Psychology department here at Hamilton. Her PhD is from Yale, so you rest assured, she is quite competent and can help you."

"Wait a minute, I came over to see you, I didn't agree to see some shrink. No offense, Ma'am, but I just don't need to see a shrink."

"No offense taken," Dr. Nance said. "Let's just make this a little chat, so we can get acquainted. You can decide, after we talk, if you'd like to see me again."

"No. No chat. I just don't want to talk to a shrink," Jim sputtered.

"Well, what are you afraid of Jim? I won't bite," Dr. Nance said, smiling.

"I am not afraid," Jim countered, "I just know already I don't need a shrink."

"Well, why don't you two just get acquainted?" the judge offered. "I will be in my office if anyone needs me."

Jim relented, and thought, *I'll be polite, but I will not see this woman again.* He and Dr. Nance sat across the table from one another and neither spoke. Jim occasionally glanced at his watch or at the clock on the wall, while Dr. Nance just looked at him.

"Aren't you supposed to be saying something?" Jim asked.

"What do you want me to say, Jim? Is there something you want to ask me?"

"Well, before we begin, I don't have any money to pay you. I have no idea what kind of insurance I have at the paper, but for sure, I don't have any money and I don't think insurance covers shrinks anyways," Jim offered.

"You don't have to worry about paying me, Jim. I am not going to charge you anything. You are a friend of the Judge, and so am I, so we can take as much time as you want or need."

"Do you think I need to be here?" Jim asked.

"Jim, on Christmas day, you were on a five-day binge; you hadn't shaved or cleaned up in over three weeks; and you were sitting in your chair with a gun under your chin. I think you need to talk about it," Dr. Nance said gently.

"You don't understand, Dr. Nance. I know what really happened to Mary, Irene, and Steve, but I can't prove it and no one, and I mean no one, believes me. They think I am nuts. And Willy, my boss even said the only person responsible for anyone dying is me. I drove the truck and Mary was killed."

Jim, eager to tell anyone who would listen, had not stopped to think whether this stranger knew who the three were. "Do you have any idea what I am talking about?" he asked.

Dr. Nance answered, "I do. I read your articles and spoke to the judge. And, Jim, I don't think you are nuts. Your theory makes sense to me. Coincidences of that magnitude don't happen, in my experience."

Jim felt incredible relief and gratitude. *Perhaps, this is one person who will listen to me without telling me to just move on.* So, Jim, started talking and went on for almost an hour telling Dr. Nance how much he loved Mary, their plans, and how much he missed her. He said he thought of her all the time, day and night. He talked about his parents who, on the way to his high school graduation where Jim was to receive athletic and academic honors, were killed in an auto accident. He told her he had one true friend, Edgar Johnson from his high school baseball days. And Edgar, who lived in the projects with his little sister and his mother, who was like a mom to Jim, were treated horribly – and Jim had never known and just found out.

And the world seemed even more wrong and unfair now that he knew. He told her he went to AA and it didn't feel right and he felt no identification with the other older men in attendance. He told her he had trouble sleeping and had little interest in anything, and the only comfort he had was when he was drinking, though he had not had a drink for a week.

During Jim's soliloquy, Dr. Nance didn't interrupt and never changed her calm expression.

When he was finished, Jim looked up at her and asked, "Aren't you supposed to be saying something?"

"I wanted to listen first, Jim. You have a lot of pain, that's obvious, and I think I can help you through the pain. I can't eliminate it. You will always feel the loss of Mary and your parents. Those are extremely deep losses, and you must recognize and respect that. But I can help you deal with it, if you are willing to be an equal partner."

"You know, I didn't want to be here. It's the last place I thought I needed to be. But when you reminded me where I was on Christmas Day and what I was doing, it shocked me into reality. It hasn't even been two weeks. I have tried to forget it, pretend it didn't happen. Sometimes, I shudder when I think of it. But I now know, I was lucky Edgar and Maybelle knocked on the door. I am still not sure if I would have pulled the trigger, but it was way too close. I am ashamed of my actions that day, and perhaps you can help me. I know what I did isn't normal. I am willing to try and work with you.

"One more thing, you are the first person who has just listened to me without saying, oh, the police investigated, and you need to move on. I can't move on when I know there are people out there walking around, who are responsible for Mary's death. I just can't.

"So, thank you for listening and not telling me I am crazy, or I should just move on."

"Jim, there are different ways to move on. If you want to pursue those responsible for Mary's death, you must be physically and mentally sound, not drunk every night. Do you understand the difference?"

"Yes, I do. Thanks for this session. I am thankful to the judge for setting this up. I would like to come back, and we can talk some more and, hopefully, you can help me through the depression. I don't ever want to sit in a chair with a gun in my hand again," Jim vowed.

FIFTY-ONE

THREE WEEKS now and nothing to drink, Jim reflected. *I've kicked the habit. My drinking problems are behind me.*

Jim still woke up thinking of Mary and Reid's role in her death, but he felt the appointments with Dr. Nance were helping. Although the basic problems hadn't changed. Mary was still dead. Those responsible were still unpunished.

Bernard won't overrule Willy and let me investigate all the incidents of that day in August. It couldn't have been a coincidence. Jim wondered if he needed a complete change of scenery. *There is not much of a future for me in this town or at this paper, if I am only going to be writing obituaries. I am going to talk to the Sgt. Major about joining the Marines.*

"You want to do what?" an exasperated Sgt. Major Harlow bellowed after hearing of Jim's plans to join the Marines.

"That's the stupidest idea you have come up with yet, and you have come up with some whoppers. Look, Jim, serving your country, especially in time of war, is the most honorable thing a man can do. You lay your life on the line to protect the freedom that this great country gives us. But you must want to join for the right reasons. And the right reason is not that you are angry and depressed about the rotten hand life has dealt you, or that you are bored with your job.

"I know what is behind this decision, but it just isn't the answer for what you are fighting. What you need to be doing, Jim, is getting yourself healthy. Cut back on the drinking and get yourself in to good physical condition. Deal with your issues, and then if you want to join, I will fully support you."

Despite Harlow's advice, Jim felt he had no other option, and he drove to the Marine Recruiting Office. His visit to the recruiting office was brief. The recruiters, surprised that someone was enlisting voluntarily rather than being drafted, told him that before he could enlist he needed to take a physical. They made an appointment for him at the Armed Forces Physical Examination Center, north of Columbus and just a few miles from Lincoln.

After his exam, the military doctor looked at Jim and said, "Son, I admire your patriotism, but there is no way you are getting into the military. Not any branch would touch you. Your right knee is in bad shape -- and that left arm. It doesn't go straight. Were you born that way, or did you have an accident?"

Disappointed, Jim told the doctor his arm was dislocated in a football game and didn't heal correctly. "Thank God it was my left," Jim joked, "or I would have been done with baseball. I was a pitcher," Jim said proudly. The doctor smiled, sympathetically. Jim asked the doctor again if there was any possible way he could get into the Marines, the Army, or any service. The doctor shook his head no.

Nothing is going right. I can't even get into the army

when they are drafting just about anyone who can walk. Willy keeps correcting my obituaries. No one believes me except Dr. Nance, and she is paid to listen. Oh, the hell with it, I am going to have a drink.

At O'Toole's Bar, Stavros was glad to see him, but warned, "No more than two drinks, Jim. That's your limit. The Sgt. Major told me what happened." "I can go to any bar in town and get what I want," Jim retorted angrily. "Give me a Bushmills on the rocks with a glass of water."

Keeping to Stavros' limit, Jim finished his drink and drove to Edgar and Maybelle's home for dinner. He didn't call; he just showed up. Pulling into the back of their unit, he was surprised at the glares of other residents. It was a new experience.

"What the hell is going on? I parked in the back and a couple of tough looking guys looked at me as if I was with the KKK," Jim asked Edgar.

"Things are getting tense around here, Jim," Edgar replied. "The more they are talking about a Civil Rights Bill; the tougher people are getting. With Dr. King's marches and the demonstrations, there is a lot of pressure on President Johnson to pass President Kennedy's legislation. Rev. Jefferson is getting anonymous threats on his phone, because he is planning a big march here in town. I warned him not to do it, but he is going ahead."

"And, Jimmy," added Maybelle, "more pickup trucks are comin' through the neighborhood throwin trash all over our yards. Some of the young men are wantin' to strike back."

"Damn right," Edgar added.

"No cursing in this house," Maybelle answered, "And you won't be one of them fools. We don't want no more trouble in this family. Your daddy and your brother are in prison and no more of my family is goin' there."

Jim had forgotten about Edgar's father and brother and didn't know how to respond, so he decided to change subjects. He told them about trying to get into the Marines and his experience at the physical. He also told them his friend the Sgt. Major went off the rails on him.

"The Sgt. Major is right, Jimmy," Maybelle said. "That's the dumbest idea I've heard you come up with. Boys are dyin' over there."

Maybelle's lecture was interrupted by yelling from the street. Jim, Edgar, and Maybelle hurried to the front porch. Three pickup trucks were parked at the curb. In the bed of each of the trucks were men throwing garbage and beer bottles over the wrought iron fence. Jim ran towards them and started throwing the trash back.

"Hey darkie lover. You need to stick to your own kind. You gonna get hurt if you hang around here. We gonna kick your ass."

Before Jim could respond, the trucks sped away, but he noticed the truck the men yelled at him from had an eagle emblem painted on the driver's side door.

"Jim, get your ass back here!" Edgar yelled.

Jim noticed the same men who stared at him when he entered the house were staring at him again. Most were shaking their heads in disbelief, but one caught Jim's eye. His eyes were hard as steel, and he stared at Jim, fearless and angry. He nodded his head at Jim, made a fist and put it to his chest. Jim nodded back.

"Edgar, who is that guy, who just nodded at me?

"That's Rufus. He thinks he's the head of the Peace Stones. Don't mess with him. He's tough as nails, but more important than Rufus, Jim, this isn't your fight. I told you before, you don't understand what's going on here," Edgar warned. "Those pickup trucks come by a couple nights a week. One of these nights, the boys out there, the Peace Stones, they are going to fight back. My brother was the leader years ago and they have been quiet for a long time, but these trucks are getting them activated. You 've got to be careful. Jim, your heart is in the right place, and I love you for it, but you aren't helping. We need you to stop this one-man fight for us. It's not working."

"I'm sorry, Edgar. God am I sorry. I hate this damn town. I hate this world – there's no justice. Nothing is fair."

"Jim, that's how it's always been. You of all people should know."

Jim went home and opened a bottle of Bushmills.

FIFTY-TWO

Jɪᴍ ᴡᴏᴋᴇ ᴜᴘ ᴀɴɢʀʏ. He was past feeling bad for throwing garbage back at the trucks, and he felt an unstoppable urge. He would fight those bastards, he thought, for Edgar and Maybelle, and Haley. And he knew, now, that the trucks were the same ones he saw when he was after Reid – they were connected with Reid somehow. *I'm a reporter*, Jim thought. *That's how I'll fight.*

At work, Jim went straight to Willy. He told him the story, and Willy simply pointed to the Obit Desk and shook his head. After the deadline, Jim walked down the stairs into Bernard's office where Audrey was meeting with her dad. He told them the story of the mistreatment of the folks in the projects. "These guys in trucks throwing garbage and stuff. It's not every night, but it happens enough to be a story."

Leaning back in his chair, Bernard, as usual, was attired in a dark blue blazer, crisp white shirt and striped tie. His silver hair was neatly trimmed and parted on the left. Bernard took off his glasses and rubbed his eyes.

He looked, Jim saw for the first time, old and tired.

"That story is as new as a story that the sun rises each morning. The only difference is, our readers don't care."

Jim was stunned. He admired Bernard but thought him a coward in that moment.

"Jim, you're not wrong. And, someday, things will change. But it will be slow, and a story like this will do more harm than good."

Jim knew the Hills made substantial contributions to the Simpson Village Community Center and he had assumed Bernard would be more sympathetic to the current plight of the community.

FIFTY-THREE

FRUSTRATED, Jim knew he had time before his appointment with Dr. Nance to stop in to visit with George Rogers,
the District Attorney. Rogers listened attentively and
compassionately.

"Jim, you know I would bend over backwards to find out
who was responsible for Mary's death. She was my most
talented assistant D.A., and a wonderful person. But what
you have is just supposition and guesswork. You have no
evidence these guys did anything."

"The truck with the Eagle emblem shows up everywhere something is wrong. How is that not evidence?" Jim
asked incredulously.

"It's just a truck, Jim, with a couple of guys drinking
beer. It doesn't prove they had anything to do with Mary's
death."

"Then what about the trash they're throwing? That's
a crime."

"It is. But we've had no complaints filed and, I promise
you, no one will testify. The black folks are scared, and they

don't trust the police." Rogers lowered his voice. "I don't blame them. We have a few bad apples on the force."

Jim was beside himself. "You're the DA," he complained.

"Yeah," Rogers replied. "And my hands are tied. You really don't know the world you are living in, son."

FIFTY-FOUR

DESPITE HIS INABILITY TO get Bernard or the DA to move forward, Jim's energy was heightened when he walked into Dr. Nance's office and began their session by telling her the events of the night before at Simpson Village.

"It was a pickup truck with an emblem on it. It was the same truck that was outside Irene's house or one just like it. It is all part of the same gang. I now know for sure it's an organized gang."

Dr. Nance listened without expression and, when he was through, said, "You, don't know it was the same truck. There could be many trucks with an eagle emblem. You look a little hung over. Did you eat breakfast this morning?"

"What, you are asking me? If I ate breakfast? And if I am hung over? I just told you, I was threatened. They are hassling the people at Simpson Village and they are throwing trash and Lord knows what else on their front yards. For God's sake, I am telling you what happened and all you are asking me is if I am hung over. What kind of shrink are you? I thought you were my friend."

"I am your therapist, Jim. Nothing more, nothing less. Are you drinking again, Jim?"

"Well, yes, last night I had a couple of beers," Jim admitted.

"You told me you didn't like beer. What was it you said? The first drink on a hot day is fine but after that it tastes like piss? You said, real Irish people only drink Bushmills. Remember, that's what you told me. Now which is it, beer or Bushmills?" Dr. Nance asked sternly.

Jim didn't answer. He just stared out the window and the resulting silence was uncomfortable.

"OK, I had some Bushmills last night. But you would, too, if you were threatened and witnessed what is going on at Simpson Village."

"Jim, I am strongly recommending you go back to AA and tell them that when you are stressed, you drink. I think their program will help you."

"For Christ's sake, Dr. Nance, I am not going to AA. I went there, and, as I told you, it is just a bunch of old men talking about their troubles. Here's a list of everyone who won't help me. Bernard at the paper, the DA, and I know the Lincoln Police won't help me. They are led by Captain Buckner and he was friends with Reid and Rev. Smallwood. They all are probably in on it. And now you. I'm on my own."

"I am on your side, and I want to help. Perhaps not as you'd like, but it is still help. Jim, you won't be able to proceed with your investigation if you are drunk. Anyone would laugh you out of their office."

Jim didn't react, just looked at Dr. Nance, then the clock on the wall, and was grateful the hour was almost up. He knew she was right and he shouldn't have drunk so much the night before. He knew he was close to knowing who was responsible for all his problems. He just needed help. He wished Mary were still with him. She would help, and she would understand.

"You know what the problem is," Jim proclaimed, standing up. "It's not just the bad actors. It's good people who do nothing. They let it happen and they're just as responsible for it."

"You echo the words of a wise and inspiring man, Jim. His name is Martin Luther King. The difference is change is his paramount priority. What's yours? Feeling sorry for yourself and drinking? Or fighting for what is right? As you drink remember this: you are another good person doing nothing."

Jim was stunned. At a loss for words, he stared out the window. The uneasy silence was interrupted by a knock on the door. Dr. Nance said, "Come in," and Judge McCallister opened the door.

"I see the hour is about up and I have some news, Jim, you may be interested in," Judge McCallister said.

"The hour was not up Judge," Dr. Nance said frowning.

"Yes, it is," Jim countered, delighted for the interruption. "We were done. What's the news?"

"Excuse me, Dr. Nance. But one of our faculty members does pro bono work up at the Ohio State Reformatory, and he just briefed me on a case I am sure Jim will be interested in.

"It seems a couple of guys up at Mansfield organized a group of prisoners, KKK fellows, to attack some of the Blacks during exercise time in the prison yard. Apparently, they didn't count well or underestimated the response. They got their asses kicked. Most of the Blacks ended up getting blamed, of course, but there is a twist.

One of the KKK fellows, who was looking at more time

on a new assault charge, made a deal and named the orga-
nizers of the attack. A few prisoners named Alex Reid and
Rev. Smallwood.

"Prison officials, faced with this clear evidence, have
reacted just as expected. They've done absolutely nothing.
But the story made its way to the local DA, thanks to our
professor. The judge up in that jurisdiction is famous for
being tough on people who cause trouble at the prison and
the DA is a good man. He is pushing for a max sentence,
and he'll get it. The judge will throw the book at Reid and
Smallwood. So, your two convicts Jim, when the judge acts,
are going to be in prison for five more years. That will put
Reid in for almost ten years and Smallwood for seven."

"Wow, now that's really good news. But I want them
nailed for what they did to Mary, Irene, and Steve,"
Jim said.

"Jim, you can't let this become an uncontrollable obsession. You have to be calm and reasoned," Dr. Nance
cautioned.

"Bullshit," Jim said. "I won't rest until I get those
responsible."

Judge McCallister, noticing the tension, took Jim by the
arm and began to usher him out. "One more thing, Jim.
Apparently, Rev. Smallwood was in the middle of the fight.
And you know, he is not in great physical shape, and apparently, he got the daylights beaten out of him. He is in the
prison hospital."

"Good," Jim muttered as he walked outside, "I hope the
son-of-a-bitch dies."

Discovering he left his favorite baseball cap in Dr.
Nance's office, Jim went back to the office. As he
approached the half-open door, he heard the judge and Dr.
Nance talking.

"I am worried about him, Judge. His obsession with finding those responsible for Mary Ryan's death is bordering on excessive. Plus, I am confident he is back drinking and that's not good. He won't consider AA, and the drinking, coupled with the obsession, is just a dangerous road he is going down."

"I was afraid that's what you would find out," the Judge lamented. "I think it is time, you, Audrey Hill, and I have a conference. Perhaps we need to have an intervention with young Jim. I would hate to see him go over the edge. He was close to taking his life, and as you know, the second time is usually fatal."

Dr. Nance agreed.

Both were startled when Jim walked into the room.

"I left my baseball cap. And let me tell you two something. I am not going to AA. I am not going to get totally drunk again. I am not going to kill myself. I am, however, going to find out who killed Mary. I would appreciate your help, but whether I get it or not, I am going to find out."

FIFTY-FIVE

SLAMMING the door to his truck, Jim was irritated and angry. Irritated at the thought he was being manipulated by Dr. Nance, the Judge, and perhaps even Audrey. Jim was angry at the world.

No one believes me. No one wants to help me. I know what happened, I just can't prove it, and no one is willing to help me. Well, screw them, I will do it myself.

"Stavros, a Coke, please," Jim said. It was April 15ᵗʰ, Tax Day, and Jim had dropped off his tax return in the mail box. More important to Jim, it was nine months since Mary died.

How can it be nine months? It seems like it was yesterday. How I wish Mary were still here.

Bantering with Stavros about the Ohio State basketball team lifted Jim's spirits. "I think with the University of Cincinnati and Ohio State, we are the basketball capital of the United States," Stavros contended.

Jim was shaking his head at Stavros reminding him Ohio State had been to the finals twice in the past three years but had lost both times to the Bearcats of Cincinnati.

He didn't notice an attractive young woman sit down on the bar stool next to him.

"Well, Jim Monaghan, are you going to buy me a drink?" asked Anna Masters, a former fellow student at Northwestern. Jim had heard through the grapevine that she was a junior stock broker at Merrill Lynch, but he hadn't seen her in a couple of years. Anna was tall with light brown hair and warm brown eyes. Her hair was pulled back in a low pony-tail and her smile was infectious.

Startled, Jim said, "For goodness sake, Anna, I haven't seen you since graduation. Of course, I will buy you a drink. I am having coke, but order whatever you want."

Under the watchful eye of Stavros, Anna placed her hand on Jim's arm and said quietly. "I have wanted to get in touch with you for a while. When I read about that horrible accident last summer, I felt so bad for you. And then I found out you and that poor girl were in love. I wanted to reach out, but I just didn't know how. We were friends at school, but not that close. Do you know what I mean? I don't know if this is a good time or not, but I just wanted to say hello."

"Surprising himself, Jim said, "It is fine. Actually, it is a good time. I have had a rough couple of days, but tonight is, well it's almost the start of a new day," Jim sputtered. "Let's get reacquainted and talk about how poorly the Northwestern football and basketball teams have played. I don't think they are getting better."

Smiling, Anna agreed.

For the next three hours, Anna sipped her wine and Jim drank cokes.

Jim found Anna easy to talk to. She told him she had just moved out of her parents' home in Lincoln and had her own apartment. She was excited about her latest promotion at Merrill Lynch and had hopes for a promising career. "Most of my colleagues are men, but I am as tough as any of them. Plus, I have an advantage. Some women only want to invest their money with a woman."

She encouraged Jim to tell her all about Mary, the copper casket investigation, and other stories he had written. It was almost eleven and Jim was about to ask Anna if she was interested in going down the street to one of the new clubs to dance. It would be the first time he asked a girl out since Mary died.

But he hesitated, wondering if he was being disloyal to Mary's memory. Staring off into space, he felt a nudge on his wrist.

"Did I lose you there for a minute, Jim?" Anna asked.

Not sure what to say, Jim just nodded.

"Well, this has been a fun evening, Jim. Maybe we can visit again sometime, ok?" Anna asked as she slid off the bar stool.

Watching Anna walk out of the bar, he turned to Stavros and asked, "Do you think I was being disloyal to Mary talking to Anna all evening. My God, I almost asked her out."

"Jim, I am your friend, and I am telling you what you did tonight was not only ok, it was necessary. You need to get out. Mary is gone, Jim. You can't live with just a memory. Call that girl up and take her to dinner."

Surprised at Stavros' fervor, Jim nodded and asked for a nightcap of Bushmills.

FIFTY-SIX

As WINTER TURNED to spring and Jim's Christmas nightmare was in the past, his life settled into a routine, or, as he described it, a rut. Not many general story assignments from Willy, just routine obits. He continued meeting with Dr. Nance and felt better. *Anna Masters has been an interesting addition to my life. Nothing serious, just fun get togethers,* he thought. *I am sticking to no more than two drinks a night most of the time. But I am not making any progress at unlocking the conspiracy. There must be a solution that I am missing. The Eagle Emblem is the key.*

"Hey Paula, do you want to play Twenty questions?" Jim asked his obituary partner. Paula trained Jim when he first arrived, and they had become friends. She was from Alabama and was a typical southern belle. She was married with two children and her husband was a high school Physical Education teacher. Dressed as if she was going to high tea, in a flowy skirt and ruffled blouse, her soft southern accent belied a fierce personality.

"It's time for lunch, Jim, and I brought a sack of goodies.

I can share with you if you like, and, sure, I would love to play a game," Paula said smiling from ear to ear.

"I am trying to figure out who owns these pickup trucks with Eagle emblems stenciled on the side. Think you can help me?

"Well, momma always said, if you don't know what's right, figure out what's wrong, and you will end up with the right answer. Pickup trucks. Hmm. Now, for sure the professors at the university don't drive them. The folks at Oberson's department store don't drive them. How about farmers? Every farmer I know has at least one pickup."

"The drivers look like farmhands or laborers."

"Well, there you go. How do they talk?"

"Like morons."

Paula laughed. "Okay, how do they dress? Dirty clothes, nice looking?"

"Dirty, like they just got out of the field. You know those Oshkosh coveralls."

"What kind of truck? Old, beat up, new, shiny?"

"Not brand new, but not old clunkers, either. "

"Then those aren't their trucks. Not on a worker's wage."

"So, I'm looking for a farmer or business owner," Jim concluded.

"You need to get a license plate number, so you can find out who owns the trucks," advised Paula.

Jim didn't have much hope for the license plate angle. Art Wilks, chief photographer for the Lincoln News Tribune had captured a license plate on a photo he took at a casket switching operation at Calvary Cemetery during the copper casket investigation. The plate turned out to have been stolen months before.

"It's funny, but I discounted farmers because every single one I have ever known was an upstanding citizen."

FIFTY-SEVEN

JIM HAD REJECTED the prospect of a farmer, he reflected, in large part because he was one. At least he used to be. He grew up on a farm, and for all his life, before college, almost everyone he knew was a farmer. And they were good people. The idea of one of them murdering someone was an impossible thought. Murders happened in cities. But, Jim reconsidered, there are bad people everywhere – a lesson he was learning all too well. *I don't know any rich farmers,* he thought, *but I know someone who knows them all.*

Checking with Willy, Jim was excused from any afternoon duty as the evening shift for the Saturday morning paper would be in soon. Jim called his brother, Hugh, and asked if he could come for supper.

Driving through Dale brought back bittersweet memories for Jim. He parked at the high school and walked over to the football/baseball athletic field complex and relived the glory days. But as he turned to the school's auditorium, he poignantly remembered the bitter night of his high school graduation. Sitting in school's study hall, joking with his friends about the right way to wear the tassel on his graduation cap, he noticed the school superintendent walking towards him with the county sheriff. He knew something was wrong but could not imagine what he was going to be told.

His dad and mom, driving to the graduation, had hit a pothole on the country road near their farm. His dad lost control of the car which slammed into a telephone pole. The car burst into flames and they both died. It has been the worst day of Jim's young life. The tragedy, however, increased the bond between Jim and his brother.

Hugh, Jim's older brother by two years, was delighted to see him. He took pride in showing his younger brother the improvements he had made around the farm and was especially proud of his new John Deere tractor. His wife cooked a delicious T-bone steak dinner. After dinner, the brothers sat in the living room with a bottle of Brandy and Benedictine.

"So, what is the reason we are honored to have the award-winning journalist from the big city of Lincoln as our guest tonight?" Hugh asked.

"You know I have always felt Reid and his crew were responsible for that truck that hit me and killed Mary. I believe Irene Dunn didn't fall down her steps and Steve didn't commit suicide."

Hugh nodded patiently. Jim had expressed his feelings on the matter a dozen times before, and every time he visited.

"The only connection I have are pickup trucks with an eagle emblem on the side. When I stayed at Edgar's, after Christmas, pickup trucks driven by white guys circled the neighborhood, and at least one and sometimes two, had the same eagle emblem. As we get closer to the Civil Rights Act being passed, Edgar tells me the frequency of the trucks driving by and hassling the folks is increasing. And let me tell you, Hugh, they are mean sons of bitches. One yelled at me to quit hanging around the Blacks or he would kick my ass. I saw pickup trucks with that same emblem on the door drive by Irene's house. Irene's house is a long way from any farm. There must be a connection, don't you think?"

"I don't know about that. Let me show you something." Hugh said seriously to his brother, "You better get another drink.'"

With that he walked out of the room and came back with a magazine. "Look at the cover."

Jim looked at the magazine, *Shelby County Farm Bureau*, and read the headline, "Outstanding Farmers." On the cover was a photo of the little man he had seen with Reid, Rev. Smallwood, and Captain Buckner at Smallwood's church and in the county jail's parking lot when Reid made bail. Jim was certain of it.

"That's him – Hugh, how did you know?"

Hugh calmly put his hand up to slow his brother down. "Read the article. You'll see."

Jim opened the magazine and flipped to the article. The background picture showed a truck with the eagle emblem, and the little man standing proudly beside it. Jim started reading furiously.

"Ronald Pugh, owner and operator of Eagle Incorporated, the largest farming operation in Shelby County just got bigger. He has purchased an additional section of land, increasing the size of his farm to three miles square."

The story went on to describe the Pugh operation, saying it was run military style, and Pugh had designed his personal headquarters, including his office, conference room, kitchen, and bathroom, on the second floor of his 20,000-square foot machine shed.

"Where is this guy's farm, Hugh?"

"It's just north of Lincoln. In fact, it borders the Simpson Village projects. That's where all the trees came from on the north end of Simpson. Pugh put them in, so he didn't have to look at the Village when he sits in his office. I was there once for a Farm Bureau meeting. The office is opulent with beautiful hard wood floors and wood-paneled walls. His desk is what is most impressive. He had it made to match the Resolute Desk, some presidents have used in the oval office. But let me tell you something, don't mess with him. From what I understand, he is one mean bastard," Hugh warned.

"What, he's a farmer. How dangerous can he be?"

"Let me tell you something. His people always cut in line at the co-op grain elevator when they bring in their crops. Everyone just gets out of their way. It's been that way since Pete Tyler, who you know from a couple of farms over, objected and wouldn't let Pugh's guy in. Well, Tyler showed up on the roof of the grain co-op building, and he had the shit beat out of him. He wouldn't say what happened, never reported it, but everyone knows who did it.

"Jim, you don't want to mess with Pugh. Tell me you will stay away from him. You are the only brother I've got, and we are the only family left."

Jim nodded agreement, but was thinking, *he's only a farmer; how tough can he be?*

After a great weekend at his brother's home, spending time with his nephew and niece, Jim decided to take a detour home. He approached Lincoln from the north. He slowed as he approached the Pugh Farm. On a whim, he pulled into the long, paved lane and approached the immense barn, but screeched to a stop, when a man with a rifle stepped out of a pickup truck that had an eagle emblem stenciled on the driver's door.

The man was over 200 pounds of hard muscle. His face was deeply tanned, and his thickly callused hands caressed the rifle. Dressed in gray one-piece work coveralls, he wore a black baseball hat with the eagle embroidered on the crown. "What do you want?" he bellowed.

"I heard about Mr. Pugh's machine shed and I was wondering if I could take a tour," Jim replied mildly.

"This is private property and there ain't no tours. Turn your piece of shit truck around, get the hell out, and don't come back," the man threatened.

Jim put his truck in reverse, backed out, and headed for Lincoln.

This Pugh is not just some farmer. No farmers I know have armed guards on their property. He must be the key to everything.

Jim's Timex watch read 5:30 p.m. His stomach rumbled, and he headed to Edgar's to see what Maybelle was fixing for dinner. He wanted to fill them in on what he learned about the trucks' owner.

FIFTY-EIGHT

"I DON'T THINK you should stay for dinner Jim. And I think you should leave now. Things got bad last night and this morning," a distraught Edgar warned.

"Jimmy can have supper, then he can leave," Maybelle said.

"What the h... heck happened, Edgar?" Jim asked, aware of Maybelle's arched eyebrow.

"Late Saturday night some hoodlums in white sheets drove into the neighborhood. Klansmen," Edgar stated. "Some teenagers were hanging out in the field across the street. Four of the Klansmen grabbed two kids, threw them in the back of their pickup, and drove off. It happened so quick, no one could do anything.

"The kids were found out by the fairgrounds and had been beaten pretty badly. The Peace Stones are getting organized, and I am afraid they are going to retaliate. And when they do, all hell will break loose. You need to leave and not spend time here until things get back to normal. You'll get it from both sides. Not every brother in this place knows you like I do. You're just a white guy. And you're a race traitor in the eyes of the Klan. Go home, Jim."

"What's normal?" a tearful Haley asked. "I don't want anything to happen to Jim."

"Nothing is going to happen to Jim," Maybelle said calmly. "Just eat your supper and go home, Jimmy. You will be all right."

Jim drove home and thought about the past 48 hours. *Ronald Pugh is the key. His trucks are at the scene when there is trouble. And, he was involved with Reid and Smallwood. Why else were they together outside the jail, when Reid made bail? Reid and Smallwood,* Jim laughed out loud bitterly. *I am glad they are in jail.*

How stupid of those two bastards to start a prison brawl – and to try to fight in it themselves. Surely, they would know they couldn't win a physical fight. Reid is weak, and Smallwood is just an overweight frump. Well, I'm glad they did and got their asses kicked.

Jim saw the dots connecting, and it all led back to Pugh and the Klan. He knew what Edgar, his family, and his neighborhood were enduring – the eagle trucks, those were Pugh's. *But is Pugh behind the Klan activity? Or is it just that some of his field hands are in the Klan? I know there are KKK people in the county, but to be brazen enough to kidnap a couple of kids and beat the daylights out of them! Why would Pugh risk be being involved in that?*

Jim conjectured that maybe Reid and Smallwood got involved with the Klan in prison, and Pugh's people were acting without his permission. For a minute, he almost believed that.

Jim arrived at work, just a little bit late, drawing a scowl from Willy. Being Monday, the obituary phone lines kept him, and Paula busy all morning, up to and past the two deadlines.

"Why do so many people die on the weekend?" he asked Paula.

"Gotta go sometime, Jim," she drawled.

After the final deadline, Jim leaned back and started to read the first edition of the paper, checking up on the Cincinnati Reds, his favorite baseball team. He was delighted his two favorite players, Pete Rose and Frank Robinson, were continuing their stellar play with both players hitting over .300. *Hall of fame numbers,* he thought. *And the Reds are still in the pennant race.*

Turning to the front page, he looked for the story from the police reporters on the attack at Fourth and Bradley and the subsequent discovery of the boys, battered and bruised, at the county fairgrounds.

It wasn't on page one or page three, where the most important local stories were placed. Leafing quickly through the pages, he found a short story on page 18.

Holding the paper, he walked over to Willy's desk. "Willy, help me understand something. How can a bunch of guys kidnap a couple of kids, beat them up, and it's not a page one story? Does the fact that the guys doing the kidnapping are white and the boys are black have anything to do with it?"

"Sit down, Monaghan. Shut your mouth and listen to me. Again, and I don't know how many times I have to tell you this, you are an obituary writer with some general assignment work. You don't decide what is on page one, page three, nor any line of any page on this paper. I do. I checked with Captain Buckner and he said, 'giving publicity to this type of action only encourages it,' so, that's why it is on page 18."

"This newspaper is taking editorial advice from Captain Buckner? You have to be shitting me, Willy!"

"Well, it's not Captain Buckner much longer. The old chief is retiring, and Buckner is going to be named Chief. I have an exclusive interview on the story and it is running on page one tomorrow, so, keep your mouth shut about it."

"Willy, give me a break. Let me write the story. Let me write a profile on Buckner." Jim had no intention of writing the puff piece he knew would be published. He would interview Buckner and ask him about Reid, Smallwood, Pugh, and that private meeting they had – for starters.

"Not a chance kid, not a chance. Now, don't you have something to do?" Willy waved his pudgy hand dismissively.

FIFTY-NINE

"I AM BEGINNING to hear some stuff." Sgt. Major Harlow looked at Jim somberly, as they sat at the bar at the American Legion Hall.

"What kind of stuff?"

"You know how guys brag, trying to impress one another. I am hearing there is an active KKK in the county. It's small, but I hear a couple of them drink here in the legion."

"Why do you think they are part of the Klan?"

"Well, Saturday night, a bunch of guys in white sheets picked up those boys up at Fourth and Bradley and beat them up and dumped them at the fairgrounds – right?"

"I'm surprised you knew. It was buried in the paper."

"I knew. And not just from reading the paper. Any word on how those kids are doing? I heard some maintenance guys found them.

"I don't know," Jim answered, thinking that he should find out. "You said you read it in the paper, but you found out another way."

"I did. Two guys, sitting at that table right there last

night, were drunk as skunks and talking louder than they realized. I overheard them, and I think they might have had something to do with it. Every other word was . . ." the Sgt. Major looked around and became uncharacteristically uncomfortable. "Nigger," he whispered. "Forgive me, that was the word they used. I almost came over to tell them about the black men who served under me in Korea. My men had more honor and courage than those two bastards. I was about to throw them out on their asses, but they were talking about those kids. And they didn't know I was listening, so I stayed quiet."

Jim was enthralled with the story but paused to reflect on what a good man the Sgt. Major was. Most people he knew never talked about race, and Jim didn't know until then where the Sgt. Major stood on it. Jim often felt like the odd man out, having a black "second family," and his admiration for his friend, the Sgt. Major, skyrocketed.

"They were laughing about one of the boys crying for his mama. They said Horace, one of their friends, must've been, came close to killing the one that gave him lip. Then one of them said the Chairman was pleased. Now, that doesn't make sense. The head of the KKK is called the Grand Goblin."

"You are kidding, Sgt. Major, one of the leaders of the KKK is called a Grand Goblin? That's rich," Jim laughed.

"It's not funny, Jim. They are serious people and dangerous, so, keep your voice down. You might want to consider hanging around here at night. I've seen those two in here before, but they keep to themselves. I expect they'll come back. I will talk to the commander and he will give you a waiver, since you are not a veteran, to be in the private area, where they'll be if they do come back. Who knows, they may be part of the same group you think killed Mary and Patrick's wife, Irene. But this is between you and me and we both are going to be careful. Got it?"

"Yes sir," Jim replied.

For the next three weeks, Jim became a regular at the American Legion hall bar. The two men had, as the Sgt. Major predicted, come back, but only occasionally. Jim came every night. He learned to sip his Bushmills on the rocks and kept his consumption to no more than two drinks a night. He was very proud of himself, but despite his efforts to befriend the two men, he hadn't made any progress. He didn't look the part, for starters.

"You some kind of hippie with that long hair? You one of them demonstrators?" was the harshest language Jim encountered, and he laughed it off. On a Tuesday night, during Jim's fourth week at the Legion, he sat with Sgt. Major Harlow complaining that this was all a waste of time. Sgt. Major answered, "Son, what do you know about camouflage?"

Jim quipped, "It's hard to see."

Harlow laughed, but pressed on, "That's the idea. It blends in, and you don't. You look, talk, and act like a college graduate. You need to give them something to relate to."

"Sgt. Major, can I ask your forgiveness in advance?"

"That depends – what for?"

"Dishonorable language."

Harlow smiled. "Camouflage. Forgiveness granted. Good hunting, Jim."

SIXTY

JIM RETURNED every night that week, ready with his plan to blend in and make a connection with the two strangers he had been lying in wait for. They did not show up until the weekend. It was one week before July 4th, and most of the legion members were planning for the annual Fourth of July parade. Jim thought of his last session with Dr. Nance. He told her he thought he was getting close to getting some concrete information, but she cautioned his drinking in a bar every night was dangerous.

The Sgt. Major had saved a barstool for him and both men sat facing the bar, where they could see the crowded tables behind them in the mirror. Conversation and laughter reverberated from the concrete block walls. Topics varied from the Viet Nam War to the Cincinnati Reds' chances of making it into the World Series. But what caught Jim's attention was the table just a few feet from where he and Harlow were sitting. One of the three men was silent and sullen, while the other two were gulping shots and beer and getting louder and louder.

Jim started a conversation with Harlow to get the men's

attention. He spoke loudly enough for the men to overhear it, but they were interrupted by the bartender, who handed the Sgt. Major the phone and told him he had a telephone call.

Harlow grabbed Jim's arm and pulled him near the phone. Holding the phone so Jim could hear and placing his hand over his other ear, he kept saying into the phone, "We have to meet soldier. We have to meet."

Because of the noise in the bar, Jim couldn't hear any of the other end of the conversation, but knew from Harlow's furrowed brow, it was an important call. When the call ended, Harlow asked for a bottle of Bushmills and two glasses and took Jim by the arm into the Commander's private office.

Shutting the door, Harlow motioned Jim to a chair and pulled his own up, so they were almost nose-to-nose.

"Get a hold of yourself son, because what I am going to tell you will change your life. Are you ready, Jim? You must be strong and controlled. Promise me, you will hear me out and help me make a plan."

Harlow wasn't angry. He was eerily solemn.

"Who the hell was on the phone, Sgt. Major?"

"I don't know. He kept his voice low and spoke rapidly. But I would recognize the voice if I heard it again. He said, 'Sgt. Major, I need to talk to you soldier to soldier. I was in Korea, too. I have done something very wrong and I can't live with myself. I know you are friends with the newspaper guy, Monaghan. Tell him the old lady was pushed down the stairs and the queer guy was murdered. The newspaper guy was supposed to just be injured, just put out of commission for a while. We didn't know the girl was in the truck with him. That wasn't supposed to happen. He was supposed to be alone. She shouldn't have died. I read her dad was a police captain and veteran, and, Sgt. Major, I feel so bad about all this, I just can't live with myself.'"

Harlow went on, "I pleaded with him to meet with me, but he kept saying 'No'. I asked him to go to the police and he said, he couldn't do that because the Chairman would kill him. He told me, Jim, you need to be very careful. This chairman is still furious with you because of Reid.

"He said this was all he could do to make things right, and then he hung up the phone.

"For God's sake, Jim, do you realize what this means? You have been right all along. I am sorry I didn't listen more carefully to you, but my God, you were right."

To his surprise, Jim's immediate reaction wasn't anger. He slumped in his chair and dropped his head into his hands.

"I am responsible for Mary dying. They were after me and she got killed. Why did she have to go with me in the truck? Why couldn't she have driven her own car?" Jim moaned.

"She was with you because she loved you, Jim. It was an accident. You didn't cause it. They did, and now we know for sure what happened. We just need to prove it. Where do you think we should start?"

Jim replied, "We need to identify the guy who called you. We need to be here every night. Can you, quietly, figure out who works at the Pugh farm and was in Korea?"

Jim suddenly jumped up, his chair tumbling backwards! "Holy shit, Sgt. Major! Do you remember that table with the three guys? Two were drinking shots and getting loud, while the third guy was just looking down at his drink. When you were on the phone, I looked over and didn't see the third guy. Then out of the corner of my eye, I think I saw him on the pay phone in the corner. I didn't think much of it at the time, but shit, that's him. Let's go get him!" Jim exclaimed.

Both men ran out of the Commander's office to the table where the three men were sitting. It was empty.

The Sgt. Major draped his arm around Jim, and with anger and resolve, he said softly, "They murdered Irene." His eyes showed a kind of surprise, like he just realized it, despite having heard minutes ago on the phone that it was true.

And, for the first time, Jim saw in him a need for support and condolence.

"I know," Jim said quietly. When you identify your informant, we can make our move. And I think we know who he is."

As Jim walked out of the room, he turned and looked at the bottle of Bushmills and his empty glass. *Didn't drink a drop. Can't wait to tell Dr. Nance.*

SIXTY-ONE

IMMEDIATELY AFTER THE LAST DEADLINE, Jim hurried to Audrey's office.

"I'm on my way to Dr. Nance's for my weekly shrink meeting, but I have to tell you what I found out on Saturday night. As Jim began to relay his story, Audrey stopped him, called her father over the intercom and asked him to join them.

Bernard listened without expression, while Audrey smiled and when Jim was through, she gave a small cheer. "Oh Jim, that's great. All this time, you have been certain, and you were right. I am so happy for you, but now, what's next?"

"Wait just a minute," Bernard warned. "What we know for certain is the Sgt. Major received a phone call. We don't know who called, or if he was telling the truth. You two need to settle down. We still don't know who did what or when. We just have a phone call. And no witness on the record – we don't even know who the witness is."

"That's true, Bernard, but at least we have a lead. We

think we know who it is. We need to be certain, but the Sgt. Major will recognize his voice when he hears it again."

"Proceed carefully, Jim. Proceed very carefully," Bernard cautioned.

"I don't care what my dad says," Audrey whispered as she walked him out of her office. "I think it is great you know now for sure. I am certain the phone call was legitimate. I can't prove it, of course, but it just feels right."

Dr. Nance told Jim she thought it was appropriate to bring the judge into the conversation. "I think he should hear what you have told me, and he will have a good idea what to do next."

The Judge and Dr. Nance sat silently while Jim retold his story.

"My goodness," the venerable Judge sighed. "That's troubling. I always felt for you, Jim. In your grief, I thought you were just looking for answers that simply weren't there. It is very frightening that such a criminal conspiracy could be going on here in Lincoln.

"But, what Bernard told you is absolutely true. The Sgt. Major received a phone call from someone he thinks he may be able to recognize. You saw a man on a pay phone, but you don't know if the man was talking to the Sgt. Major. It strains belief someone would make up a story and call him with it, but the phone call is all we know. If he can identify the caller and then get the caller to talk to the District Attorney, we have something. But until then, we really have just a phone call and suspicions."

"That's more than I've had until now. Before the phone call Saturday night, it was just me, who suspected a conspiracy, and everyone thought I was full of crap. Now, I am ever more committed to finding who is responsible," Jim contended.

"One more thing," added Jim, "the chances that this guy who made the phone call and his accomplices are the leaders seems remote. If it is all connected to Reid, then someone is pulling the strings. That's who I must identify. The others are just thugs."

"But, they are dangerous thugs, so be careful. If you think you are getting close, call the police," Judge McCallister counseled.

"One last thing," the judge said. "I have been dilatory, and I have not kept you up to date on another development. Remember when we were in the cemetery and digging up the graves. I told you and Mary that, with the evidence we uncovered that day, we would need an excellent plaintiff's attorney to sue Reid for damages, because I knew Reid and his legal team would fight hard.

"When Mary died, I just put everything on the back burner. But things have changed. I hosted a meeting with twenty families I identified as potential victims. I asked Brian Franko, the most highly regarded plaintiff's attorney in town, and maybe the best in the state, to join us.

"He eagerly accepted our case and he immediately started discovery proceedings. He and his team have gotten a lot of Reid's accounting papers and his bank statements. He called me today and said, it's a treasure chest of information, and he feels the financial complexity Reid had is amazing. He also told me there are other partners in Reid's organization, but it is going to take time to identify them. But that's all good news, Jim."

SIXTY-TWO

"Jimmy, it ain't' safe for you to be stopping by," Maybelle warned over the phone. "It's gettin' bad here. Civil Rights bill been passed, and President Johnson say he gonna sign it. If you come, make it early and leave before dark. Those trucks keep coming by, and the Peace Stones is gettin' restless. I will have Rev. Jefferson stop by, and maybe you can convince him not to march – 'specially on July 4th. I been tryin' to tell him, and so have others, but he ain't listening."

Despite Maybelle's warning, Jim joined them for supper bringing ice cream. "It's butter pecan, the best," he smiled. "You are the only one who thinks butter pecan is the best," Haley said, "but I will have some later."

He told Maybelle, Edgar, and Haley about the telephone call the Sgt. Major had on the telephone at the Legion hall Saturday night. Jim was measured in his conversation, trying not to sound too excited.

"I am pretty certain I saw the guy on the pay phone. I know, it's not for certain, but I sure feel it's him."

"It's good to know what happened, Jim, but it's also bad to know. Do you realize who you are dealing with? Let's say everything that guy told the Sgt. Major is true. These thugs are brutal," Edgar warned.

"I can take care of myself," Jim bristled, and he and his old friend exchanged a charged stare.

Rev. Jefferson entered and broke the tension in the room. He hugged Maybelle, and Haley, shook hands with Edgar and then Jim.

"Jim, it's good to see you."

"It is good to see you, too, Reverend," Jim answered. "I owe you a debt of gratitude. You pushed me in the right direction when we talked after Christmas. I have been seeing Dr. Nance regularly, and our frequent conversations have helped. My drinking is under control, and I am taking better care of myself. Most important, I think I have them." Jim recounted for Rev. Jefferson all the information he had collected, most notably the call to Sgt. Major Harlow. Rev. Jefferson leaned back in his chair and rubbed his chin.

"It's good to know your enemy, but you still are a long way from really doing anything about it. You can't provide any proof and, for something like this, your facts have to be airtight."

"I'll get there," Jim answered confidently. The Reverend patted Jim on the knee, and said, "I believe you will, son. I truly do." His tone grew solemn and his lips turned downward. He looked deeply at Jim and said, almost in a whisper, "What happens when you do, son, is truly frightening. May the Good Lord shepherd you, for your path ahead is through darkness where you will face the fallen." The room became hauntingly quiet. Jim, for the first time on his quest to avenge Mary, felt afraid.

Maybelle interjected, "Tell him to be careful, Reverend. He don't listen to a word no one says. Maybe he'll listen to a man of God."

The Reverend smiled, turned to Jim, and said, "I am sure everyone has told you to be careful and when you think you can prove who is responsible, you go directly to the DA, and have your friends at the newspaper on your side. No vigilante business. Hear me, son, no vigilantism," Rev. Jefferson warned.

"I notice you left the Lincoln Police Department off the list of people to see," Jim smirked.

"Yes," Rev. Jefferson answered earnestly. "I did. There are plenty of good men on the force, but I don't trust the new Chief."

Maybelle pulled a steaming, fragrant apple pie from the oven, and Rev. Jefferson joked about his impeccable timing. He went on to say how excited he was that President Johnson was going to sign the Civil Rights legislation on Thursday. "I talked to Dr. King today and congratulated him. He reminded me that the bill is a small step and we have such a long a road ahead. He asked me what I planned to do to walk that path. I was very proud to tell him that we have a march planned, a march of celebration on July 4th after the Legion parade is over. I am not going to interrupt their parade. We will begin an hour after their parade ends. I know you are worried, Maybelle, but it will be peaceful – no civil disobedience."

"I'm going to be in the front row of the March carrying a picture of Dr. King," Haley proudly announced.

"No, not going to happen," Maybelle sternly answered.

"Momma, I am 18 years old and a high school graduate. I am an adult and I can make up my own mind. I am going to march with Rev. Jefferson. There is nothing you can say that can change my mind."

"It could be dangerous, and you still my little girl," Maybelle pleaded.

Haley and Maybelle locked eyes, both frowning with determination.

Finally, Rev. Jefferson said, "Maybelle, your little girl is growing up. She will be safe in the march. I will keep an eye on her and so will Edgar. Actually, Maybelle, why aren't you marching?"

"Edgar, you marchin' too?" Maybelle asked. Edgar just smiled at his mother and nodded.

"Well, Lordy, Lordy, Lordy, I guess I am going to be in my first march on July Fourth. Who woulda thought?" Maybelle chuckled, smoothing her apron.

"You know, what I have just witnessed would make a great story for the paper. A family deciding to walk in the civil rights march. But, I know Willy would never print it. Perhaps I can weave part of it into the story I am writing about the march," Jim said.

SIXTY-THREE

It was a Wednesday morning at the obit desk. Mid-week was usually slow, but they were so busy Jim didn't have a chance to talk with Willy about the Civil Rights march on Saturday until late afternoon.

Willy asked, "Do they have a permit? Because if they don't have a permit, they can't march. I wonder if Chief Buckner knows about this parade. I am going to call him."

"Willy, it's a march, not a parade. And I would like to cover it. President Johnson is signing the civil rights legisla-tion tomorrow and we can run a story about the march as a sidebar to the legislation. Willy, both our Senators voted for the legislation as did every one of our Congressmen, except one. And his district is a long way from here. Everyone is getting behind this legislation, Willy, and it's about time, too."

"All right, Monaghan, talk to Rev. Jefferson. Get his take on the legislation, his relationship with Dr. King, and all that crap and I will find a place for it. We will run it as a follow-up to the civil rights legislation. You might call our Senators and Congress people and get some quotes. Don't forget to talk to the one who voted no. Find out why he is the only one in Ohio who voted against it. But be fair about it because, to some people, he is a hero. And don't expect it on page one."

"Oh, and one more thing, Willy, I am getting close to finding out who was behind Mary's death. We don't know who it was, but someone called the legion on Saturday night and essentially confessed," Jim said smiling.

"Just keep to the facts on the Reverend's story. Keep your pie-in-the-sky theories out of it, or I will kill the whole story. Just facts, Monaghan."

Feeling better than he had in months, Jim skipped down the stairs and ran into Bernard and Audrey as they were headed for lunch.

"Jim, we are going to the new restaurant opening on Main street. Want to go with us?" Audrey asked.

A beaming Jim answered, "Yes Ma'am. I am having a wonderful day. Best day in a long time, and I have news for you.

It was a festive atmosphere at the opening of the newest restaurant in Lincoln, La Cucina. Jim was surprised to find it had an Italian motif. Red and white checked tablecloths and chianti bottles with candles in the necks decorated the tables, and an Italian opera played softly in the background. The only Italian food Jim had ever eaten was spaghetti. Bernard told him to order the veal scaloppini. He did but butchered the pronunciation. The waiter was gracious and told Jim it was an excellent choice. Jim had no idea what he had ordered.

Jim brought the Hills up to date on the civil rights march Rev. Jefferson planned on July 4th and said how pleased he was that Willy assigned him to cover it.

"More important, he asked me to do a profile on Rev.

Jefferson. It's about time. He's been active in the civil rights movement for some time and has participated in some of the marches in the South. Dr. King called him yesterday to chat about what to do after the legislation is signed. Rev. Jefferson was with Dr. King in jail in Birmingham and was injured by Bull Connor's dogs and fire hoses. I think few people in town even know he exists."

"That's great, Jim. I am surprised Willy assigned you, but you must have worn him down. And it is about time we had some positive coverage of that part of town," Audrey said.

"That's not all. Judge McCallister has engaged a plaintiff's attorney whose team is going over Reid's financial documents. They are finding some interesting entries.

"Plus, I am spending nights at the legion with the Sgt. Major to see if he can recognize the guy who called him on Saturday night."

Before the Hills could react, Jim noticed five men sitting two tables away.

"Isn't that Chief Buckner at that table over there. And is that Ronald Pugh sitting with him? I recognize the mayor, but who are the others?

"Jim, if you are going to be a reporter here in Lincoln, you have to get to know the players. Yes, that's Chief Buckner, Mayor Scott Weir, and City Manager, Arlen Davis, and you are right, that is Ronald Pugh. The other man is Judge Lawlor." Bernard informed.

"What's the story on Pugh? I understand he is a big farmer?"

"He farms about 2,000 acres. He belongs to the Country Club, but never plays golf and is rarely there for dinner. I think I met his wife once or twice but haven't seen her in years. They don't have any children. Pugh keeps a very low profile but is involved in a lot of businesses here in town. In fact, I heard he is the money behind this restaurant," Bernard said.

At that point, Pugh turned in his seat and stared at Jim. Pugh appeared to be about five feet five or six inches tall and probably didn't weigh more than one hundred and forty pounds. His gray thinning hair was losing the battle to baldness. He was impressively dressed, Jim thought, admiring his blue blazer with gold buttons, white shirt, gray trousers, and black highly polished cowboy boots. He wore a bolo tie with an engraved eagle on the clasp.

Pugh's withering stare was one of pure hatred. Jim stared back thinking, *Are you the son-of-a-bitch responsible for Mary's death? Were you mixed up with Reid? Are you the one, you filthy son-of-a-bitch?*

As Pugh looked away, Jim felt a hand on his arm.

"Jim, you look like you are ready to jump out of your chair. What is it?" Audrey asked.

"You couldn't see, Audrey, but Pugh is sitting right behind you a couple of tables away, and he was staring at me. I just stared right back. Now, he is pointing towards me and everyone at his table is looking at me.

"They may be the most powerful people in this town, but I am not backing down from them. They are not intimidating me. Do you suppose they are all connected in this conspiracy?"

Bernard leaned across the table and spoke quietly, "Jim, you aren't suggesting the Mayor, the Manager, the Judge and the Police Chief are involved with Reid, are you? That's ridiculous. I have known Scott Weir his entire life, and I knew his father. Heck, his father started the country club thirty years ago. You are barking up the wrong tree, son. I know you are convinced there is a vast conspiracy out there, but trust me, that table is not involved. I am not a fan of Chief Buckner, and frankly I don't understand why the Manager named him Chief. But they are both from Alabama, so perhaps they knew one another down there. Audrey, maybe I should have one of the police reporters do a thorough profile on Buckner."

"Oh, please let me do the profile," Jim begged. But Bernard smiled and shook his head. "No, do the Rev. Jefferson profile first, Jim, then we will see."

SIXTY-FOUR

Jim finished his work on the obit desk and immediately started his editing on his profile of Rev. Jefferson. "Paula, would you mind reading copy on this story? I need to get it to Willy as soon as I can.

"President Johnson is going to sign the civil rights act tonight on television and we are going to have a lot of stories in the paper tomorrow. If I get this to Willy early, maybe it will get better play."

"My grandmother would be turning over in her grave if she knew I was helping you write a story about civil rights. You know she grew up in the deep South when times were very different. Well, it's about time these changes were made. Let me help you, Jim," Paula said.

Jim handed the story to Willy, then he called Rev. Jefferson and told him the story was submitted and chief photographer Art Wilks got some great pictures. "He also made copies of some of your photos with Dr. King, and Willy said, he might use them. Not sure what 'might' means, but at least we have a chance for a nice spread."

"Jim, we are putting a television up in our sanctuary

tonight and I expect a large crowd to watch the signing. I called Chief Buckner and told him we are going to have a crowd, probably overflow, but I promised him everyone would be peaceful. He told me he would hold me personally responsible if things got out of line."

"I would love to be there, Reverend," Jim offered. But Rev. Jefferson demurred. "Just let us celebrate by ourselves, Jim. This is our night to celebrate."

Not bothered by the non-invitation, Jim ambled down to Harlow's café for his usual evening dinner of a cheeseburger, fries, and a coke.

"Hey Sgt. Major, I had lunch the other day at the new Italian restaurant and had some veal thing. Not sure what Bernard called it, but it was decent. You ought to put in on your menu," Jim said laughing.

They chatted about the civil rights act. Jim knew Harlow's position of support, bolstered by the Sgt. Major's next comment. "See that hunk of a man sitting at the end of the counter. That's Johnny Washington and he is my best friend."

Jim looked at Washington, a man at least six feet six tall and weighing over 250 pounds. His ebony skin and dark eyes exuded strength. His white curly hair showed his age and his quick smile told Jim he had a mischievous side, too. "You talking about me, Sgt. Major?" Washington grinned as he elbowed Jim and squeezed into the booth with him.

"Sorry, little guy, but the Sgt. Major likes to sit by himself. You know, that Sgt. Major crap, and me just a plain Sgt.," Washington chuckled, looking directly at Harlow.

Harlow nodded, "Johnny and I were in Korea together, and we can't count the number of times, we saved one another. To me, Jim, Johnny is my brother and I don't give a shit what color his skin is. Let me tell you why.

"It was August 1951 -- the Battle of Bloody Ridge. The big shots were all meeting at Kaesong trying to negotiate a cease fire. But that didn't matter to me and Johnny; we were in a shit fire fight. The Ridge was taken by our guys, then lost. It rained buckets for days. I got hit in the leg and couldn't move."

Pointing at Washington, Harlow continued, "This man picked me up, slung me over his shoulder and carried me, over a mile, over steep and slippery terrain back behind the lines, where the medics took care of me. 2,500 of our guys died taking that damn Ridge."

"Yea, Sgt. Major, but 15,000 North Koreans died. But, what about a year before that at the Naktong Ridge. You did damn near the same thing for me. I would have bled out..."

But before Washington could finish, Harlow said, "That's enough war talk. Now, let's talk about something more important.

"You haven't been to the legion the last couple of days, Jim. I think I have our guy identified. We are going to have the tv on tonight to see our President sign that bill, and I expect there will be differing opinions. So, finish your supper and let's go down to the legion."

"Let me explain why I haven't been there, Sgt. Major. I met a girl. She went to Northwestern with me. She's fun. We have had a couple of dates, nothing serious, just friends."

"That's great, Jim, but we have serious business tonight, so keep your head screwed on right and don't be thinking of that girl. Things could get tense, if I have the right guy picked out. I have asked Johnny to be there tonight, just in case we need some back up. I doubt it, but it's good to have a backup, right Johnny?"

"Nobody's going to mess with you guys tonight. By the

way, kid, why don't you get a haircut and shave? You look like shit."

"Last summer, my hair was short, and I didn't have a beard. I don't want anyone to recognize me from last summer, so I let my hair grow and have this nice beard. Besides, I might play Santa Claus this Christmas," Jim bragged.

"What a bunch of bullshit," Washington moaned.

SIXTY-FIVE

THE SGT. MAJOR was correct in the reaction of a smattering of people at the Legion Hall to Johnson's signing of the Civil Rights Act. There were mutterings around the room. The voices were low, Jim thought because of the presence of Johnny Washington, who positioned himself in the middle of the 30-foot bar. Perched on a bar stool with his back to the bar, he had an unencumbered view of the entire room.

Jim and Harlow sat at the end of the bar, purposely separating themselves from Washington. "Are you surprised there are so many supporters of the legislation here?"

"Not to me," Harlow said, "a lot of these guys served with Blacks in Korea. You gotta remember back then, the Army was not that integrated. There were a lot of objections to the integration, but old Harry Truman made sure it happened.

All the concerns ended when the shooting started. Black soldiers were just as brave as the white ones. And when a Black soldier saved a white guy, word spread about it quickly. That's when the bitching stopped.

When you are in a foxhole, Jim, the next guy's skin color, or where he went to school, or who his father was doesn't mean shit. Remember what I told you about Johnny hauling my ass back behind the lines. Do you think I cared he was Black? In tough times, all you care about is, does he have my back? Will he cover me? There are a lot of guys like me whose best friends are Black. They may not advertise it, but they are friends. Of course, there are bigots in the service just like everyplace else, and there are a few bigots in the crowd tonight."

Nursing his first drink of the evening, Jim felt Harlow's sharp elbow in his side.

Harlow whispered, "That table over by the bathroom. Those are the same three guys from the other night. The one with the gray baseball hat, the one with the seed corn company logo. Is that the guy you saw on the pay phone? He keeps looking at me, but when I make eye contact, he turns away. "

"I think you are right," Jim said.

Harlow walked over to Washington and arranged a signal if he needed help.

"Let's grab that table next to them and start talking some trash," Harlow suggested to Jim. "I will sit where I can make eye contact with the guy. You sit near to one of those two big bruisers, so they can hear you talk."

Harlow and Jim sat down and started a loud conversation. Using the N word, they blamed all the problems in Lincoln on the Blacks and thought Johnson should be thrown out of office for even thinking about the Civil Rights bill. "Where are our Congressmen and Senators? Why are they all voting for this shit?" Their conversation continued in this vein for several minutes, when Harlow whispered to Jim, "He's going to the bathroom, keep talking to yourself."

While Harlow was in the bathroom with the man in the gray hat, Jim continued his soliloquy, acting drunk, slurring his words, and talking to himself about how the Blacks belonged on the plantation and why the hell was his home town named after Lincoln. "Son-of-bitch Lincoln, he freed the slaves and that started all of our problems," Jim said loudly, hoping the guys behind him heard.

"Hey Long Hair, come join us," one of the big men said.

"Thanks brother," Jim said as he sat down. *Jesus*, Jim thought to himself, *these guys are huge*. Both men were over six feet tall, broad at the shoulders with huge beer bellies. Their denim work shirts were bulging at the biceps and were stained with dirt and grease as were their camo pants. Both wore baseball caps -- one a green John Deere hat and the other a red International Harvester one. They smiled revealing yellowed, crooked teeth. Jim pulled up a chair and said, "That damn Johnson, next thing you know, he will want one of those Blackies to marry my sister."

"Damn right, Long Hair, said the man with the International Harvester hat. "This shit is getting out of hand. I can't believe a man from Texas would sign such shit legislation."

"Who's from Texas?" the green hat man said.

"You dumb shit, Johnson is from Texas."

"Why do you wear your hair like that, Long Hair and why the beard? Don't I know you from somewhere?" The man in the red hat asked.

"Yeah, I have seen you guys here in the Legion a lot. I do odd jobs around, some here at the Legion, and no one really cares what I look like. Plus, I save a lot of money. You guys must get yours cut twice a month," Jim joked. "By the way guys, my name is Mitch. Let me buy a round of drinks for some real Americans."

The man in the red hat said his name was Clyde and the man in the green hat said his name was Buck. Both thanked Mitch for the drinks.

"Well, Buck and Clyde, nice to see you in the Legion," the Sgt. Major said as he pulled up a chair. "I am running a survey. Do you think we should fly the Legion flag, not the American Flag, but the Legion flag at half-staff tomorrow?"

"Hell yes," Buck replied. "This is a sad night for white Americans. A sad night. But we don't intend to take it lying down. In fact, in an hour or so, a bunch of us guys are going to go over to Fourth and Bradley and kick some ass. We got a truckload of nasty trash and we gonna spread it all over those Blacks' front yards."

Clyde laughed and said, "Those assholes just look at us, and don't do a damn thing."

Jim continued the Black bashing, ordering drink after drink. Jim knew the duo were already inebriated when he sat down and hoped the drunker they got, the more they would talk.

Neither Buck nor Clyde, so engrossed in the conversation, noticed that Jim only pretended to drink. And neither remarked on the absence of their friend who had been at the table with them.

"Now, where in the hell did Delmar go?" Clyde finally asked. "You mean Delmar Batcher," Harlow asked, as he sat down at the table. "How the hell do you know Delmar?" a suspicious Clyde demanded.

"His sister comes into my café. I met Delmar a couple of weeks ago," Harlow answered. "He's a good guy, a real American, a stand-up guy."

"Yeah," Buck said, "but you know he is acting strange lately. Oh, screw him. He's got his own truck and he wasn't going with us tonight, so the hell with him. Now, I want to talk to my new friend, Mitch, about how the hell did this town got named after that asshole Lincoln.

"Sure, Buck, and I've got a question for you," Jim said, "but first, Bartender, a round of shots for my new friends!"

As the evening progressed, Clyde and Buck got drunker and Jim and Buck got friendlier. "Mitch, you are one standup guy. You know I like you. Would you like to join me and Clyde and throw some trash on some Blacks tonight?"

Jim punched Buck in the shoulder and said, "Absolutely, I would. I got to clean up the bar tonight after it closes, and I could get a shitload of trash for your pickup. That way, I ain't no freeloader like them Blacks, I'll be contributing."

"You got a gun, Mitch? Buck asked.

"Damn straight, I do," Jim said, "and it's a beauty, it's a 22 caliber Browning pistol with a hand-carved walnut handle."

"That ain't no gun, Mitch," Buck argued. "That's a pistol. I mean a gun. If we goin' hunting Blackies, we need a big gun. Some of them boys are big, and your little pistol won't do shit. When we go hunting, I'll get you a gun. You ready to do some huntin', Mitch?"

"Shut up, Buck, yer gitten' too drunk," Clyde growled.

"I can drink your ass under the table," Buck challenged, and Jim waved to the bartender, "Four more shots for my warriors!"

When the shots arrived, Jim downed his, saying, "Ok, let's see who can drink and who can't."

The other three followed suit, and Jim ordered another round.

Deliberately slurring his words, Jim looked at Buck and Clyde and said, "Guys, I gotta be straight with you. I ain't got no problems with throwing trash on front yards or even beating the shit out of a nigger, but I'm not sure I could shoot one.

"I'm a church- goin' man, and they may be black, but they're human, just barely, but they're human."

"Well, Buck does a lot of big talking," Clyde confided and then belched so loud, guys from three tables over yelled for him to shut up.

"Screw them," Clyde said.

Jim continued, "Now there's one group of people that I wouldn't have any problem putting down and that's them fags, them queers. That screwball Johnson is probably going to get civil rights for queers and that will be the last straw."

"Oh, yeah," Clyde stuttered, "Mitch, you right. The one thing that's worse than the Blacks are them queers."

"Rights for queers, that will be the last straw," Buck said. "I hate them Blacks and would love to see them go back to Africa or just die. But, if I see one of them queers, it just turns my stomach."

"You know guys, added Jim, I wouldn't mind killing one of them queers. Fact is, couple of my friends and I were in a bar, and one of those bastards grabbed my ass. I turned around and cold cocked him."

"Right on, Mitch," Buck said, clapping Jim on the back. "I bet it felt real good."

"Yeah, you're right, Buck, in fact, it isn't even a sin because it says in the Bible, they are the real sinners. Says, right there in the Bible, they're going against God's law."

Buck, Clyde, and Harlow all voiced their agreement and Buck stood up and yelled at the bartender, "More shots for my warriors."

"Hey, Buck, that's my line," Jim joked.

"Well, ain't we brothers, Mitch?" Buck asked.

"Damn, straight, we are," Jim said.

"Wait a minute, guys," Jim said, "I am going to nominate a queer for fag of the year. Do you guys remember last summer, they found one of them queers up at Crystal Park with a gun in his hand and a suicide note. Stupid bastard killed himself. Probably just wanted to put himself out of his misery. Well, I am glad he did it. One less queer to grab my ass."

Buck leaned over grinning conspiratorially and said in a low voice "Are you sure he killed himself?"

Jim reared back in his chair. "What the... do you mean, am I sure he killed himself? Of course, I am sure. He had a gun in his hand, he wrote a suicide note, and it was right there in the newspaper. It said, he committed suicide."

"Are you sure?" Buck asked, now more serious.

"Shut up, Buck," Clyde snarled.

"Wait a minute," Jim said. "Are you saying what I think you are saying? Someone killed him?" Punching Buck in the shoulder, Jim continued "Man, if that's true, I would buy that guy three shots."

Buck looked at Harlow and then at Jim and sat straight up in his chair. "Mitch, my new friend, why don't you order me three shots and get three shots for Clyde and Harlow here. Shit, man, let's order four for you and me."

"Absolutely, yes, Buck, you the man. And you ain't in any trouble with the Good Book.

It says in the good book, they are sinners and are going to hell. Shit, man, you just sped the process along," Jim said, jubilantly.

Clyde's face turned red and he twisted Buck's arm. "Shut up, or I'll tell the Chairman. He'll be pissed at you and you know what happens when he gets pissed."

"Well screw the chairman," Buck retorted. "We did our

part and he promised us a bonus. But where the hell is the money? I ain't seen none of it. He welched on the deal. I did the hard work. You held him, and I put the gun in his hand and pulled the trigger. That took skill. All you did was grab that old woman and push her down the stairs."

"Shut up, Buck!" Clyde shouted and started to stand up.

Harlow told Buck and Clyde to settle down. "It's the booze that's got you two guys fighting with one another. It's time to switch to beer."

Standing up, he shouted, "Hey, bartender, we need four Budweiser's over here."

That was the signal Washington was waiting for and, with two men almost his size, he slowly advanced to the table.

Jim took a deep breath, leaned across the table, and said, "The Sgt. Major and I each have a question for you." "Fine, Mitch, let's hear your question. Is it about what the queer said before he died? He begged like a baby."

Neither Jim or Harlow reacted.

In rapid fire, Harlow and Jim asked almost simultaneously,

"The old lady was her name Irene?"

"Which one of you bastards rammed my truck into that pole and killed Mary Ryan?"

SIXTY-SIX

"Who are you, punk?" Clyde shouted as he reached across the table and squeezed his beefy fingers around Jim's neck. "Who the hell are you?"

Jim fought to pry Clyde's deadly grip from his throat. He was choking. Harlow jumped up, grabbed Clyde by the shoulders, threw him to the ground. Clyde's grip was like a vise on Jim's neck, and as he fell, he pulled Jim across the table and onto the floor.

Johnny Washington put his massive arms around Clyde's chest, while Harlow wrenched back Clyde's beefy fingers from Jim's neck, leaving bright red welts.

The two other men pinioned Buck's arms.

"Call the police," Harlow shouted to the bartender. "They killed Patrick's wife! Hold them down, guys." Buck and Clyde lay face down on the concrete floor, restrained by Johnny and his buddies.

Bar patrons crowded in for a closer look.

"These two bastards killed Patrick Dunn's wife, Irene. They pushed her down the stairs and she broke her neck." Harlow's voice rang with emotion.

Buck and Clyde squirmed and tried to get up, yelling insults to Harlow and Jim. "You stupid bastards, you don't know who you are dealing with. We have powerful friends, and you guys are screwed!" Clyde yelled.

Washington loomed over the men writhing on the ground. "Either one of you assholes move and I will belt you."

"I thought we were friends, Mitch," Buck pleaded.

Jim just stared at the two. "No, we are not friends, you pile of shit. Which one of you drove the truck that hit me. Was it you, Clyde? Was it you, Buck? Come on tough guys, admit it. Who did it?

It didn't take long for the wail of sirens to pierce the air. Jim continued to stand over Buck and Clyde and stare at them.

After all this time, I am looking at the faces of the people who killed Irene and Steve and probably rammed my truck and killed Mary. Why do I feel so numb? I thought I would be jumping for joy. But I just feel like shit. Those assholes.

The police arrived in force, led by the eleven-seven shift commander, Lt. Everett Malcolm.

Harlow explained that Buck admitted shooting Hampton and reported Clyde pushed Irene Dunn down the stairs. Both victims had been scheduled to testify in the Alex Reid trial. Both died within 24 hours of one another and only a week before the trial. Harlow went on to tell Malcolm that Monaghan was to testify, too, and when Monaghan asked them, "... and I remember it exactly, 'Which one of you bastards rammed my truck into the pole and killed Mary Ryan?' this prick, pointing to Clyde, here lunged at him and grabbed his neck.

"Look at Monaghan's neck. It is red and obviously, Clyde tried to strangle him."

Clyde and Buck protested. They argued they were misunderstood, and that Monaghan started the fight, and they were just defending themselves.

Based on Harlow's recounting of events, Lt. Everett handcuffed Buck and Clyde, and he ordered four of his officers to escort them to a police car. Jim watched with grim pleasure.

Finally, justice, he thought.

As Lt. Everett started to leave, one of his officers came in and whispered in his ear. Turning to Jim, he said, "Those two fellas are insisting you started the fight, so we have to take you in for questioning. As Jim was being handcuffed, many of the Legion members protested. "No, he didn't start the fight," several contended.

Lt. Malcolm, surrounded by some 50 veterans of Korea and World War II, paused and turned to Harlow.

"Sgt. Major tell me the truth. How did the fight start?"

"That guy, Clyde, grabbed Monaghan by the neck and tried to choke him. That's how it started."

"Is that right, Monaghan? Is that what happened?" Lt. Malcolm asked Jim.

"It's exactly how it happened." And a chorus of Legionnaires shouted agreement.

Malcolm removed Jim's handcuffs and told him and Harlow the detectives would be in touch with them in the morning to get their statements. "Right now, we are just arresting them for disorderly conduct and fighting. After you talk to the detectives, there may be more, but that's it for tonight."

SIXTY-SEVEN

When the police left, there was loud muttering in the room about Irene Dunn's murder. Her husband, Patrick was a popular former commander of the Legion Post and decorated war veteran. The muttering turned to talk of revenge, but Harlow calmed the group by saying, "Let the police and the prosecutors handle this. No one here gets out of line. Patrick would not want anyone to do anything that would violate the law. You all know that."

The room settled down and men clapped Harlow and Jim on the back. Jim went to Washington and his two friends and thanked them for having his back. "That guy had such a grip on my neck, I almost passed out. Thanks guys."

"No problem," replied Washington. "I told you and the Sgt. Major, nobody was going to mess with you tonight."

After the crowd dissipated, Jim and Harlow had a private moment.

"Well, Sgt. Major, this long journey is almost over. But we are still far from total justice. There is no question that if those two guys killed Irene and Hampton, and they sure as hell rammed my truck. I now know, for sure, it wasn't an accident, and the guys responsible are behind bars. But Clyde and Buck are dumb as a sack of bricks. They would not have done those things on their own. Someone is behind all this and I need to identify him or them.

"And I am so grateful to you Sgt. Major. Without you none of this would have happened. But we still have a trial to get through."

Both men paused, reflecting on the evening, when Jim turned to Harlow and asked,

"How in the hell did you know the third guy's name was Delmar Batcher?"

Grinning with mischief, Harlow turned and said, "I was wondering if you were ever going to ask me about my time in the bathroom. Let me tell you, it was something."

"What happened? Did he tell you his name? Did he admit to everything he told you on the phone?" Jim sputtered his questions rapid fire.

"When I followed him into the bathroom, he was waiting for me and he looked scared shitless. In fact, the first words out of his mouth were, 'I am scared shitless, Sgt. Major.' And when he spoke, I immediately recognized his voice.

"I told him, 'I know who you are, and I know you called me. I need your name and how do I get ahold of you?'

"He was just shaking, and told me, 'I can't do that Sgt. Major, he'll kill me. He is evil and powerful. He is worse than anything we saw in Korea. I can't give you my name.'

"So, I pushed him up against the wall and told him I wanted his name and wanted to know if everything he told me on the phone was true. He said it was the God's truth, but still wouldn't give me his name. Then, he said his sister was Sally Batcher, and she lived over near the university, and she could get ahold of him.

"I asked him if he killed Irene or Hampton and was he driving the truck that hit you. He said he didn't do any of it but was there. He told me it was Clyde and Buck and they were sitting at his table. So, I told him to get the hell out of the Legion.

"When Clyde asked where Delmar went, I just guessed his last name was Batcher, like his sister, and I was lucky. So, we know his name and how to get ahold of him. But I bet those two bastards are suspicious of him, so he may go into hiding. He sure is afraid of this guy they call, the Chairman."

"Son of a bitch, what an evening," Jim sighed.

SIXTY-EIGHT

AFTER JUST A FEW HOURS' sleep, Jim ran up the steps to the city room and plopped down at the obit desk. He decided to play it cool. Two of those responsible for Mary's death were in jail. Rather than tell Audrey and Bernard or rub it in to Willy, he decided to let them read it in the paper.

Finishing up his last obit, he waited for the first edition to be printed and dropped off in the city room. When it arrived, he poured through every page and found nothing about the arrests.

Controlling his fury, he walked to the police reporters' desk. "There were two guys arrested at the Legion last night, but I don't see anything in the paper about it," he asked calmly.

"There was nothing on the overnight reports about it. There was a drunk-and- disorderly arrest at the university," the most senior veteran said. "What do you know that we don't?"

"I was at the Legion last night. There was a fight, and two guys were arrested. They told me and Sgt. Major

Harlow they killed Irene Dunn and Steve Hampton. When I asked them if they rammed my truck into the utility pole, one lunged at me and grabbed me by the neck. Lt. Malcolm and four of his officers arrested the guys. I know that for a fact," Jim said with conviction.

"Sorry, Jim, but there was nothing in the reports about any of that. I will check later, but if it wasn't in the overnight reports, it didn't happen."

Jim went down the street to O'Toole's and called Harlow. The server at the café told him the Sgt. Major was at the grocery store, but she would have him call Jim. After ordering a Bushmills, he told Stavros his story.

"I simply can't believe this shit. I stopped at the cop shop and talked to the day shift and no one there knows anything about last night. I even stopped in at the Chief's office, but he was too busy to see me. Tonight, I am going to go see Lt. Malcom and the night shift people and find out what happened.

SIXTY-NINE

As Jim contemplated ordering his second drink of the afternoon, he thought of George Rogers, Mary's boss and Shelby County District Attorney. *He will act on this information, I know he will.*

The Shelby County District Attorney's headquarters occupied the entire second floor of the County's new steel and glass building. Climbing the steps to the second floor, Jim thought back to his first trip when he sought the advice of an attorney about the potential crimes of Reid's casket switching operation. That was when he met Mary Ryan.

The receptionist, who acted like a drill Sargent at Jim's first visit to the DA's office, now greeted him warmly. She said that Mr. Rogers was available and for Jim to walk back to his office.

Jim hesitated because he knew he would be walking past Mary's old office. Would it be occupied, he wondered? Jim paused at the door and looked in. It was bare. No papers on the desk, no files on the credenza. As he paused, he felt an arm across his shoulder.

"We don't have the heart to move anyone in," George

Rogers spoke softly to Jim. "Everyone here knows how much you loved her, Jim, but Mary was very special to us, too. Someday, we will move someone in, but not for a while. Now, how can I help you?"

Rogers looked impressive in a blue suit, white shirt and red tie. His dark brown hair was becoming flecked with gray. Jim noticed Rogers had lost some weight. *Probably getting ready for his run for Congress,* Jim thought.

Jim relayed the story of the previous evening. He was furious that the men at the Legion bar bragged about fooling the police, who called Hampton's death a suicide. Jim went on, "I'm glad those two who said their names were Clyde and Buck, are in jail, but our police reporters told me this morning there was nothing on the overnight reports. Not even a mention of the arrests. And a guy, who tipped off the Sgt. Major, and admitted to knowing about Irene and Hampton's murders, has the information we need to send them to prison permanently. His name is Delmar Batcher.

He called Harlow, a day or so ago, on the phone and said he couldn't live with himself and had to tell someone about Irene and Steve being murdered. Then, last night, Harlow met him in the bathroom at the Legion. Batcher told the Sgt. Major, it was Clyde and Buck who killed Irene and Steve and they were driving the truck that rammed me.

"He told Harlow, he was sorry Mary died, but they didn't know she was going to be in the truck. They just wanted to hurt me and put me out of commission. I want your office to investigate and bring him in for questioning."

"We just can't bring people in off the street and start questioning them, Jim. We need a charge. We could have a grand jury, but who is going to testify? They could say it was all bar talk and then where would we be?" Rogers counseled.

"If we get Batcher to come in and talk to you, will that help?"

"Absolutely. That would make a huge difference," Rogers nodded.

"Then we will find him and bring him in," Jim said.

"Now be careful, Jim. He must come in on his own volition. You can't coerce him, or you will be in trouble."

"I will handle it," Jim said.

"Jim, I appreciate your passion and I know you are a serious and intelligent young man. I am encouraging you to keep looking but be careful. If you are correct, these people are dangerous and can hurt you. When you find out anything concrete, or if you can get this Batcher fellow to talk, call me immediately and I will get one of the sheriff's deputies to help you. Call me anytime day or night."

Jim was gratified by Roger's encouragement and even more so when Rogers gave him his home phone number.

SEVENTY

BACK AT O'TOOLE's, Jim chatted with Stavros until it was time for the late shift to convene at the cop shop. Jim prided himself on drinking cokes. He thought about the tension and excitement of the past few days and, other than the one drink earlier in the day, he had his drinking under control. Plus, he knew it wasn't smart to show up at the police station at eleven at night with booze on his breath.

The first-person Jim saw at the station, just before the night shift went on duty, was Lt. Malcolm.

"What the hell happened to those two guys you arrested last night at the Legion?" Jim questioned.

"I figured you would be here tonight," Lt. Malcolm replied. "We brought them in and put them in the night lock-up. I was out patrolling when the duty officer called me around four in the morning and said the Chief was in the building. I couldn't imagine what had happened, so I came back to the station as soon as I could. When I got here, the Chief was walking the two guys out, and he told me, 'I talked to those guys and they were just bullshitting that kid and the Sgt. Major. They didn't have anything to do with anything, so we are cutting them loose. You can't arrest someone for bullshitting at a bar. And so, what if there was a little pushing and shoving? No big deal.'

"I told the chief they were arrested for disorderly conduct and he told me, 'Oh, hell, Malcolm, boys will be boys. We have more important things to investigate.'"

"You have to be shitting me, Lieutenant. Is it normal for the Chief to come in at four in the morning? Did those guys make any phone calls? I mean this is just wrong. They admitted killing Irene and Hampton. And Clyde tried to choke me; I couldn't breathe."

Lt. Malcom lowered his head and stared at his shoes and didn't comment for a moment. In a soft, almost inaudible voice, he said,

"The old Chief never came in at four in the morning. I have been working the eleven to seven shift since I was a rookie. I never saw the old Chief except on ceremonial days. I don't know the new Chief as he rarely showed up on my shift when he was the Captain. This is the first time I have ever seen any Chief in the building at four in the morning."

"I don't know if they made any phone calls. It would be their right to do so, but I don't know. I will ask around, but I must get out on the street. I can talk to you tomorrow."

Totally depressed and angry, Jim drove back to his apartment. He realized he hadn't watched Johnson sign the landmark civil rights legislation. He realized he didn't care. He opened his cabinet where there was a half-bottle of Bushmills.

He drank it all.

SEVENTY-ONE

"I've got a touch of the flu and won't be in," Jim told Willy, who replied, "Bullshit, Monaghan, you're hungover. I doubt it is the flu, but make sure you are here Saturday morning. We are having wall-to-wall coverage of the Fourth of July Parade in the Sunday paper, so plan on being here all-day Saturday. I want you get reaction from the Legion guys in the parade. Oh yeah, you need to cover Rev. Jefferson's parade, too."

"It's a march, Willy, not a parade," Jim rejoined.

"Whatever."

Jim focused on what he knew about the murders. The one common thread in was the eagle emblem. Jim was sure that Pugh was the force and money behind it all, but he needed to discover who was called The Chairman.

Jim recalled that one of the deputies said that Reid, when he was arrested was belligerent during his first phone call, but when he spoke to someone he called 'Chairman' he was meek and apologetic.

And Clyde told Buck, the "Chairman" would be pissed if

he knew Buck was talking about killing Irene and Hampton, Jim thought. *Who the hell is the Chairman? Is it Pugh?*

Jim was sure Delmar Batcher would be able to offer solid information. *We have to get Batcher to talk.*

Gathering his notes, Jim called the Judge and asked him to meet him at Dr. Nance's office. He told him he had some information he wanted to pass by him and Dr. Nance. Arriving early at Dr. Nance's office, Jim was chatting with the Judge in Dr. Nance's outer office when Audrey walked out with Dr. Nance.

"I thought you had the flu, Jim," Audrey sheepishly said, her eyes lowered and her cheeks turning red.

"I feel better. I didn't know you were a patient of Dr. Nance's," Jim countered, and an uncomfortable silence lingered.

"We all have issues, Jim. I have worked with Dr. Nance for a couple of years, but like your sessions, mine are private.

"Well, I am glad you are both here, and as you can see, I have asked the Judge to join us. Let me tell you about the past 48 hours.

Jim recounted the events at the Legion Hall and Harlow's conversation with Delmar Batcher. He told of being handcuffed and being blamed for starting the fight but was released when Lt. Malcolm listened to Harlow. He told them about the unusual visit by Chief Buckner to the police station at four in the morning and the men named Buck and Clyde being released.

"The Chief said it was just boys being boys and barroom talk. Such bullshit. And Lt. Malcolm told me the old Chief never showed up at four in the morning and couldn't explain why Chief Buckner was there. He told me he didn't know Chief Buckner that well."

He told them about his visit with George Rogers and his interest in talking with Batcher and how he hoped he and Harlow could find him and convince him to turn state's evidence.

Jim noticed Judge McCallister stooped over in his chair, shaking his head from side to side.

"This is just terrible. Who can believe such activity is going on in our town. I am a retired federal judge. I have adjudicated countless cases of crime and corruption. And tomorrow is the celebration of our Independence. I wonder sometimes, just how far we have come. We are a nation of laws and the system should, it must catch lawbreakers and put them away. But I know that is idealistic. I know there are criminals walking the streets. It just bothers me when it happens. What in the world was the Chief of Police doing at four in the morning interviewing two thugs arrested on battery charges. It doesn't make sense. And all this malicious activity at Fourth and Bradley. Perhaps, it is time for me to step up and be more active."

Dr. Nance, Audrey, and Jim nodded in agreement.

"And I think the newspaper can do more," Audrey said.

"Well, we can talk about all of this another time," Dr. Nance said, "but this is Jim's time and we have some ground to cover today."

After Audrey and the Judge left, Dr. Nance turned to Jim and asked, "How much did you have to drink last night?"

"Oh, I had a couple of beers," Jim replied.

"Jim, we have gone through this before. You didn't have a couple of beers last night. You know it and so do I. Now, answer me, how much did you have to drink last night?"

"I drank a half bottle of Bushmills and, yes, I was hung over this morning. But last night, I just didn't give a shit.

When I found out the Chief let those guys out of jail, I just didn't care about anything. Can you understand that?" Jim asked.

"Of course, I can," Dr. Nance said. "But you have to learn to deal with life without giving in to depression and getting drunk. It will kill you. I am going to suggest again you go to AA. I think you are an alcoholic, and I think you suspect you are, too." "I am not going to AA. I can stop any time I want to," Jim replied, while looking away.

"Yes, Jim you can stop any time you want, except when things don't go your way."

SEVENTY-TWO

JIM ROSE EARLY on the Fourth of July. He felt good. He wasn't hung over. He didn't need to drink water to hydrate his dry mouth and he didn't need an aspirin for a headache.

He thought his appointment with Dr. Nance went well. She listened and didn't challenge him too much. Jim was bothered by the AA recommendation, but knew he could control his drinking, so it was no problem. After all, he didn't drink last night.

He remained curious about Audrey's presence. Jim had heard Audrey had problems with her husband, Jasper. The stories were he couldn't keep a job, drank too much, and ran around with other women. Jim remembered Mary talking about how much she admired Audrey. *Well, if she is having problems, Dr. Nance may be helping her.*

He got dressed and ready to go to a parade and a march. *I could have three byline stories in the paper tomorrow. Willy told me he was holding Rev. Jefferson's profile for Sunday's paper. That and my coverage of the Legion's parade and Rev. Jefferson's Civil Rights March, should make for my best day at the paper.*

He thought of Anna Masters. For the past few months, their frequency of meetings was increasing. Usually at O'Toole's or Harlow's for dinner and then dancing. The relationship was evolving, Jim thought, or was it.

There had been some serious fooling around lately, but Jim knew it wasn't the same as with Mary. In fact, he often thought Mary was in the room watching, and he felt guilty.

The last time they were together Anna brought it up. Her words still stung.

"Jim sometimes when we are together, you aren't here. Your mind is someplace else. I can't compete with Mary, and I am not trying. But sometimes, you are just impossible to be with because you are not present. Do you understand? Sometimes, I feel like I am kissing someone who isn't kissing me back. It seems like you are just going through the motions. And it hurts, Jim. It hurts."

Jim liked Anna and didn't want to hurt or insult her. He was doing his best, but he still missed Mary intensely and thought about her all the time. Jim and Anna were to meet after Jim wrote his stories on the parade and the march and Jim hoped he could be more attentive and put her at ease.

SEVENTY-THREE

It was a perfect day for a parade. The sun was shining, the humidity was low for a July day in central Ohio, and a slight breeze ruffled the leaves.

Jim met up with the Sgt. Major at First and Main, the gathering spot for the start of the parade. Impressed Harlow could still fit into his army uniform, Jim asked him about the various ribbons on his chest. He was especially impressed with two medals, the Silver Star and the Distinguished Service Cross.

"Did you get both in Korea or was one in World War II?" Jim asked.

"I got them at the Army PX. They were having a sale," Harlow grinned. Johnny Washington, watching the exchange, pulled Jim aside and said, "He got them both at Heartbreak Ridge in Korea, but he will never talk about it, so don't ask him. He did unbelievable things that day, but lost half of his team. Never ask him about it, ok?"

"Yes, sir," Jim almost felt the need to salute the imposing ex-soldier.

"Sgt. Major, did you hear Chief Buckner released Buck and Clyde at four a.m.?"

"Yeah, I heard that, but it's worse. I went to Delmar Batcher's sister's house and asked her where I could find Delmar, and she slammed the door in my face.

"The parade is about to start. We can talk later," Harlow said.

Jim thought the parade was spectacular. The five Lincoln High school marching bands were resplendent in their uniforms. Various organizations had floats, and the best, in Jim's eyes was the one provided by the Daughters of the American Revolution. It was decorated in red, white, and blue ribbons and featured women, young and old, in colorful period costumes, including bonnets and high-button shoes.

The DAR float paused right next to where Jim was walking. He found himself staring at one of the young women. She smiled and waved. Jim waved back and yelled over a compliment about how great the float was and how nice she looked.

"Thanks. We are hosting a reception at the end of the parade. "Why don't you drop by?" the pretty young woman invited.

"I'll be there," Jim answered. Well, he thought, there is nothing wrong with me. I just made a date for after the parade and I don't feel guilty about it.

The streets were lined three and four deep with families waving American Flags and cheering. At the end of the parade, Jim was impressed with the solemn presentation of arms by the Legion. Mayor Scott Weir called for a moment of silence, which was pierced by the sound of taps from a lone bugler.

Jim looked for the DAR reception and found it to be a

popular gathering spot.

"I'm glad you stopped by. My name is Jenny Fowler," the pretty young woman said.

"Well, after that smile and that invitation, of course I am here," Jim said as he admired the tall, nearly five-foot eight, slim blonde with sparkling eyes.

"That dress looks uncomfortable. "You must be sweltering under the sun today," Jim said.

"Oh, it's not bad, and it's only once a year. Mother is related to both the Cabot and Lodge families back in Massachusetts, so this is a big deal to her. I am a senior at Hamilton University. Who are you and what do you do? Were you involved in the parade?" Jenny asked smiling.

"I am Jim Monaghan and I am a reporter for the News Tribune. Why don't you give me some quotes for the story I am writing, and I will put them in the paper."

Spying Art Wilks, the News Tribune's chief photographer, he asked him to take Jenny's picture near the float.

"Hope the picture gets in the paper," Jim said. "I have to go back and write my story."

"Thanks, Jim Monaghan, call me some time," Jenny smiled and waved goodbye.

Jim jogged back to the newspaper office and completed his story with quotes from bystanders, the Legionnaires, and others marching in the parade. For reasons, he didn't understand, he made sure Jenny Fowler's quotes were in the early part of his story. He noted she was related to the Cabots and the Lodges of Massachusetts and hoped Willy would know who they were.

Willy will be pleased, Jim thought. *Everything in the story is positive.*

I wonder what the reaction to Rev. Jefferson's March will be?

SEVENTY-FOUR

TRUE TO HIS WORD, Rev. Jefferson started his march one hour after the main Fourth of July Parade, right in front of Lincoln's City Hall. The march was scheduled to wind its way to Fourth and Bradley, at the entrance to Simpson Village and near the Reverend's church.

Jim reached the head of the march and spied Rev. Jefferson. He was surprised to see Judge McCallister standing at the front of some 500 marchers talking with Rev. Jefferson.

"I am surprised to see you here, Judge," Jim commented.

"I told you I was going to get involved. I called Rev. Jefferson and asked if I could join him in the march. He invited me to walk with him. I said I would be honored.

"You will find a number of my colleagues from the University in the group marching today. I think it is a great day for Lincoln. We just had a wonderful Fourth of July parade and now Rev. Jefferson's. Soon, I hope both events happen together," the judge opined.

Jim noticed the crowd from the Fourth of July parade

had dwindled, and of those still on the sidewalks, some looked on with curiosity, while others stared malevolently.

Jim filled his notebook with comments from the marchers. As the march left downtown and headed towards Rev. Jefferson's church, the sidewalks were mostly empty until it edged closer to Fourth and Bradley. There, families held hand-made signs: "Freedom", "Thank You Congress", "God Bless Dr. King," and other supportive comments.

Jim noted the crowd had swelled to almost 1,000 when Rev. Jefferson stood on a makeshift podium, made from a bale of hay, and addressed the crowd.

"Today, on the 188th anniversary of our nation's founding, we declare July 2, 1964 a day we will never forget. It is not the end of our struggle. It is only a beginning. But it is a beginning with hope, not hate. Let's continue our vigilance and our prayers. Remember, Dr. King's words, 'Let us not seek to satisfy our thirst for freedom by drinking from the cup of bitterness and hatred.'"

He went on to thank Judge McCallister for being there, along with all who participated. "One last quote from Dr. King, 'Are you ready to be a better person?'"

The crowd cheered and crowded around Jefferson.

Believing he had a great story, Jim hurried back to the newspaper, office typed his story, and handed it to Willy.

"I think this has been a really great day for Lincoln, Willy. So many good things happened. I feel pretty good about it."

"Well hot damn, Monaghan, that's the first time I have heard you being positive about anything in about a year. No pickup trucks, no conspiracies. Maybe this **is** a great day," Willy replied.

"Oh, there are pickup trucks, and I will prove the

conspiracy to you someday, Willy, but not today. This was a really good day."

Willy looked at Jim and shrugged his shoulders dismissively.

SEVENTY-FIVE

Jim couldn't figure it out. He felt good. Anna looked especially beautiful tonight. Dressed in a Cincinnati Reds tee shirt and dark brown pedal pushers, her hair pulled back in a ponytail.

Stavros even convinced him to have a real dinner of steak, mashed potatoes, vegetables, and a salad. Anna teased, "Imagine this, Jim not having a cheeseburger."

"Let's get a booth tonight." Jim suggested, "We have a lot to talk about and we can have more privacy."

As they sat across from one another in the back booth, Anna reached over and held Jim's hand, "Jim, I know the last time we talked I was hard on you. I didn't mean to be hurtful, but every time I think we are making progress in our relationship, you just seem to tune me out. Your mind seems to be somewhere, I don't know where, but I suspect you are thinking about Mary Ryan.

Under the watchful eye of Stavros, who was paying more attention to the back-booth customers than to anyone else in the bar, Jim and Anna delved into their relationship.

"It hasn't been a year since Mary died, and you knew

when we first met, that Mary and I were in love. You can't imagine what it is like to be totally in love and then bam, that person is dead. I am doing my best, Anna. But I know I can do better, so I hope you will let me have the opportunity."

Smiling and gripping Jim's hand tighter, Anna said she would.

They finished their dinner and for the next three hours, Anna sipped her wine and Jim drank cokes.

Jim found Anna easy to talk to.

Jim was having such a fun and relaxing time, he had almost forgotten about Buck, Clyde, and Delmar Batcher. It was almost ten and Jim was about to ask Anna if she would like to go dancing. He was certain of her response. Just as Jim was about to ask, Stavros shouted that he had a phone call.

Irritated by the interruption, he pulled the phone from Stavros and barked into the phone, "Monaghan."

"Jim, you gotta get here right away. They tried to kidnap Haley, but Edgar stopped them and beat the daylights out of them. Now the police are trying to arrest Edgar. You gotta help me, Jim. I can't raise Rev. Jefferson. You gotta help me!" Maybelle screamed into the phone. Then the phone went dead.

"Maybelle! Maybelle!" Jim yelled into the phone, but there was no answer.

He slammed the phone down and ran out of O'Toole's.

Anna walked up to Stavros and asked, "Was it something I said?"

"No, Anna, trust me, it wasn't you. That was his friend Edgar's mother, Maybelle, who lives in the projects. Something bad is going on and Jim went to help. Just be patient, young lady. Just be patient with Jim. He is carrying a huge burden. I am one of his best friends and I'll tell you, I have not seen him smile and laugh like he did tonight for months now. So, you just be patient, ok?"

"Well, I haven't paid a bill on a date ever, but there's always a first with Jim Monaghan, so how much do we owe you for tonight?" Anna asked.

"No problem, Anna, Jim has a tab here. It's taken care of," Stavros said.

SEVENTY-SIX

Jim raced to Fourth and Bradly, skidded to a halt at the stop sign, and pulled in front of Number Eight Simpson Village. Six police squad cars, lights flashing, straddled Bradley Avenue. As he raced to Edgar's front yard, where all the policemen were standing, Jim noticed a group of young men milling around the vacant lot across from Simpson Village. Rufus made eye contact with Jim, and with his fist closed rapped his chest.

Jim found Edgar lying face down on the ground. His hands were handcuffed behind his back. Maybelle was talking to a police officer, and Haley was curled up on the front stoop, her eyes wide with fear. When she saw Jim, she raced over and jumped into his arms. A policeman tried to separate them, but Haley screamed, "He's my cousin." It was a private joke started years before when Jim would come for supper and Haley would ask, "Why is he here for supper all the time?" Jim told her he was her cousin and families often ate together.

A stern Lt. Malcolm walked up to Jim and said,

"What's your connection to this incident, Monaghan? You seem to show up at all the wrong places."

"How the hell is this the wrong place? Edgar is my friend and has been for years. Maybelle called me asking for help. Now, maybe you can tell me what happened."

"I'll tell you, Jim," Edgar shouted. "Haley was coming back from Bible Study and these two assholes stopped their truck, grabbed her and threw her in their cab."

Jim stepped over to where two men were face down on the ground with their arms tied behind their backs. Jim leaned down and looked at their faces.

"Well, son of a gun! It's Buck and Clyde. Hello, assholes. And you are telling me, Lieutenant, that I am always in the wrong place. What about these two bastards?"

"All I know is we got a call saying there was a kidnapping at Fourth and Bradley. I ordered all available to proceed with lights and sirens. When we got here, these two men are on the ground were surrounded by those guys across the street. Edgar was yelling at them, and both guys had been roughed up badly. I've ordered an ambulance crew to look them over to see if they need to go to the hospital," Malcolm said.

"These bastards jumped us, that's what happened," Clyde yelled.

"Quiet, Clyde, we are going to get this sorted out and I want you to keep your mouth shut. And you, Monaghan, stay the hell out of the way."

Rev. Jefferson, fumbling to tie his bathrobe, hurried to the scene accompanied by several women who had filled him in on what they had seen.

"I can tell you, Lieutenant, that young Haley was at Bible study tonight, and I can tell you she is a good God-fearing young woman. Whatever she tells you will be God's truth.

"And that truck," Jefferson pointed to a pickup with an eagle emblem stenciled on the driver's side door," has been harassing this community for weeks. They throw trash, feces, and Lord knows what else on our front yards. We have complained, but nothing has ever been done. What have they have done to poor Haley?"

Lieutenant Malcolm motioned Haley over and said, "Young lady, I want to talk to you, and I want the truth."

"I'm not talking to you unless Jimmy, my Momma and Rev. Jefferson are by my side," Haley defiantly answered.

"Ok, Monaghan and Reverend, please come over here."

"I was walking back from Bible study. I was just crossing Bradley when their truck came flying around the corner and screeched to a stop. I thought they were going to throw garbage on me. But that one," pointing to Clyde, "jumped out of the truck, picked me up, and threw me in the cab with that one, who was driving." Haley pointed to Buck. I started fighting them and scratched that one, the one who grabbed me. That's why his face is bleeding. Then he slapped me hard across the face and I spit on him. Then he hit me with his fist. I can't see out of this eye and my lip is bloody."

"I knew what was going to happen, so I started to pray.

"Then I saw this fist come through the window. It was Edgar. He grabbed the steering wheel and hit the driver in the face. He must have knocked him out, because his face slammed down on the steering wheel. Edgar opened the door, pulled the guy out into the street. Then he grabbed the other guy. Edgar belted him until he went down.

"Rufus and his friends came over and held them down. Someone got some rope and tied them up, and Momma called the police. No one touched those two men, because Edgar and Momma wouldn't let them. And Rufus and his guys left just as soon as you and the other policemen got here. That's what happened, so help me Jesus,'" Haley's slight body shook, and tears streamed down her cheeks.

Lt. Malcom shook his head and said "Ok, we will arrest them for kidnapping and assault." Turning to Jim, he smiled and said, "It will be hard for the Chief to say this was just bar talk.

"But I have to take Edgar in. These two have been battered and he is the only one here who says he did it."

"You can't take him in, Lieutenant, he was protecting his sister from being assaulted," Jim pleaded.

Rev. Jefferson waved at six women, who were across the street. "Lt. Malcolm, these fine women are part of my Bible Study. They were walking behind Haley and they can account for everything Haley has said. We have seven witnesses who will say Edgar was just protecting his sister."

"Ok, uncuff him," Malcolm said. "But Edgar, we will want you and your sister to come down to the station tomorrow and tell the detectives what happened tonight. Can I count on you to do that?"

"Yes, sir," Edgar said.

"What the hell kind of white man are you," an enraged Clyde yelled.

"Cuff'em and take them in," Malcolm ordered. "I will fill out the paperwork myself."

Turning to Rev. Jefferson, Maybelle, Edgar, Haley, and Jim, Lt. Malcolm said,

"See folks, sometimes the system works."

Jim smiled, then slapped himself on the forehead, "Oh shit, I forgot about Anna."

SEVENTY-SEVEN

Jim was in a deep sleep at five am when he was jarred by the telephone.

"Jimmy! Jimmy! The police came. Chief Buckner hisself came and arrested Edgar. They said he beat up two defenseless white guys and he was gonna to join his daddy and brother in jail. This is terrible Jimmy, help us! Please help us!

"You've got to be shitting me. Tell me exactly what happened, Maybelle."

"After you left, Rev. Jefferson came in and we prayed. Then, since we all go to get up early in the morning, we went to bed.

"About a half hour ago, we was all asleep and I heard this crash. I started to run downstairs. Edgar was right behind me. I just had my pajamas on. Two policemen with guns were coming up the stairs.

"They pushed me down, stepped on my back, grabbed my Edgar and pulled him down the steps. They throwed him on the floor in the living room. They put him in hand-cuffs and started to take him away.

"Haley and me were both screaming and that's when the Chief came in. He said Edgar assaulted two men who were just mindin' their own business drivin' home from work.

"We said it weren't true. Edgar was protecting his sister, but the Chief wouldn't listen. That's when I noticed our front door was broken. I asked the Chief, actually I screamed at him, why did you break down the door and all he said was he wanted to make sure Edgar didn't escape.

"I said, escape, he was asleep," and the Chief just laughed at me. Can you help us Jimmy, we ain't got money for no lawyer or anything!"

"I know people who will help," Jim assured Maybelle.

It was too late to go back to sleep and too early to call Audrey or the Judge, so Jim decided to go down to the police station and see what he could learn.

SEVENTY-EIGHT

As Jim walked into the police station, he found Chief Buckner and Lt. Malcolm in a heated argument.

"I'm the chief and I have the final word," Jim heard Buckner yell to Malcolm.

It was Jim's first up close view of Buckner. The chief was a tall man, at least six feet five and well over 240 pounds. He looked about 50 years of age. He was nearly bald and the first thought that came to Jim's mind was "bullet head." He had an unusually large nose and almost no chin. His deep Alabama drawl seemed totally out of place in Lincoln, but the word was he was the favorite of the city manager, who was also from Alabama, and his relationship with the manager was how he got the job as Chief.

"Tell me, Chief," Jim asked, "Why was Edgar Johnson arrested and why was his home's front door broken down? Did you have a warrant?"

Buckner stared down at Jim. "You aren't the regular News Tribune reporter. I only talk to the regular guys. Besides, who said, we busted through their front door?"

"Maybelle Johnson told me. You and your guys scared

the daylights out of that family, especially Haley, who had been assaulted and kidnapped by Buck and Clyde last night. Why did you have to do that?"

Buckner just stared at Jim.

Realizing he wasn't going to get an answer, he called Audrey and the Judge and briefed them on what had happened. Both indicated they would go down to the police station immediately.

Audrey was the first to arrive. She was wearing a sweat suit workout outfit. It was the first time Jim had ever seen her without her trademark tailored suit.

"I talked to the Judge and we agreed we needed the best defense attorney in town. So, I called, Aaron Williams. He told me not to worry, he would be down in half an hour."

Soon, the Judge arrived and unlike Audrey, he was dressed in a dark suit, white shirt, and tie.

"Thanks for coming Judge. You are the only lawyer person I know, and I really appreciate you being here. I need the moral support."

By the time Attorney Aaron Williams arrived, the outer office of the police department was filled with Audrey, the Judge, Jim, Maybelle, Haley, and Rev. Jefferson. The Judge and Audrey asked to speak to the Chief but were told he was not available.

After talking with Maybelle and Haley, Aaron Williams was allowed back in the lockup to interview Edgar.

Williams told Lt. Malcolm it was a bullshit arrest and Buckner and his crew could be charged with a false arrest, but he was more interested in getting Edgar out of jail.

Malcolm told Williams, it was the Chief's arrest and he had to talk to him. Together, Malcolm and Williams walked into Buckner's office. Jim and the crowd in the outer office could hear yelling from behind the closed door.

"I will sue your ass for false arrest," they heard Williams threaten.

After ten minutes of shouting, the door opened, and Williams walked out while Malcolm walked back to the lockup. Within minutes, Malcolm walked out with Edgar.

SEVENTY-NINE

A SOLEMN EDGAR walked into the reception area of the Lincoln City Police Department Jail and was surrounded by, Jim, Haley, Maybelle, the Judge and Audrey. "I don't know you, Mr. Williams, but I am grateful," Edgar said hugging Williams, "thanks for what you all did. Thanks to all of you for being here and supporting me. It was rough back there. There are three cells and they put me in the one next to those two.

"Those two guys threatened me and told me they were going to cut my balls off, excuse me Mom, when they got out. They told me they would be out before me because they were connected to powerful people.

"I am so relieved to be out of there," Edgar concluded.

Maybelle told the group, "remember people, today is the Lord's day. When you all go to church, thank Jesus for Edgar's release and that those horrible people are behind bars."

As he was leaving, Jim asked Lt. Malcolm if Edgar's arrest would be part of his permanent record? "An arrest for fighting would be a black mark on his record. I know for a fact he has never been arrested for anything, so hopefully, this won't show up either," Jim pleaded.

Lt. Malcom reached behind the desk and picked up some sheets of papers, pulled two out, and tore them in half. "It never happened Jim. I have a sister, too, and I would have done the same thing he did. Tell your friend, it never happened. I'm sorry, but I can't explain why the Chief did what he did. It just blows my mind."

Jim thanked the lieutenant and asked when the two men would be transferred to the Shelby County Jail.

"With the seriousness of the crimes they are being charged with, probably around noon. It will take us that long to get all the paperwork together, but I want to get them over to county as soon as possible."

Catching up to Audrey in the parking lot, Jim thanked her for all her help. "I know you are tired, but I have a great idea. Why don't you call George Rogers and ask him to meet us at the county jail when these two get transferred there around noon today. I will have the Sgt. Major there and we can put pressure on Rogers and his investigators to really go after these guys and see if we can get them to admit to anything."

"That's a great idea, Jim. As long as you don't tell Maybelle I am going to miss church today, I think I can get George to show up. Jim, maybe this nightmare is going to be over."

EIGHTY

An irritated George Rogers met Audrey, Jim, and Sgt. Major Harlow at the door to the county jail. "For God's sake, Audrey, couldn't this wait until Monday? You know I play golf on Sunday at the club, and I was looking forward to playing on such a beautiful day. Why couldn't this wait until Monday?"

"Because it can't, George," Audrey said. "We need to strike while the iron is hot. What these guys did last night was horrible, but Jim has a more compelling reason.

"George, these are the same two guys from the fight at the Legion. One of them admitted to the Sgt. Major and me he shot Steve Hampton and told us the other guy knocked Irene down the stairs. I suspect they drove the truck that killed Mary. And Delmar Batcher told the Sgt. Major the same thing, and he said they were driving the truck, and he was with them when they did. So, let's get them to admit it."

"And one more thing, George," Audrey said. "Do you have those interview rooms in there with the two-way mirrored glass? Can we watch the interrogations?"

"Whoa, slow down Audrey," Rogers said. "Yes, we have those types of interview rooms, but I am not sure about having the three of you back there."

Jim countered, "George, Mary told me once, material witnesses were allowed to watch the questioning, so they could help out. It would be the same as a line up. We would be allowed to pick them out of a line up. It's the same thing, George," Jim pleaded. "Besides, Mary had said, we can be helpful to the interrogators," Jim argued.

As George was mulling over his dilemma, Jim watched Audrey form a smile. "George, I bet our paper would look favorably on a creative District Attorney, who used every tool in his tool box to find truth and justice. Especially one who might be looking to run for higher office."

Perplexed, but smiling, too, Rogers looked at Audrey and said, "I don't suppose it would make any difference if I called your father, would it?"

"No, George, it wouldn't."

Clyde, who Jim suspected was the strongest of the two, was the first to be interrogated. With Jim, Audrey, Rogers, and Harlow watching, the DA's chief investigator started by asking, "What happened last night, Clyde?

"A bunch of them Blacks jumped me and my friend, Buck, and they beat the hell out of us. Don't know why we were arrested, but you need to get us out of here as soon as you can. Damn Blacks."

"Not so fast, Clyde. We have six witnesses who saw you jump out of the truck, grab young Haley Johnson, and throw her in the cab of your truck. What do you say to that?"

"Never happened. You know those Blackies. They stick together. They made all that crap up."

"Well, Clyde, what about that young woman's black eye and bruises on her face, what do you say to that?"

"Don't know nothin about that," Clyde said.

"And how did you get that nasty scratch on your face?"

"Hell, that's easy. I told you we were jumped by that gang of Blacks. They beat the shit out of me, that's how I got the scratch," Clyde replied.

"The witnesses said it was just Edgar Johnson, who pulled you and Buck out of the truck. And it was just him, not a gang as you said. Are you saying it was a gang or was it just Johnson, like the witnesses say?"

"You shittin me, of course it was a gang. No one guy is going to take me and Buck out. No way," Buck angrily responded.

"One last question, Clyde, what were you doing in that neighborhood last night. Your driver's license address says you live out on the west side of town. Doesn't make sense you being there at night? Did you move into the neighborhood?"

"Hell no, I don't live there. I was just cutting through that neighborhood going to work. And I am done talking. This is such a shit waste of time. What kind of white man are you? The Blacks attacked me, and you are asking me all these questions. You're acting like what happened is my fault. Bullshit! Me and Buck are the victims here. This is bullshit. I'm done talking," Clyde slammed his fist down on the table.

The chief investigator got up to leave and then said, "Clyde, one final question. I am confused. What do you do, going to work at ten o'clock at night? Do you work the night shift? There are no factories in that part of town."

"Ah, I was just going to get some stuff done, I didn't get done earlier. I work days.

Oh, shit, I am not saying any more. I'm done. Don't ask me no more questions."

Buck, in the adjoining interrogation room, was going along the same lines. He blamed Edgar and his friends for attacking him for no good reason. He told the investigators he and his Clyde were just cutting through the neighborhood to get back to work but refused to say where he worked. Like Clyde, he said he didn't know who owned the truck.

As Jim observed Buck, he gestured for Audrey and Harlow, to come over quickly.

"Listen to this:

"You know, Buck, there are various charges we can level at you. It's one thing to be in the truck when someone jumps out, scoops up a girl and throws her in the cab. It's another thing to be the person who did it. The person who jumped out is charged with kidnapping and assault. And, Buck, there are six witnesses to that crime. The young girl who was the victim is ready to testify.

"Kidnapping and assault carry long sentences up at Mansfield, while the guy just sitting in the truck could have much lesser charges. And if they cooperate, maybe hardly any jail time at all," the investigator said as he leaned back in his chair.

"I wasn't the one who jumped out grabbed and slapped that girl. I was just sitting in the truck," Buck blurted out.

"Maybe Clyde was just getting the girl for you Buck. Is that what happened? Was Clyde just getting the girl. What were you two planning to do with her?"

"It was all Clyde's idea. We were just going to hassle the Blacks, but Clyde told me to stop and next thing I know, he jumps out and picks that girl up and she's in the cab, yelling and scratching him. But I had nothing to do with it. I was just driving the truck."

Leaning across the table, the investigator stared into Buck's face "Were you just sitting in the truck or were you driving the truck when you rammed Jim Monaghan's truck last summer and the girl flew through the windshield and died?"

"I wasn't driving! No, I didn't mean that, I don't know nothing."

Jim was jubilant and hugged Audrey and Harlow, but their joy was interrupted by a loud noise from down the hall.

"What is going on here? Are you bastards talking to my clients without a lawyer present? What the hell is wrong with you, George? You know you can't interrogate them without a lawyer," said Wilber T. Waters.

Jim remembered the Columbus based attorney who represented Alex Reid and was brutal in his cross examination of Jim at the trial.

"We asked them if they had wanted an attorney, but they said, no," Rogers replied.

"Well, everything they have said will be thrown out," Waters declared straightening his tie and squaring his shoulders. "These men are not sophisticated and don't understand what is going on here. So, for now, no more questions until I get a chance to talk to them. You will not interrogate them again unless one of my colleagues or I am with them. Is that understood?" Waters demanded.

"Of course, Wilber," Rogers replied.

As Waters turned to leave, he looked at Jim, Audrey and Harlow. "And what are these people doing here?"

Jim stared at Waters for a moment before answering, "We were just listening to two guys confess to three murders and watching a corrupt slime ball lawyer show up to try and get them off."

Harlow and Audrey grabbed Jim by the arm and hurried him out. At the door, Jim turned to Waters, "Who's paying you?".

With a broad grin, Waters answered, "Wouldn't you like to know."

EIGHTY-ONE

THERE WERE few obituaries to write on Monday morning, giving Jim time to read Sunday's paper. He was thrilled to see his profile on Rev. Jefferson prominently displayed on page three and his sidebar on the Fourth of July parade and a photo of the Legionnaires on page one. The sidebar on Rev. Jefferson's parade was also on page three. *This is great,* Jim thought, *seeing my byline on pages one and three. I am enjoying this job again. These general assignment stories are a lot better than writing obituaries.*

Turning to page five, he saw it was devoted to pictures from the parade and the march. Prominent in the middle was a four column wide six-inch-deep picture of Jenny Fowler standing on the DAR float. The caption mentioned she was related to the Cabots and Lodges of Massachusetts and her ancestors were active in the American Revolution.

"Paula," Jim asked, "Do you see this picture on page five. It says Jenny Fowler is related to the Cabots and the Lodges. Do you have any idea who they are?"

"I have no idea, Jim, but they sound like Republicans."

"Actually, they are. The original Cabots and Lodges go

all the way back to the American Revolution. They are as close to American Royalty as you can get."

Jim stared at the photo for a while thinking Jenny Fowler was a very good-looking woman, when he remembered he needed to talk to Willy.

Jim told Willy how much he appreciated the placement of the stories.

"You know Monaghan, those stories were pretty good. Not great, but pretty good. They were factual and tightly written. Keep it up," Willy said.

Grabbing a cup of coffee, Jim waited for the first edition of the Monday paper to be delivered to the newsroom.

"Holy shit," he said to Paula. "Look at this story on page one." Paula leaned over Jim's shoulder and read the headline.

EIGHTY-TWO

Kidnapping, Assault at Fourth and Bradley

THE STORY, written by the senior police reporter, was a factual chronicle of the events which started with Haley Johnson's abduction. It quoted the six women who witnessed the event, as well as Edgar Johnson's account. Conspicuous by its absence was any comment from Clyde or Buck. Jim's role in the events was absent as well.

"Wow!" Jim exclaimed. "Audrey said the paper was going to be more aggressive in its coverage. Well, she sure was true to her word."

"Things, they are a changing," Paula replied, "and it's about time."

Jim told Willy, he had an appointment with Dr. Nance and an idea for a story and would not be back for a while. As Jim left, Willy, with a mocking smile, yelled across the city room, "Hey Monaghan, tell that shrink she is doing a good job with you. You are improving. Now, if you would just cut your hair and your beard." Others in the newsroom laughed and looked surprised. Jim's visits with Dr. Nance had been known only to a few.

Well, screw Willy, Jim thought. *Just when I thought he was being decent to me, he pulled that shit. Asshole.*

Jim's appointment wasn't until later in the day, and he knew what he was about to do before then was fraught with peril.

The lane to Pugh's farm was a quarter mile long and lined on each side with Poplar trees. The road was paved with asphalt. As Jim approached, he was impressed by the meticulous attention to detail everything seemed to receive. There was not a weed in sight.

As he approached the end of the drive with Pugh's huge machine shed directly in view, Jim screeched to a halt as two pickups came barreling down the lane at him.

They stopped directly in front of his truck. Two men, one in denim overalls and the other in camo pants and a brown t-shirt, both armed with rifles hopped out of their trucks.

"State your business!" the man in denim overalls asked while the other leveled his rifle at Jim.

"I would like to see Mr. Pugh," Jim answered.

"Why do you want to see him?"

"It's none of your business. It's between him and me," Jim answered.

"Well you ain't going to see him unless you tell me what it's about."

"I am Jim Monaghan from the Lincoln News Tribune and I want to talk to Mr. Pugh about his two employees who were arrested at Fourth and Bradley. Also, I want to find out what Mr. Pugh thinks about his trucks frequently being at crime scenes."

"This is private property. Turn your truck around, and

get out of here, and don't come back. Mr. Pugh doesn't have time for you today or ever, so just leave. If you come back, we'll call the police and you will be arrested for trespassing," the camo man snarled, spitting a wad of tobacco at Jim's feet.

Oh well, it was worth a try. And I want that bastard Pugh to know, I am on to him, Jim thought as he drove to Dr. Nance's appointment.

EIGHTY-THREE

Dr. Nance's bow was furrowed and her eyes wide.

"You did what? You drove to Pugh's farm. What were you going to do if you saw him? That was foolish.

"Those men could have shot you and said you were trespassing. What you did was irresponsible and dangerous. Jim, you just keep pushing the envelope and living on the edge of danger."

Slamming his hand on the table, Jim raised his voice saying, "But I know he is the one responsible." Dr. Nance interrupted him. "Stop it. Do you think he is going to admit anything to you? Do you think you are going to make a citizen's arrest? Jim, get with reality. Sometimes, you are just unreasonable, but your obsession is getting out of hand. Please take a deep breath and get control of your emotions and your actions."

Shocked by the criticism, Jim said,

"I don't think you and I are going to agree on Pugh and what I am doing. But trust me, I am going to be careful. After all, he is just a farmer, right?

After looking around the room, Jim said, "let's switch gears. There is something else I want to talk to you about. It is a long way from Pugh and pickup trucks.

"I have told you I have been dating Anna Masters. We are getting along pretty well, but sometimes, I feel Mary is in the room watching. I don't want to be disloyal to Mary, but she is gone, but I still can't accept that fact. Anna is a beautiful woman and a lot of fun. But the other night, when I was kissing her, I was thinking of Mary. That can't be normal, can it? What do you think?"

"The fact you brought it up means it is important to you. Why do you think it is happening? I never met Mary, of course, but I have talked to the Judge about her. And what I have learned is that she was a beautiful and very smart young lady, who loved you. I think Mary would be delighted you were with someone, Jim. She would want you to be happy and if you can have some fun with Anna, then if Mary was the person you have described to me, Mary would be the first person to encourage you."

"Well, I am not totally dead emotionally. As I was walking along the parade on the Fourth, the DAR float stopped right next to me. I couldn't take my eyes off this one young woman. I stared at her and when she looked at me, I waved, and we started talking. She invited me to their reception after the parade and I met her there. We chatted for quite a while. I made sure one of our photographers took her picture. I brought a copy of Sunday's paper and here she is, right in the middle of the photos from the parade. And all while I was talking to her, I didn't think of Mary and I didn't feel guilty about it afterwards. So, I am making progress.

"Yes, Jim, I think you are. But remember you are a multi-faceted guy. You are trying to get back to a normal life after Mary death; you are trying to uncover a conspiracy and find those responsible for her death; you are trying to help your friend Edgar and his family. You have a lot going on. I just want you to be careful and sober.

EIGHTY-FOUR

JIM CALLED Anna at the Merrill Lynch office and invited her to meet for dinner at Harlow's.

Harlow's café was noisy as Anna walked in. Attired in a pale green suit with matching high heel pumps, she had a beige chiffon scarf tied fashionably around her neck. Her soft brown hair fell easily to just above her shoulders. She spotted Jim in the back booth and smiled. As she walked towards him, the crowd quieted.

Harlow, sitting with Jim, said "Jesus, that's quite an entrance. Hey, she is walking towards us."

"Sgt. Major let me introduce you to Anna Masters, my dinner date for the evening. Do you have any of that veal scaloppini on the menu tonight?"

"Don't be a smartass, Monaghan," Harlow replied.

"I lied and told her, this was the best place to eat in town, so we expect good service and good food," Jim winked.

The Sgt. Major slipped out of the booth and Anna slipped in. "Nice to meet you Sgt. Major. I have heard many good things about your café and of course your service to the country," Anna smiled.

"Thanks for the comments, young lady, but the question is what in the world is a beautiful and obviously smart young woman doing having dinner with this guy?"

"Well, Sgt. Major, we all make an occasional mistake," Anna said mischievously. "Actually, we went to Northwestern together and we recently reconnected. We have been seeing one another a bit. Just friends."

The evening with Anna exceeded Jim's expectations. He found himself fascinated by her stories about the stock market, about which he knew little. He was impressed with all the licenses Anna needed to legally sell stocks and bonds. He was also surprised at Anna 's compassion when she reached across the table and place her hand on Jim's.

"I know it hasn't been a year yet since you lost Mary. I want to be here for you, if you want to talk. I want to be your friend. And as your friend, I want to be honest with you."

"And I want to talk to you, Anna. Remember when you told me sometimes I tune you out. Well, I talked to a trusted friend about your comments. This is a great time to talk about it."

Leaning across the table, Anna spoke in almost a whisper, "Let's talk, Jim."

Jim looked around the diner, then leaned across the table and whispered to Anna. "I told you when we first met that I was no prize. In fact, Anna, I am a mess. My parents were killed on the way to my high school graduation. I fell in love with Mary and she's dead. Everyone I have ever loved, except my brother Hugh, has died.

"I am obsessed with Ronald Pugh. I know that Pugh and his people are probably responsible for Mary's death, but I can't prove it. And what's frustrating is I can't get anyone to believe like I do. They say I need more proof. I can't get it if people won't help me. Sometimes, I just feel so alone."

Looking around the room again, Jim made sure no one could hear him and in an almost inaudible voice said, "What I am about to tell you will probably cause you to get up and leave, but here goes.

"Do you know where I was on Christmas day? I was on a five-day drunk, and I was sitting in my chair in my apartment with my dad's loaded pistol in my hand, thinking about suicide. I don't know if I would have pulled the trigger or not, but Edgar and his mom showed up and I have been getting better ever sense.

"You said, you wanted to know about me, well what I have told you is known only by Edgar, his mom, Maybelle, Audrey Hill and a few others.

"I told you I was no prize and if you want to get up and leave, I totally understand."

Anna's mouth formed a silent oh. Her expression never changed while Jim talked. When he finished, she withdrew her hand and leaned back in the booth. This is a shock, Jim. I can't imagine anyone wanting to kill himself.

"But, you have been through so much. It is understandable you are reluctant to be close to anyone. I appreciate your honesty and forthrightness. Have you thought about talking to someone, like a professional, a psychologist? I know they can be very helpful. I know people don't like to say they are talking to a psychologist, but I know some people who do, and they tell me, it was the best decision they ever made."

Jim leaned over to Anna and told her he was seeing a psychologist, who helping him through issues.

"Right now, Anna, as I told you, I am not a prize. I have lots of issues, but I would love to have you as a friend. If we can continue to spend some time together, that would be great."

"Of course, Jim, let's take it a step at a time.

EIGHTY-FIVE

JIM WROTE his last obituary of the day, leaned back, and smiled at Paula. "What an interesting morning.

When Jim arrived at work at seven a.m., he saw a Lincoln Police squad car parked in front of the building. Lt. Malcolm stood beside the car drinking a cup of coffee.

"Thought I would make your day, Monaghan. We made an arrest last night you might be interested in."

"Tell me about it, Lieutenant. Hope it wasn't one of my friends," Jim answered.

"Don't think he is a friend, but you do know him. You talked about Delmar Batcher being at the Legion the night we arrested those two guys. Well, Delmar had a little too much to drink last night, and he was driving down main street when he ran a red light right in front of one of my cruisers.

"The officer stopped him and was just going to give him a ticket for running a red light. Then, the officer smelled liquor on Delmar's breath. He looked in Delmar's car and there was an open beer can on the seat and several empty cans on the floor.

"The officer told him he was going to be arrested for drunk driving, having an open beer in his car, and running a red light. Delmar said he wasn't going to jail and started to run, but the officer tackled him. Delmar slugged the officer. So, your friend is going to spend some time in jail. You hit a cop, you do some time. I thought you would want to know."

Thrilled, Jim left a note for Audrey on her desk and called Harlow and brought him up to date.

Then, in the middle of the morning, Paula told him a young woman was on the phone and it wasn't an obituary.

Jim picked up the phone and to his pleasant surprise, it was Jenny Fowler.

"I don't know if you remember me, Jim, but we met at the parade and you put my picture in the paper and some of my quotes. I just wanted to thank you and I was wondering if you could send me a copy of the picture?"

Jim told her he was still working on a deadline, but he would get a copy of the picture and send it to her. Jenny gave him her address and told him, "Now, if you want to deliver it personally, this is my number."

Jim and Paula talked about how great the morning was and whether Jim should deliver the picture. "I think things are going pretty well with Anna, maybe I should keep things simple."

Their laughter was interrupted by a shout from Willy.

EIGHTY-SIX

"WHAT THE HELL were you doing at Ronald Pugh's farm yesterday?" Willy's florid face and cracking voice greeted Jim as he approached his desk.

"Jesus Christ, Ron Pugh is one of the biggest and most successful farmers in central Ohio. He's also one of the richest. He invests in businesses all over town. For goodness sake, he is one of the most important people in our community.

"I was beside myself trying to explain to him, you were acting on your own and were not representing the paper. I had to apologize repeatedly to him. I kept telling him I was sorry. You put me and this newspaper in an awful position. Do you understand that? What you did was irresponsible and wrong."

Willy stood up and as he continued, he stuttered with spit flying. The other reporters in the news room were silent. Some chuckled as the confrontations between willy and Jim had become great theater.

"I told Mr. Pugh you would be disciplined, and you

would never show up at his farm again. And you won't will you, Monaghan?"

"Sorry, Willy, I didn't know Mr. Pugh was a big advertiser like Alex Reid," Jim retorted.

"Don't get smart with me, kid, you are back on thin ice and your friends downstairs will back me on this. You were out of line. Now, get to work."

Surprised at how little Willy intimidated him lately, Jim smiled at Paula, frowned. "Jim, he is your boss, you can't keep pissing him off like that."

Reading the first edition and eating his lunch at his desk, Jim was gratified to see more coverage of the hassling at Fourth and Bradley. *Audrey must be really pushing Willy to get more of these stories in the paper. That's good.*

A couple of people had been charged with disorderly conduct for throwing trash on the street. *Must be more than Pugh's people or does he have an organization? Couldn't be the KKK, or could it? I would love to interview the Grand Goblin,* Jim thought chuckling to himself.

Jim was concerned about the number of young men from the Fourth and Bradley neighborhood who had been arrested. The charges ranged from disorderly conduct to assault. *I trust Maybelle is keeping Edgar out of trouble. Maybe it's time for lunch with Edgar out at Hansen's manufacturing. We could talk baseball, if nothing else.*

Jim's thinking was interrupted by the presence of Sgt. Major Harlow who walked into the city room, past Jim and up to Willy's desk.

"Willy, the District Attorney is demanding Jim Monaghan be in his office as soon as possible. I told him I would tell you, but if you doubt me, you can call him," Harlow said.

"No problem," Willy said. "Monaghan, you are excused, but come back when you are done. I want to know why the DA wants to talk to you. Maybe, you are going to be arrested for trespassing on Pugh's farm," he smirked.

EIGHTY-SEVEN

"Now, WHAT'S THIS ALL ABOUT," Jim asked.

"Just wait until we get there, I am not saying anything until we are with the DA," Harlow answered tersely.

Harlow told D.A. Rogers,

"Delmar Batcher's sister, Sally, came to my café about an hour and a half ago and whispered Delmar wanted to visit with me and Monaghan. Then she turned on her heel and walked out."

"Can Delmar have visitors?" Jim asked.

"I don't see why not, said Rogers. "Neither of you are lawyers, and he just got transferred over here and doesn't have an attorney and hasn't asked for one. He's in rough shape, been throwing up all over his cell. I'll see if he is in condition to talk, and if he is, I can see no objection. His sister said he asked for you, so why not? By the way, Sgt. Major while you are here today, I want one of my investigators to interview you, so you can give us your testimony on your conversation with Batcher in the bathroom that night."

Jim and the Sgt. Major were escorted back to the interview room by the same deputy who had told Jim and Mary

Ryan of Alex Reid's conversation with the so-called Chairman, the night of his arrest.

Has Delmar making any phone calls?" Jim asked.

"No, but you should have seen the reaction of Buck and Clyde when we brought Delmar in. They asked him why he was being brought in, but Delmar didn't respond to them. That really pissed them off and they started yelling at him to keep his mouth shut. Since there was so much hostility, we put Delmar in one of the back cells. It's hard enough to keep peace back there, we didn't need the hassle."

"What do you suppose Delmar wants to talk about? I hope he wants to come clean and tell us what he told you, Jim asked the Sgt. Major.

"Not a clue," Harlow answered as the door opened and Delmar Batcher walked in.

"I don't have a lot of time to talk to you guys, and I'm hoping no one knows I am doing it. I think even my sister would be in danger if they knew I was talking with you guys. But I want you two to know, I am scared to death. You two don't know how big this is. You don't know, Monaghan, that you are in danger. They hate your guts and blame you for screwing everything up. I have heard him say things were running smoothly before you came to town," Johnny said.

"Who is they? Who is him?" Jim asked.

Beads of sweat collected on Delmar's brow and he fidgeted in his seat and looking at the door. "I don't want to give you any names, but Sgt. Major everything I said in the bathroom is true. Monaghan, I was in the truck that..."

Just as Batcher was about to finish the sentence, the door banged open and a flushed and furious Wilber T.

Waters stormed in and slammed his manicured fist down on the interview table.

"This conversation is over and you, Batcher, you don't talk to anyone unless an attorney is with you. Is that understood? Now, Deputy, get this man out of here.

Jim rose and confronted Waters. "Just a minute, counselor. We are not lawyers, we are not the police, we are not with the district attorney's office. We are just friends with Delmar and we were just visiting with him and helping him pass the time in jail. We have every right to be here and he has every right to have friends visit him."

"Delmar is this man your lawyer?" Jim asked.

"Don't answer that, Batcher, I have been retained to be your lawyer. Don't say another word. Deputy get this man out of here."

Looking down at the diminutive Waters, Jim said, "Let the man answer the question, asshole. Don't move him, Deputy, until Delmar answers the question. He didn't have a lawyer ten minutes ago, and just because this slime ball says he is the attorney doesn't make it true."

With his head down, Delmar got up and walked out of the interrogation room saying nothing to anyone.

"I know who you are, Monaghan. You are a damn reporter. My clients do not talk to the press and they especially don't talk to you. I don't know who you are fella," looking at Harlow, "but you can't be here either."

Harlow stood up towering over Waters and said, "I am a friend of Delmar's family, and you, Waters, are a slimy bastard."

As all three men glared at one another, the deputy told Jim and Harlow they had to leave but whispered that DA Rogers wanted them to stop by his office.

EIGHTY-EIGHT

Jim again pleaded with Rogers to bring Pugh in for questioning, as Batcher all but named him as the force behind the criminal activity.

"Jim, damnit. Don't you think I want to nail the people who killed Mary? For Christ sake, they killed an Assistant District Attorney. Like you, she was a principal in a criminal trial. You, Mrs. Dunn, and that Hampton fellow were the key witnesses, and someone tried to take all of you out.

"But, we are a Country of laws and there is not one bit of evidence that Ronald Pugh is involved in any of this other than those two guys were driving one of his trucks."

"Well, that would be enough for me," Jim said clenching his fists. Rogers lowered his voice and said, "I know, Jim, but that's simply not enough, son. This guy can say Pugh is behind everything, but without proof, it means nothing. I am sorry."

Jim left Harlow to be interviewed and took the city bus back to the newspaper, where he found a note in his typewriter from Paula.

"Jim, an Anna called and asked if you wanted a pizza for dinner. Go have the pizza Jim and then tell me all about Anna tomorrow morning."

EIGHTY-NINE

As the trial date for Buck and Clyde approached, the hassling at the Simpson projects intensified. Those arrested for disorderly paid their fines and were back hassling a few days later.

Jim spoke with the police reporters and was told the cops were getting concerned about the Peace Stones. It appeared they were sometimes confronting the pickup drivers with rocks and baseball bats. Several headlights had been broken. A few of the drivers were bloodied when rocks flew through their windshields.

The reporters said the cops were frustrated because, after the attacks, the Peace Stones melt into the projects and couldn't be found. None of the truck drivers or their passengers could identify any of the Peace Stones. And no one from the Simpson projects would cooperate with the police. The consensus among the police was something bad would happen sooner or later, probably right around the trial date.

Concerned about Edgar, Jim called Donald Hansen, Edgar's employer and owner of Hansen Manufacturing company. Hansen was Edgar's American Legion baseball coach when they competed against Jim and his Legion team.

"Hey coach, would you and Edgar be available for a late lunch? I need to talk to him and would love to visit with you, too," he asked.

"Love to see you, Jim. Maybe you can tell me again, how you managed to hang that curve ball so often," Hansen, laughed jovially.

Jim smiled as he thought of Hansen. At six feet seven and over 300 pounds, his physical presence and booming voice dominated anyone in his world. He kept his hair in a flat top and always wore collared golf shirts, khaki pants and cowboy boots.

As Jim was about to leave, he thought of Anna. *She is always asking about my friends and what I do. I think I will ask her if she wants a late lunch. It will be interesting to see her reaction to Edgar.*

Anna jumped at the chance for a late lunch. The markets were closed, and she told Jim she was just doing paperwork, which could wait.

It was difficult to determine who was more surprised when Jim showed up at the diner, next to Hansen's manufacturing operation. Both Edgar and Donald gaped when Anna, as usual dressed impeccably, walked in with Jim.

"Fellows, this is Anna Masters, a friend of mine."

Anna shook hands with Hansen and gave a slight wave to Edgar.

"Edgar, what's going on in the neighborhood and how serious are the confrontations getting between the pickups and the Peace Stones?"

"It's getting bad, Jim. Those pickup guys are getting more aggressive. The Peace Stones started hitting back with rocks and baseball bats and now the pickup guys are brandishing guns. I think someone is going to get seriously hurt or even killed. The police have avoided our neighborhood for years, so the boys think they have to enforce the law themselves."

"I'll tell you how serious it is, Jim," Hansen added. "I spoke with Maybelle, and we talked about putting Edgar on the night shift, so he can avoid some of these confrontations. I also offered to hire a few more of Edgar's friends to keep them out of trouble. We damn near have a baseball team working here now, but to help out, I can hire some more."

"Putting me on the night shift isn't necessary boss," Edgar added. "I know enough to stay inside. But Jim, I have to tell you, the night Haley got attacked, a few of the Stones helped me keep those two guys on the ground. One was especially helpful tying them up. I still don't know where they got the rope.

"They listened to me, Jim. Rufus wanted to beat the shit out of them, but after I asked them to back off, they just stood in a circle and made sure those two guys didn't move. It was tense. Haley was crying and some of the neighbors came over to comfort her. Rufus was hot and arguing with me and those two guys on the ground kept yelling insults. They called us every name in the book, but the Stones just stood there and took it. I was very impressed. They aren't gang Jim. They are just kids trying to protect the neighborhood.

"But I have told the Stones, I can't be a part of what they are doing. They respect me for that, or at least they let me alone because they are afraid of Maybelle," Edgar laughed.

Anna, who had been quiet, but listening attentively,

through lunch, finally piped up and asked, "Who's Maybelle?"

Hansen, Edgar and Jim laughed.

"If Jim hasn't introduced you to Maybelle yet, you are in for a treat," Hansen said.

"Maybelle is my mom," Edgar said, "and she has been taking care of Jim since his parents' died five years ago."

NINETY

AFTER LUNCH WAS OVER, Anna suggested she and Jim go to O'Toole's. "I am fascinated by what you do and the people you now. Can we talk some more this afternoon?" she asked. "We can stop at my apartment. It will give me a chance to get out of my business clothes. I am more comfortable in slacks and a shirt."

Their conversation at O'Toole's lasted through dinner with Jim and Anna filling one another in on their life's history and their hopes for their professional careers. The time flew by. Interesting, Jim thought, the previous discussions about Jim's troubles and him seeing Dr. Nance never came up. They decided they would try the new club down the street for dancing to end the evening.

Outside, sirens blared as police cars and fire engines raced down First Street, just one block south of O'Toole's.

"Something big must be going on. Want to play reporter and see what is happening, or do you want to dance?"

"If I don't go with you, you will probably get a phone call and leave me like you did the last time." Anna smiled.

"Yea, well it's one thing to leave you with Stavros, but

it's another to leave you in the middle of a dance floor. It wouldn't be a second before someone would be asking you to dance."

"And would that bother you, Jim Monaghan?" Anna asked.

Cheeks flushing, Jim said, "Let's get into the truck and see where the emergency vehicles are going." Anna smiled, then took his arm and said, "Let's go cover the breaking news."

They ran to Jim's truck and followed a fire truck as it sped towards the northeast section of town, where Simpson Village was located. He hoped he was wrong, but he had a bad feeling about what they were about to find.

NINETY-ONE

STOPPING a block from the intersection of Fourth and Bradley, they got out of the car and counted five police cars, three firetrucks, and two ambulances. As they got closer, Jim saw firemen hefting huge hoses spraying water on Rev. Jefferson's church.

"Stay close to me, Anna, and if anyone asks, tell them you are helping out the News Tribune." Grabbing Jim's arm tightly, Anna murmured, "Thank God, I changed clothes."

Flames erupted through the roof and windows of Rev. Jefferson's church as firefighters struggled to control the raging inferno. Jim glanced across the street at the barren field and saw six young black men sitting on the ground with their hands handcuffed behind their backs.

Jim spotted Lt. Malcolm, asked him, "What the hell happened?"

"Damn, Monaghan, you seem to be everywhere these nights. It got bad tonight. Apparently, someone firebombed the church. I think they used a Molotov cocktail."

"What is a Molotov cocktail?" Anna asked.

"They stick some sort of wick in the top of the bottle

filled with kerosene, light the fuse and throw it on the roof. The bottle breaks, kerosene is everywhere, and the lit wick ignites the kerosene.

"The Stones over there say two guys, who were taken away in an ambulance a few minutes ago, threw the bottle on the roof. The Stones stopped their truck, pulled the two guys out, and just beat them pretty badly."

"Where's the pickup?" Jim asked.

"Sorry, Jim, I know you are looking for an eagle emblem, but it's not there. I know the two guys. I have arrested them before. They work at Hansen's Manufacturing, or at least they did. When Don finds out about this tonight, he will fire their asses."

"Sorry Miss," Malcolm said, looking at Anna, "forgive my language."

"That's the least of your problems, Lieutenant. I am fine. I have heard such language before. Hell, I am with Jim," she said and playfully poked Jim in ribs.

As Jim and Anna were leaving, Jim heard his name being called. It was Reverend Jefferson.

"Jim, this is terrible, but fortunately Bible Study was over, and no one was in the church. I was visiting with the ladies from Bible study in front of the church, when that truck," Rev. Jefferson said, pointing to the truck Lt. Malcolm had identified, "came roaring down the street and pulled onto our front yard, just missing the ladies.

"Two men jumped out with what looked like beer bottles, but with fire coming from the top. They each had two bottles and one guy threw his bottles on the roof and the other guy tossed his through our open door. The fire just exploded everywhere. My church is ruined Jim. It is gone.

"The Peace Stones came running over and the two men rushed back to their truck, but they couldn't get it started and the boys pulled them out and started beating them up. But, I stopped them before those two thugs were really injured.

"But this is terrible, Jim."

Jim introduced Rev. Jefferson to Anna and extended his sympathy for what happened and hoped the church would be able to rebuild. Anna was silent but nodded to acknowledge Rev. Jefferson.

"We can hold the service under a tent if we have to," Rev. Jefferson said as he turned, shoulders drooping and head down, and walked back to the gathered crowd.

"My goodness, you have an interesting life," Anna said as they drove home.

NINETY-TWO

THE NEXT MORNING, Jim had never seen such hectic activity in the newsroom. Audrey and her father were both at the city desk, talking with Willy. When Chief Photographer Art Wilks, showed the Hills and Willy some of his photographs from the night before, Willy yelled, "Monaghan, get your ass over here!"

Paula said quietly, "Jim, I hope you are not in trouble again."

"Monaghan were you at Fourth and Bradley last night when they were fighting that fire?" Willy asked.

"Yes, sir," Jim answered.

"Well, why didn't you tell me. Paula can take care of the obituaries. Write up what you saw, who you talked to, and get it to me quick. We had two people badly injured and a number of people arrested and of course the church burned. Oh, and call your friend Rev. Jefferson and ask him how badly the church damage is and what plans he has."

Excited Jim started back to his desk, when he felt a tight grip on his arm. It was Audrey Hill holding a photograph of Jim, Anna, Rev. Jefferson, and Lt. Malcolm. "Ah, Jim, we are using this picture on page three today. Just who is the young lady? I don't think she works for the paper."

"Her name is Anna Masters. She works at Merrill Lynch, and she is a friend of mine," Jim said surprised at how warm his cheeks were getting. "And if we are going to use that picture, I have to ask her if it is okay."

"I am sure she won't mind, Jim," Bernard said. "My experience is people don't mind having their picture in the paper but give her a call. And Jim, write a good tight story."

Anna was thrilled to have her photo in the paper. She invited Jim to dinner at her apartment and asked if he could bring some extra copies of the paper and a copy of the photograph that was going to be in the paper and any others.

Jim called Rev. Jefferson, who was distraught.

"Who would have thought something like would have happened? The firemen did a great job, but we have a lot of damage. Fortunately, the good people of my congregation were here early this morning. The men have already moved the debris out to our front yard. The women are scrubbing and cleaning everywhere. Everything is so dirty and covered with soot.

"Later today, some of the men, who are carpenters will start the rebuilding work. I shouldn't tell you this, but your publisher Bernard Hill called me this morning and he told me he was going to make a deposit in our checking account at First National to help with the repairs, but he doesn't want anyone to know about it. But I can trust you, not to say anything. can't I, Jim?

"With everyone working together, we can put our church back together. It will be hard, but my people are dedicated. We will have our Sunday services outside for a while. Mr. Hansen said he would provide us with a tent.

Jim, you know my favorite expression, "We will prevail.' We will prevail Jim, with God's grace, we will prevail."

Jim assured Rev. Jefferson he wouldn't say a word about Bernard's donation, but he wasn't surprised at his boss's generosity.

"One more thing, Jim, I talked to Dr. King this morning and told him what happened. He is considering coming to Lincoln. Wouldn't that be wonderful?"

"If Dr. King comes to town, I want an exclusive interview, Reverend. I would love an exclusive interview."

"Ever the reporter, eh Jim?" the Reverend answered with a smile.

NINETY-THREE

As the deadline passed, Jim turned to Paula, "You know, I am enjoying my work lately and my life is finally turning around. Those bastards are in jail and I hope one of them breaks and tells the truth about last summer. I have had several byline stories, so I feel like a real reporter. And, Paula, I have been invited to dinner at Anna 's apartment tonight and I feel good about it. I know Mary would not object."

"No, Jim, she would be happy for you. Now, you make sure you clean up real nice before dinner. Why don't you shave that ugly beard, get a haircut, and make sure you bring that young lady flowers?"

"Paula, you are acting like my mother," Jim joked.

"I am just your very good friend, Jim," she smiled.

As the afternoon paper was delivered Jim's jaw dropped when he saw the front page.

News Tribune Demands Blue Ribbon Investigation

THE RIGHT-HAND SIDE of the front page featured an editorial by Bernard Hill. The editorial demanded Mayor Weir appoint a blue-ribbon panel, headed by Judge Douglas McCallister, to investigate the ongoing conflicts centered near the intersection of Fourth and Bradley.

They suggested the panel be comprised of seven citizens appointed by McCallister. The editorial had two suggestions. One, they recommended Rev. Jeremiah Jefferson be a member of the panel, as well as a young person, from the Simpson Village community. The balance of the panel they would leave to Judge McCallister's discretion.

"I am so damn proud of the Hills. This is a great newspaper to work for," Jim told his fellow staffers who had gathered to read the paper.

At dinner that night, Jim told Anna how happy he was to be working at the News Tribune. He was so effervescent, Anna asked him if he was high on something.

"No, just excited. And the trial is coming up and I hope they throw the book at those two bastards. And if we can get Delmar Batcher to talk, then finally justice. Mary would be so excited. If she was still in the District Attorney's office, she would be right in the middle of getting ready for trial and encouraging Delmar to talk. Finally, justice for Mary, Irene and Steve."

Taken aback by Jim's reference to Mary, Anna tried to change the subject telling him, how pleased she was about her picture being in the paper and it made her a bit of a celebrity at work, but each time she tried to talk about her day, Jim would acknowledge, but then go back to tell how excited he was about how things were going at work and how justice was finally going to be achieved.

They started to fool around, but Anna abruptly stopped and said, "Jim, you aren't with me again. I am glad things are great at your job. But isn't this our time?"

Jim apologized and put his arms around Anna and started to kiss her, but she stopped him telling him, "Sorry Jim, but this just isn't working tonight."

NINETY-FOUR

THE EXCITEMENT of the previous day was dampened for Jim, when the city hall reporter told Willy and the staff that Mayor Weir nixed the News Tribune's suggestion of a blue-ribbon panel.

The entire newsroom was quiet as he reported to Willy. "Read the quotes, so everyone can hear and then, everyone, get back to work," Willy barked

The city hall reporter quoted Mayor Weir: "'We appreciate the suggestion by The News Tribune for a Blue-Ribbon panel, but we do not see a need for it at this time. We have confidence in our Police Department, led by Chief Buckner, to investigate the incidents at Fourth and Bradley, including the unfortunate fire at the Fellowship of the Disciples of Christ Church. We believe the Chief will thoroughly investigate and bring those responsible for the incidents to justice."

Jim joined the reporters in the newsroom who booed.

The reporter added, he had a statement from Judge McCallister:

"I totally support the News Tribune's editorial calling

for a Blue-Ribbon Panel to investigate the unfortunate and tragic incidents centered around the intersection of Fourth and Bradley. I am especially saddened by the fire which damaged Rev. Jefferson's church. I am personally donating to a fund which will help him and the members of his congregation to rebuild. While I am supportive of the News Tribune's editorial and believe there is a demonstrable need for such a panel, I respect the mayor's decision."

Jim's fellow reporters mostly shook their heads sadly. Several made comments echoing his thoughts that Judge McCallister's statement proved he was the best qualified person to lead the panel. While most, including Jim, could not understand his decision to respect the Mayor's, but because of judge's stature in the community, Jim surmised, most would respect his decision.

"All right, everyone, back to work," Willy shouted, as the obituary phone line rang.

NINETY-FIVE

Jim's anticipation was sky high. The trial for Buck and Clyde was scheduled to begin the next day at nine a.m.

They were charged with disorderly conduct, assault, battery, and kidnapping, and conspiracy to commit kidnapping, assault and battery. The courthouse reporters told Jim they could be sentenced to up to 25 years at the infamous Ohio State Reformatory in Mansfield, if they were convicted.

I hope they get the book thrown at them. It is the same judge who sentenced Reid and Smallwood, but I hope he is tougher on these guys.

Jim finished his last obituary for the day, when he saw Willy walk over to his desk.

"It's not your beat, Monaghan, but I know you have a personal interest in the trial tomorrow. I just got a phone call from our courthouse guys and they told me DA Rogers is having a news conference at 2 p.m. today. I think you ought to go over there, and if there is a sidebar, you can write one. I will consider putting it in the paper tomorrow but let the courthouse guys write the main story. Remember, keep emotion out of it, just a concisely written story on reaction to whatever Rogers has to say. Typically, a news conference the day before the trial means a settlement, so be prepared."

Thrilled at the assignment, Jim cleaned up his desk. But he was bothered by a feeling in the pit of his stomach that something wasn't right. He called Anna and they met for an early lunch at Harlow's.

"I saw Dr. Nance yesterday and she cautioned me not to be emotionally involved in the trial, but it is hard for me not to," he confided.

"Jim, I know how much this trial means to you. You can't help but be emotionally involved. I am not a shrink, but I think I know you pretty well. I know you are disappointed the DA hasn't gotten a confession out of them about Mary and the other two, but if they go away for 25 years, that will be good, don't you think. Won't that be at least partially just?"

"You know, Anna, you are smart. You do know me. I just hope they get at least 25 years and join Reid and Smallwood in Mansfield."

NINETY-SIX

Jim joined the crowd of reporters, including television crews, in DA Roger's conference room. When many citizens, including Rev. Jefferson, Maybelle, and Haley showed up, Rogers moved the news conference downstairs to the atrium of the Shelby County Government building.

Jim tried to make eye contact with Rogers, but when their eyes briefly met, Rogers turned away. Jim turned to Harlow and said, "Something's wrong, I can just feel it."

At two p.m. sharp, Wilber T. Watson and Rogers approached the podium. The reporters hushed when Rogers began talking. Jim had his notebook out and was ready to take notes when Rogers shocked the room.

"We have reached a settlement with the two men charged with the various crimes, who were scheduled for trial tomorrow morning. You are all familiar with the original charges. Both men have pled guilty to disorderly conduct, assault and battery, and have accepted a sentence of three to five years. We feel this is a just resolution to the case. In addition, we have saved the taxpayers a great deal of money by avoiding a trial. We hope this brings closure to a most unfortunate incident."

"You have to be shitting me, George," Jim yelled out. "What about the kidnapping. How is this justice for Haley Johnson?"

Before Rogers could respond, calls from the citizens gathered behind the reporters, shouted "Cover up! Cover up!"

Soon, the sheriff's deputies were swarming the atrium attempting to calm the crowd. When unsuccessful, they ushered the noisy group out the front door.

Rogers retook the podium but was elbowed out of the way by Waters.

"Settlements usually don't satisfy either side. Speaking on behalf of my clients, I can tell you they believe, and I agree with them, the sentence of three to five years is a lot for what was a misunderstanding," Waters said with his usual smirk.

"How the hell can it be a misunderstanding when an 18-year-old girl is abducted, thrown into the cab of a truck and gets punched? How can that be a misunderstanding?" Jim shouted.

Waters glared at Jim and said, "We have a settlement, so let's all move on."

Jim and Harlow walked over to the jail and asked to visit with Delmar Batcher, who was still incarcerated for his drunk driving, resisting arrest and assault of a police officer. The deputy sheriff on duty told them Delmar didn't want to talk to anyone.

As they were leaving, one of the younger assistant district attorneys, who was a classmate of Mary's and a friend of Jim's pulled him aside and said. "This isn't over. What they didn't tell you at the press conference is that sentencing is set for 4 p.m. Judge Lawlor is a last-minute substitute for Judge Stuart. It is very unusual for the switch. Stuart has handled everything up to now. And frankly, I don't trust Lawlor. He is often too lenient."

"Why does the name Judge Lawlor sound familiar?" Jim muttered to Harlow.

NINETY-SEVEN

CHECKING his watch and noting it was ten minutes to four, Jim and Harlow hurried to the courtroom.

Entering the nearly empty courtroom, Jim saw Rogers and his chief assistant prosecutor standing and waiting for the judge to enter. On the other side of the courtroom were Watson, Buck and Clyde. When Jim and Harlow entered, all three turned and glared at them.

Other than the lawyers and the defendants, the only other people in the courtroom was the clerk, the bailiff and two Shelby County deputy sheriffs.

"This has to be routine, doesn't it?" Jim asked Harlow.

"I have no idea," the Sgt. Major answered.

The Judge called the session to order, reviewed the charges against Buck and Clyde, and asked them how they pled. Both men said they were guilty.

The judge then asked District Attorney Rogers and Defense counsel Watson if an agreement on sentencing had been reached. Both men affirmed.

"Your honor, the state asks both men be sentenced to

three to five years to be served at the Ohio State Reformatory in Mansfield."

"Does defense counsel agree?" the judge intoned.

"We do your honor," Watson answered.

"Then I sentence both men to three to five years in the State Reformatory in Mansfield."

As the judge paused, Jim's heart sunk. No, no, this isn't going to happen, and he rose to his feet.

The judge before continuing, caught Jim's eye and Jim was certain he thought a slight smirk appeared on the judge's face.

"I have reviewed these men's records. There is nothing serious in their backgrounds. They served their country in the United States Army. They are both employed and are making contributions to the community," the judge said and paused.

"No, you can't do this," Jim yelled.

"There will be order in my courtroom. Any more outbursts like that, young man, and you will be in contempt of court, and you will go to jail. Do you understand me. You will not interrupt me again."

Harlow put his arm around Jim and pulled him back in to his seat.

"As I was saying, these men have no serious infractions in their record. They are making solid contributions to the community and are gainfully employed. I see no purpose in sending them away for three to five years for what is really a misunderstanding. Sentence is suspended." And he rang his gavel down, "Case closed."

DA Rogers jumped up and shouted, "Your honor, we had an agreement. Defendant's counsel agreed as did the defendants for a plea of guilty to the lesser charges. They accepted the sentence of three to five years. This is outrageous."

"Be careful, Mr. Rogers. You could be in contempt yourself. Let me remind you, you are the district attorney and I am the judge. You made a recommendation and I don't agree with it and I have the final word, not you. I don't want to hear another word from you, do you understand me."

"Yes, your honor," a downtrodden Rogers quietly replied.

As the judge left the chambers, Watson, Buck and Clyde patted each on the back and exchanged high fives. Buck and Clyde turned to Jim and both men gave Jim the finger and shouted, "Screw you, Monaghan." And then they walked out of the courtroom free men.

NINETY-EIGHT

JIM AND HARLOW hurried up to Roger's as he was picking up his papers.

"How the hell could something like that happen, George," Jim asked. "And why was there a switch in judges. Did you see this coming?"

"Jim, I am just as shocked as you are. No, I didn't see this coming. I understand Judge Stuart suddenly took ill. It happens."

"Then can you retry them for the other charges?" Jim asked.

"No, I can't. It's over Jim. The reason I didn't charge those two men with the original charges and take them to trial was, because I saw the jury pool. They were all white. And 90 per cent of them were men. I am not sure I could get a conviction, so I got the plea agreement. Three to five years is appropriate for their guilty plea. Jim, I am just sick about this, but there is nothing we can do about it. The judge was right, he has the final word.

"But, now these guys have felonies on their record.

They won't be able to get a job and there are other problems people face when they have felonies. They can't vote."

"Oh, for Christ sake, George. You think Pugh is going to fire them? Hell, he probably will give them a raise. And they won't be able to vote? Shit that won't bother those two. I can assure you the folks who live in Simpson Village are going to be livid."

Rogers turned and walked away, his head down.

Jim stopped in the DA's office and called Rev. Jefferson, who was outraged by the suspended sentence.

"It was bad enough they reduced the charges, but to have suspended sentences, that is just not right, Jim. It's just not right."

They agreed to meet later that evening and Rev. Jefferson promised to try and keep his congregation calm.

Jim called Willy and told him what had happened at the news conference, then at the sentencing hearing. Willy praised Jim for his enterprise reporting by going to the hearing. He told Jim to come back and write the story of the sentencing hearing and Rev. Jefferson's reaction. He encouraged Jim to talk with the regular courthouse reporters and ask them if they could find out why the judge switch was made and how unusual it was. They could include it in their story on the press conference.

Chagrined at the outcome of the hearing, but encouraged by Willy's comments, Jim went back to the newspaper and wrote up his story.

NINETY-NINE

Jim picked Anna up after finishing his story and they went to Harlow's.

Seeing Jim's dark mood, Anna tried to be positive and funny and told him, "You know I am getting addicted to these cheeseburgers. If we keep eating here, I am probably going to put on some weight. Hope you don't mind Jim?"

Jim didn't respond to Anna's attempt at humor and throughout dinner, he was unusually taciturn. As hard as Anna tried, Jim switched between grief and anger, and cussed like Anna had never heard. She had never seen Jim act this way before. She even asked the night manager to call the Sgt. Major and ask him to come and help her with Jim, but was told, he was at an important Legion meeting and wouldn't be back until closing time.

"Jim, you are scaring me. Why don't we go to my place and we can talk this through?" You need to have some privacy now. You can't go to Rev. Jefferson's church in the state you are in."

"A damn suspended sentence. How can you not be just as upset as I am? It is just ridiculous. I don't want to go to your place, Anna. If you don't want to be with me tonight, then I will take you home," Jim snapped.

Pulling into the driveway of Rev. Jefferson's church, Jim was overwhelmed by the crowd milling around. As he and Anna climbed out of his truck, he noticed they were the only white people there.

They walked towards where they believed Rev. Jefferson was standing and soon realized they were surrounded by a group of young Blacks, who were glaring at him and Anna with stone cold angry faces.

Jim and Anna found their pace was slowed as the group pressed closer and closer to them. Soon, neither could move. Suddenly, Anna grabbed Jim's arm and whispered, "Jim I am scared. We need to get out of here."

"It's all right. We will be with Rev. Jefferson soon, and he will take care of us," Jim said as he put his arm around Anna and held her tight.

None of the young men said anything. They just stared with venom. They were all wearing black tee shirts, and scowls, and the closer they pressed in, the more concerned Jim was.

Suddenly, one of the young men, standing in front of Jim, shouted, "What the hell you doing here, white boy?"

"We are not here for any trouble. We are here to see Rev. Jefferson. I am Jim Monaghan from the News Tribune. I am just as upset as you are about what happened today but hassling us isn't going to do anyone any good."

Anna grabbed Jim's arm tighter.

"Oh, shit, are you crying white girl. How about our Haley? She was jumped by two white guys? And those white boys got away with it."

"Jim, we have to get out of here!" Anna screamed.

Jim's confidence that he made the right decision in coming over was shattered. He didn't see Rev. Jefferson, Maybelle, Edgar, or Haley. Like Anna, he was scared, but he couldn't let her know. As he and Anna tried to inch their way towards the front of the church, he heard a loud voice yell, "Stop it! Stop it!"

A large arm came around Jim and the voice belted out, "Back off! I mean back off now!" Immediately the gang surrounding Anna and Jim stepped back.

"You made a mistake coming here tonight," the unfamiliar voice said to Jim. Jim turned and was face-to-face with Rufus, the leader of the Peace Stones, who was calm and totally in control.

"You're Edgar's friend. The guy who threw trash back at those rednecks earlier this summer. Man, you got no business being here tonight."

Turning to Anna, Rufus said quietly, "Ma'am, you ain't in any danger. I'll make sure you two get back to your car safely."

"What are you boys doing? You leave these two-fine people alone. They are our friends," Rev. Jefferson yelled as he, Maybelle, and Haley ran over.

"It's okay, Reverend, I got control of the situation. They safe now," Rufus said.

"They ain't our friends, Reverend," one of the young men yelled.

"You shut your mouth, Tommy," Maybelle yelled back at him and grabbed him by his shirt collar. "This is Jimmy Monaghan and his friend. They have been friends of mine for years. You don't even know Haley that well, so don't go talking about how much you are upset about what happened to her. Jimmy is closer to Haley than you ever will be so, you leave these good people alone.'"

Anna shaking with fear continued to cry and Jim held her tighter.

"Jim, I appreciate you and Miss Anna being here," Reverend Jefferson said, "but I think it best you go home. Things are very tense because what happened today is not right. But as I have told you many times, we will prevail. I don't want anything to happen to you, so let's go to your truck."

JIM, arm and arm with Anna, was escorted to his truck by
Maybelle, Haley, and Rev. Jefferson. Jim asked where
Edgar was, "When Mr. Hansen heard about the settlement
and then the suspended sentence, he ordered Edgar to work
a double shift. Mr. Hansen probably will have him stay at
his house tonight. Say a prayer for all of us, Jimmy. Everything is so tense. People are so upset."

Jim hugged Maybelle and Haley and shook Rev. Jefferson's hand. "Make sure you thank Rufus for me, Reverend.
He didn't have to do that, and I hate to think what would
have happened if he hadn't stepped in," Jim said.

Rev. Jefferson agreed and told him he was proud of
Rufus. "He is a good boy, just misguided. No father at
home, you know. Such a familiar story," the Reverend said,
shaking his head.

Jim climbed into his truck, where he found Anna,
crying and trembling. She glared at Jim. "That was awful,
Jim. We never should have been here."

Anna sat as far away from Jim as she could, almost

hugging the door. And she continued to cry. Jim pulled away and drove for six blocks to the parking lot of the First Lutheran Church. Jim tried to hug Anna, but she pushed him away.

"I was so scared. I thought I was going to be raped, Jim. Why did we go there? Why did you take me to that Simpson Village area? Why do you have to be involved in everything? We should have gone to my apartment."

"I didn't think it was going to be that bad. I have always been comfortable in that community. I have stayed overnight there dozens and dozens of times and never have I seen it like it was tonight. I am sorry Anna. Why don't we go to O'Toole's and get a drink?"

"No, I just want to go home. I have booze there if you need to drink," Anna said.

Jim brought Anna into her apartment and while she went to the bathroom, he found an open bottle of Bushmills and poured himself a half full glass. After about fifteen minutes in the bathroom, Anna came out devoid of make-up, but still in her slacks and shirt and joined Jim on the sofa. She sat as far away as she could, folded her arms and glared at Jim.

"I was so scared. You don't know what it is like to be a girl and think you are going to be raped. You simply don't understand, so don't say you do."

"I wasn't going to say I understood. Anna, I can only say I am sorry. But I don't think you were going to be raped."

Jim moved to Anna's side of the sofa, but she put her hand up and said, "Stay on your side, Jim. You don't understand. What do you know? You aren't a woman. That situation was ridiculous. Why did you take me there, to that neighborhood, to be with those people? Why, Jim, why did you do it?"

"What do you mean by those people, Anna? Do you think they are different than you and me? Some of them are my friends and Maybelle, Edgar, and Haley are like family to me. What do you mean by 'those people?'"

"I don't want to talk about it anymore Jim. I want you to leave Jim. I want you to leave now. I am going to call my dad and go to my parent's house."

"I can take you Anna. I hate to see you so upset. Let me drive you to your parent's house."

"No, I am not riding in that truck again. What is that truck, Jim, your personal monument to Mary? You haven't fixed any of the dents and that replacement door, it isn't even painted. It looks stupid. What is it? You don't want to change anything about the truck since Mary was in it?

"And why are you still wearing that beard and your hair so long? Do you still think you are working undercover as an investigative reporter? For God's sake, you are an obituary writer.

"We have been going out for over three months. You slept over one night and it was great. But do you know what you do in your sleep, Jim. You talk. And that one night, which I thought was a great night. I thought maybe we had something really going. But no, you talked in your sleep about how much you love Mary Ryan. That's what you said, when you were in my apartment and in my bed.

"For God's sake Jim, she is dead. I can't compete with a ghost.

"Sometimes, like tonight, I just don't know you. At dinner, you were angry, you cussed, you were just unreasonable. Then you take me to that place, with those people, where I was nearly raped.

"Just leave Jim, please, just leave now."

Jim just looked at Anna not believing what he just

heard from someone, he thought he had a future with, or at least a friendship.

As he walked to his truck, he thought, *Anna said she didn't know me. Maybe I don't know her.*

ONE HUNDRED ONE

JUST AN OBITUARY REPORTER, *so that's what Anna thinks I am. Well, I am not going to be writing obituaries forever. What a shitty twenty-four hours. Clyde and Buck, who I know are responsible for Mary's death get a suspended sentence, then Anna kicks me out of her apartment. I can't blame her for being pissed, but I had no idea we would face what we did at Rev. Jefferson's church. I can understand how scared she was. But what did she mean by 'those people.' I know she was upset and scared. I wonder how I can make it up to her. I wonder if I want to. But she seemed really pissed that I talked in my sleep about loving Mary. Well, I did love Mary and maybe I still do. There is nothing I can do about that. For Christs sake, I was asleep.*

Jim pulled into one of the reserved spots at the newspaper parking lot and sat. *What the shit. I don't care what Dr. Nance says, I am going to get drunk tonight.*

Fortunately for Jim, the backlog of obituaries was not great, and he was able to get them all completed before the first deadline. Between deadlines, he talked to the police reporters about what happened at Rev. Jefferson's church.

"I didn't see one police car around there last night. Where were the cops patrolling?"

"From what I heard, the Chief ordered everyone to stay out of the area because he didn't want any confrontations. They knew the people would be angry, so the Chief just decided to avoid it," the veteran police reporter said.

"Wow, so much for the Civil Rights Act making everything better," Jim muttered.

Willy waved his hand beckoning Jim to his desk.

"I have DA Rogers on hold and he wants to talk to you. He knows you are pissed at him, but he has a story. He won't tell me what it is, but he wants only you to have it. It will be an exclusive, so I am going to go along with him. If you see the courthouse guys there, tell them to call me. Be professional when you are talking to the DA, understand?"

Punching in on the phone, Jim was about to say hello, when Rogers started talking.

"Look Jim, I know you are angry at me, but I had no idea the judge was going to suspend the sentence. As I told you, with the jury pool we had assembled, I wasn't sure we could get guilty verdicts on all counts. Actually, I wasn't totally confident, with the jury pool, I could get a conviction on any of them. So, I settled. I know you are upset, but I did the best I could. I just can't control a judge and as he told us, he has the final word."

"Tell that to Haley," Jim said. "I wasn't the one assaulted and kidnapped."

"I know, Jim, and I am sorry. But Jim, I want you to come to my office and bring the Sgt. Major. I have a story for you and maybe something else. Can you come this afternoon?"

"We'll be there," Jim said and hung up the phone. *Can't imagine what this is about, but what the hell.*

ONE HUNDRED TWO

At the Shelby County District Attorney's office, Jim and Harlow were ushered immediately into Rogers' office.

"Jim, I talked with Bernard and Audrey Hill this morning and then I called Mayor Weir. I told the Mayor I was taking the editorial to heart. With all the activity going on at Fourth and Bradley and throughout the county, I told him I thought it would work best if I formed a Shelby County Community Relations Commission. Their charge would be to ensure all citizens of Shelby County are treated fairly, and no government agency exceeds its authority over any citizen. I think we can do more to help all the citizens of the county improve their lives.

The Mayor agreed that he could support it, if the emphasis was county wide and not just Lincoln. "I have no problem with his concern and in fact, I think it is better to have the commission look at the entire county.

"I have talked with Rev. Jefferson and he has agreed to sit on the panel. I told the Mayor I wanted Judge McCallister to be the chairman of the commission. But, I was surprised to find the Mayor objecting. In fact, he said if McCallister was the chairman, he would not support creating the commission and besides McCallister had already declined to head the panel the News Tribune proposed. So, I asked him if he had anyone in mind, and, to my surprise he did.

"He wants a professor over at Hamilton University to be the chairman. The guy's name is Harrison T. Fowler, who is chairman of the History Department. He is from Boston and, according to the Mayor, he has a PhD from Harvard, so we know he is smart. And he has a stellar reputation. He has published magazine articles and books. Plus, he is related to the Cabots and the Lodges, so he comes from good stock. I know him a little bit from the Country Club. He's not a golfer, so I don't know him that well. But the good news is, Jim, we will have a commission and you can announce it in tomorrow's paper. I hope this news helps you to feel better about yesterday."

"George, I appreciate you creating this group and giving me the exclusive story, but for God's sake, those bastards killed Mary. They killed Mary and they slipped through our hands. They slipped through your hands. How can you sleep?"

"Jim, as I told you, I am convinced I did the right thing. You just have to trust me. But I couldn't control the judge."

"I suppose I will get over it, but it is going to be hard."

"He will manage, George, I will help him through it. I have a lot of experience dealing with death, unjust death, and I know how hard it is. I will help our young friend," said Harlow draping a muscular arm over Jim's shoulders.

"What did you say the professor's name is and who is he related to?" Jim asked.

"His name is Harrison Fowler and he is related to all the big shots back in Boston. Do you know him, Jim?"

"No, but I think I met his daughter at the Fourth of July parade. Don't really know her other than she is pretty," Jim said.

"One more thing, George. What is the Mayor's problem with Judge McCallister? I didn't think there was a soul alive who didn't admire the judge."

"No clue, Jim, but he was adamant."

As Jim and Harlow were getting ready to leave, a deputy from the jail poked his head in Rogers' office and said, "He wants to see them, if we can do it quietly. His sister is with him."

"Are there any lawyers in the building?" Rogers asked.

"None that matter," the deputy answered.

Rogers smiled, "Sgt. Major and Jim, let's take a walk. I think there is someone who wants to talk to you."

ONE HUNDRED THREE

JIM AND HARLOW were escorted to the county jail. "Any idea what this is about?" Jim asked Harlow.

"None."

In the interview room, Jim was surprised to see Delmar Batcher and a woman, Jim didn't know.

"Hello, Sally," the Sgt. Major said. "Let me introduce you to Jim Monaghan."

Jim thought Sally Batcher looked frightened. She was sitting beside her brother and simply nodded at Jim.

Batcher started talking rapidly, barely catching a breath between thoughts. "I only have a few minutes, but I need to talk to you guys. There is a lot I need to tell you, but I'm afraid. I'm afraid they'll go after my sister. I pled guilty to drunk driving and could have gotten just a few days for that. But they insisted on hard time because I slugged that cop. It was stupid, but I didn't want to get arrested and thought I could run away. But the cop wrestled me to the ground. I am being transferred to Mansfield tomorrow. I am so scared to go to Mansfield. I know he's got people up there at Mansfield, both inmates and guards."

"You never should have gotten mixed up with that bunch, Delmar, I told you that many times, but you wouldn't listen," Sally said, shaking her head mournfully.

"If you tell us what I think you want to, we can go to DA Rogers, and he can provide protection for your sister and for you. If this conspiracy is as big as you say it is, I know we can get you both protection. But you must tell someone in authority, not just the Sgt. Major and me," Jim offered.

Shifting in his seat, Delmar abruptly stood up and started pacing the small room. His scrawny frame was barely concealed by the ill-fitting jail-issued denim. His bony wrists protruded from the rolled-up sleeves of his baggy shirt. It was obvious, he hadn't shaved in days and his shirt was misbuttoned. Beads of sweat dotted his forehead. He muttered to himself. At one point, he walked into the corner and started beating his head against the wall.

Jim jumped up to help him, but Harlow stretched out his arm and gently guided Jim back into his chair.

Finally, Delmar sat down, looked around the room, jumped back up, opened the door, looked outside, closed the door and sat back down again.

"It's Pugh, he's behind it all. He heads up the KKK in this county and is one of the Klan big shots in the state." As Delmar continued, the sweat trickled down his face.

"He was involved with Reid and he hates you, Monaghan. He is out to get you one way or the other and he has lots of people in town on his team. He has secret meetings in that machine shed of his, and you wouldn't believe who goes to those meetings. I mean you wouldn't fricking believe who goes there.

"He wanted Reid out of jail and back running the funeral business because that's where he got a lot of his cash. That's why they went after the old lady, the queer, and you. I was there when it all happened, but I never did nothin. I was driving the back-up truck. We weren't sure if the truck Clyde was driving would be drivable after he hit you, so we had a back-up truck. I wanted to help when I saw the girl go through the windshield. But Buck and Clyde, they wouldn't stop. We had to get back to the farm and fix the truck. We had a winch on the front end and had to take it off. That's what hit your door, it was the winch.

Monaghan, I'm so sorry. I heard she was your girl and her father was a veteran. I'm just so sorry."

Jim steeled himself. His instinct was to leap across the table and throttle Delmar, but he knew he needed him to keep talking.

"This is all well and good, but you need to talk to the DA. And Delmar, this is important: Was Pugh there when you drove the truck back to the farm?" Jim asked.

"You guys don't understand. Pugh has people everywhere. I know he has some deputies in this building on his payroll. He is an evil man and dangerous. If he knew I was talking to you two, he would kill me."

"Guys like him don't scare me, Delmar", Harlow said. "I dealt with tougher guys than him in Korea and World War II. Let's get Rogers in here and you can talk to him. And answer Jim's question, was Pugh there when you brought the truck back."

At that point, the door opened, and a deputy Jim had never seen before, looked in and asked, "Everything ok in here?"

"Yeah, and we don't want to be disturbed," Jim said pointedly.

Delmar's face turned ashen and he jumped up and said, "That's it, I ain't saying anymore."

"Delmar, did that deputy frighten you? Why? Is he one of Pugh's guys in here?" Jim asked.

Delmar just looked down at the table, hands shaking.

"Answer him, Delmar. Tell him the truth," Sally begged.

"Listen, Delmar, I can assure you, if you talk to Rogers, he will get you a new attorney and get you in some protective custody. If he won't get you an attorney, my newspaper publisher will. Please, Delmar, let's get Rogers in here," Jim pleaded.

"Listen to these two, Delmar. They are trying to help you. I believe them. They will get us protection, and maybe we can move back to Nebraska," Sally argued.

"I'm done talking." Delmar's voice was high pitched. He jumped up from the table and fumbled at the doorknob and hurried out the door.

"You men have to help Delmar," Sally begged. "He's not a bad man. He just got mixed up with the wrong people."

"You have to help us convince him, Sally," Harlow said.

ONE HUNDRED FOUR

Jim and Harlow raced backed to Rogers' office and briefed him on their conversation with Delmar.

"Tell us, you have those rooms wired for recording conversations," Jim asked.

"Yes, we do, but we have to turn them off when they are visiting with their attorneys. I called down to the deputy on duty and told him to make sure they were turned on. So, let's go downstairs and see what's on the recorder.

Rogers and his chief investigator walked Jim and Harlow back to the jail where they asked the same deputy who interrupted the conversation with Delmar to open a locked door.

"It's in here, and I can't get wait to get my hands on it. It will be his testimony, and even if he denies it, we can get it out of him again, whether he likes it or not," Rogers said.

But his chief investigator warned, "Not so fast, Boss. We can ask him about it, but we can't use anything that's on the recording in court. He didn't know he was being recorded. You know that."

"Yes, of course," Rogers said, "but that doesn't mean we can't really press him on what he told these two men."

Rogers' assistant walked in the room where the recorders were housed and shouted, "Oh shit, that can't be."

Rogers, Harlow, and Jim crowded into the small room which had numerous recorders on the shelves.

"Look," the assistant said as he pointed to the main electrical bar where all the plugs from the recorders had been pulled out. None of the recorders were operational.

An outraged Rogers turned to the deputy, "Didn't I tell you I wanted to make sure the recorders were on. Didn't I make that clear?"

"Sorry, sir, I thought you said, you wanted them turned off. I guess I misunderstood you."

Rogers and the deputy stared at one another and finally Jim said,

"Were screwed, again."

ONE HUNDRED FIVE

Jim dropped Harlow off at the café and he went directly to Bernard and Audrey's office.

"Can a guy get a drink around here?" Jim asked Bernard as he plopped down in the chair opposite his publisher.

Audrey walked in and sat down beside Jim. "The Sgt. Major called and asked me to watch out for you, Jim. He said, you had quite the past twenty-four hours."

"Yes, I had quite the afternoon and quite the evening last night. Last night Anna and I were surrounded by a group of young guys in Simpson Village. Anna was terrified, and I was scared, but we survived. I am not sure I can survive this afternoon."

"Of course, you will, Jim, tell us what happened," Audrey said.

Jim relayed the story of Batcher's confession and naming Pugh as the force behind everything. "He stated unequivocally he was there when Irene and Steve died. He told me he was in the truck behind Buck and Clyde when they rammed me into the utility pole. They even had a winch on the front of the truck, so their front end wouldn't get damaged. Then they took the truck back to Pugh's farm, took the winch off and fixed any damage. What assholes." "Rogers told us the conversation was taped, but when we got to the recording room, the recorder was unplugged. I suspect the deputy on duty unplugged it, but like everything else in this bullshit story, I can't prove it. So, we have nothing. We are screwed again."

"Not so fast, Jim, Bernard cautioned, "I talked with Judge McCallister this afternoon. Do you remember he and the other victims retained Brian Franco, the plaintiff's attorney? Franco has over 50 clients signed up to sue Reid personally and the Reid Funeral Homes for what he did with their loved ones by switching the caskets.

"Apparently, Franco has quite an operation and in his initial discovery efforts, he has, what he thinks are most of Reid's financial books including all his bank statements. Reid has accounts all over the state, in Chicago, New York, and even Zurich. The guy had Swiss bank accounts! Franco believes there are more accounts, but it is going to take time to investigate. The judge said he has a couple of his law school colleagues, who are tax experts and CPAs to help Franco out. He said it is going to take him some time before they can begin to make sense out of it. So, we still have something, Jim, even if this Batcher fellow won't talk," Bernard gently said.

As Jim was digesting Bernard's comments, a secretary buzzed on the intercom saying Jim had an urgent call.

ONE HUNDRED SIX

"You CAN TAKE it in my office," Audrey said.

Jim picked up the phone and was stunned to hear Anna's voice.

"Jim, I want you to just listen. I don't want you to come over tonight. I am moving back with my parents. Last night, I was so terrified. I was frightened twice. At dinner and when we were driving to Rev. Jefferson's church. You were so emotional, you scared me. I never saw you so angry, so out of control. Such mood swings! You were up, and you were down. Then at the church, when I thought those guys were going to rape me. I was panicky. I don't think you understood how I felt. You said, it wasn't going to happen. How the hell could you say that? Then when I sought your comfort last night you just wanted to tell me you were friends with those people.

"Then, you talk in your sleep talking about how much you love Mary Ryan. You did that while you were in my bed, for Christ's sake. She's dead Jim, but you are still in love with her.

"I don't want to be alone, Jim, and I don't want you to

be with me. I talked to my dad and mom and they want me to come home. I need their support.

"I think we need to be apart for a while. I like you, Jim, I really do. But I can't be drawn into your emotional roller coaster. Sometimes, I don't know who you are. And Jim, I can't share you with a ghost. I just need some time. I am going to hang up now."

Then the phone went dead.

Jim dropped the phone on Audrey's desk and put his head in hands.

Audrey watched as Jim was listening to Anna. She touched him gently on the shoulders.

"What now, Jim? What has happened."

"Anna wants some time apart. She was frightened last night by what happened at the church. And she said I frightened, her, too, with my anger and mood swings. She told me I wasn't supportive, and I was still in love with Mary. What's the hell is wrong with me, Audrey? Why does everything I touch end up like this?"

"Don't get depressed, Jim. This will work out. Anna just needs some time. It happens," Audrey counseled.

Breathing deeply, Jim said, "I am going to write the story on Rogers' new County Community Relations Committee headed by some guy named Harrison Fowler. Do you know him?"

"Yes, he belongs to the club. I don't know much about him other than he is rich or at least according to the gossip, his wife is. Write your story, then maybe you can come over to the house for dinner."

"Not tonight, Audrey, I just want to go home."

Finishing his story, Jim thought about going to O'Toole's but went directly home, finished a bottle of Bushmills, and fell asleep on his couch.

ONE HUNDRED SEVEN

THOUGH HE DRANK ENOUGH to be hung over, Jim woke without his alarm at 5:30 a.m., which was a half hour earlier than usual.

Still depressed from the past 48 hours, he managed to clean up and walk into the office before six-thirty in the morning. *Well, at least Willy will be impressed,* he thought as he turned to walk up the steps to the city room.

"Hey there, you Monaghan?" the night security guard called to him.

"Yes, what do you want?" Jim barked.

"Well, you got a phone call about two in the morning from some guy named Delmar. He said he was being moved out at noon today and he needed to talk to you. He said he was ready to get a new lawyer and make the deal. He said he wanted to talk to you as soon as possible. He wanted your home phone, but it's against policy to give those out, so I didn't"

"Jesus Christ, Jim muttered, "tell Willy I have an urgent meeting over at the county jail.

Grateful there were few cars on the street, Jim sped

through town to the county jail. He hit the brakes when he saw the coroner's hearse parked at the side entrance.

No, this can't be happening, he thought as he ran to the back of the hearse. The Coroner's assistants were loading a body into the hearse as Jim ran up. "Is that Delmar Batcher," Jim frantically asked. "Not sure," the attendant asked, "You want to look?"

Jim pulled back the cover and to his intense dismay, he stared at the face of Delmar Batcher. The right side of his face was bruised, and his lip was cut. But what got Jim's attention most was the circular bruising around his neck.

"Poor bastard hanged himself with his bedsheet," the attendant said.

"Bullshit!" Jim said, "What did he do, punch himself in the face first. This is bullshit" and he sprinted to the main entrance of the county jail.

As he ran in, he found the County Sheriff and Rogers conferring.

"What the hell happened?" Jim asked.

"According to the deputies, last night he was telling them how scared he was about going to Mansfield. Can't say that I blame him, it's a tough place. So, apparently, he hanged himself with a bedsheet," the sheriff answered.

"That's such bullshit. Did you see the bruises on his face and his cut lip? How the hell do you get bruises and a cut lip when you hang yourself? Someone did this to him. Are you investigating anything?" Jim shouted.

"Now, just settle down, young man. We are doing an investigation. We will find out what happened," the sheriff replied.

"George, we should have put him in protective custody yesterday. What about the stuff he told me and Harlow. Can we do anything with that?"

"Jim, this is tragic, from so many perspectives. Let's see what our investigation finds out, then we will talk. I must get ready for an early court call. Perhaps we can talk later today or tomorrow," the District Attorney said averting his eyes.

As he drove back to the newspaper Jim wondered what more can go wrong.

He told Willy what he witnessed at the county jail and that Batcher was dead. "They said, he hanged himself because he was afraid to go to Mansfield, but I don't believe it for a minute. He had bruises on his face and his lip was cut."

"Write the story that he is dead, and the sheriff said he committed suicide by hanging. But add that there were bruises on his face, and there will be an autopsy. But keep your opinion out of it. Just the facts, Monaghan. Then get to the obit desk," Willy charged.

After the deadline, Jim visited with Audrey and Bernard telling them of the phone call at two in the morning, the bruises on Batcher's face and his cut lip. Jim insisted Batcher could not have hanged himself.

"If he was going to hang himself, he wouldn't have called me at two in the morning. And those bruises. There has to be an autopsy. Bernard is the paper going to demand one?"

"I can do better than that. I can call the corner and tell him if there isn't an autopsy, this paper will be all over it demanding one," Bernard said.

ONE HUNDRED EIGHT

It had been a week since Batcher died and it was getting close to a year since Mary's death. Jim showed up for work every day, but still hadn't shaved or gotten his haircut. His mood cycled from deep depression to mild depression, but he couldn't climb out of the dark fog.

He continued meeting with Dr. Nance, but Jim just couldn't find much to be optimistic about. The only bright spot was he didn't get drunk every night. A couple of Bushmills, but that was all. He hadn't eaten a dinner at home in a week. Paula, the Judge and the Hills, all took turns hosting him.

He was sad the Johnsons were not comfortable with him coming over for dinner as things were still very tense at Fourth and Bradley. His calls to Anna at work were unanswered and his messages were not returned.

When the last deadline passed, Jim picked up yesterday's edition of the Columbus Post-Dispatch. He had enjoyed his internship there and was disappointed there were no openings on the staff when he graduated, but was grateful to the editor Charlie Sloan, who called Bernard and helped Jim get the position at the News Tribune.

Leaning back in his chair with his feet up on his desk, he was startled to find a smiling Haley twisting his foot. Standing beside Art Wilks, Haley said,

"Jim, I have a surprise for you.   Please tell him Mr. Wilks."

"Jim, I want to introduce you to our newest employee. Haley is going to work in our darkroom, processing film and printing pictures. It's entry level, but after working with her this morning, I think she has a future here."

"Wow, that's great news, Art, and congratulations, Haley."

Jim sat back down, when one of the county courthouse reporters yelled at him.

"Hey, Monaghan, don't know how you knew, but you were absolutely correct."

"What are you talking about?"

"The autopsy on Delmar Batcher just came in. He had two broken ribs and blunt force trauma to his head. The coroner is equivocating in saying whether he died from hanging or from the blunt force trauma. He may have been dead before he was hanged. This is one hell of a story, and we have you to thank for it. Well done, rookie."

Jim's emotions seesawed. Happy for Haley and elated with the compliment from one of the veteran reporters, Jim immediately felt sad for Batcher. *He was just a guy who got in with the wrong people and was in the wrong place at the wrong time. A horrible way to die. But Irene, Steve, and Mary had horrible deaths, too, and Batcher was there, and he did nothing.*

His phone rang, and it was Audrey asking him to go to lunch with her father.

ONE HUNDRED NINE

TOGETHER THEY WALKED to Harlow's and the Sgt. Major joined them in the back booth.

"You actually going to eat the food, they serve here?" Jim teased his friend.

"Listen, kid, I know you have had a tough week and there is an anniversary coming up, but don't you talk about my food, or I will bop you in the head or have Sgt. Washington take you outside and give you a whipping."

Audrey and Bernard smiled at the bantering between the two unlikely friends.

Bernard looked Jim squarely in the eye and in a serious voice said, "Jim, I had Audrey ask you to lunch here at the Sgt. Major's café, because we want you to know we support you. The autopsy report is going to initiate an investigation. Brian Franco, the plaintiff's attorney, and Judge McCallister's colleagues are going to thoroughly research Reid's bank records and all his finances. If there is a link to others, they will find it. And I suspect they will find others. The initial look at the books shows a very tangled web of corporations and partnerships, but no names. The investigators will uncover those names. Both those investigations are going to turn the heat on those behind the scenes.

"Trust me, I know how these conspiracies come apart. Eventually people will start to turn on each other, because they don't trust one another. Holding on to information that can implicate themselves is always a heavy burden. And always, always follow the money. I suspect we will find some very interesting information when Franco completes his investigation.

"So, it is not over, Jim, and you can't get depressed about it. These things take time. You are an impatient young man, and that's one of the many things I like and respect about you.

"You have the makings of a good newspaper man. You are the youngest winner of the AP award in the AP's history. I want you to be proud of yourself and what you have done."

"Thank you, Bernard, I appreciate your kind words," a humbled Jim replied.

"I'm not finished, Jim, please hear me out. Audrey and I had lunch with Charlie Sloan of the Post-Dispatch the other day. He is a big fan of yours. He asked us a question that I am ashamed to say, I didn't have an answer for.

"Jim, he asked us why did we have an Associated Press Award winning reporter writing obituaries and occasionally some feature stories? Why wasn't that reporter working on bigger stories?"

"I know Willy has kept you on a very short leash, but I think it is time, we took you off the leash. Willy won't like it," Bernard said with a twinkle in his eye, "but I am still the publisher and I am changing your assignment.

"Jim, effective now, your new assignment will be politics with some police coverage. And your first assignment is to cover the Lucas Anderson fund raiser at the Hilton Hotel tonight. This assignment will broaden your scope and allow you to continue your investigation into other stories here in Lincoln and the county.

Jim's mouth dropped open, and he was unable to speak. As he started to talk,

Bernard held up his hand.

"I have asked Ed Norman, our chief political writer to take you under his wing. Ed's health is not the best and he is anxious to mentor you, so you can take some of the burden off him.

"And one final thought. You have my word and Audrey's word we will stay on this investigation until we are successful, and until we uncover what I think, and quite frankly what I fear, is a very corrupt operation here in the county. When they make a mistake, and they will make a mistake, we will be ready.

"Can I count on you, Jim, to be there when they make a mistake?"

Jim was speechless. Harlow put his arm around him and said he was proud of him and Audrey grinned and congratulated him.

"Bernard, what can I say? You bet your ass I will be here when they make a mistake. And what an assignment! I am so very excited. I don't know Anderson, but in 24 hours, I guarantee you I will know everything about him. Thank you so very much!"

"Jim, a couple of things. Covering politics for my newspaper is a very different job than writing obituaries. You might want to clean up your language a little bit. And that beard and your hair, you might consider getting them trimmed."

"Bernard, I hate to leave this lunch early, but I am headed for the barber shop. But, I can't thank you enough."

As Jim walked out of the diner, his feet hardly touched the ground. *Mary would be so proud*, he thought.

THANK you for reading The Copper Casket! Find out what happens to Jim Monaghan on his next adventure...One-Click THE INCIDENT now!

An armed robbery goes bad. Wrong people are suspected. Can Jim Monaghan uncover the truth without losing his life?

It's 1964. Lyndon Johnson is president and the Civil Rights Act is signed into law.

Jim Monaghan's career is on the rise, but his personal life is in shambles. He's in love with a girl who is well above his station. At least, that's what her country club father thinks. **He needs a story to prove his worth so that he can propose.** This can't be it, though, can it?

It's supposed to be an open and shut case. Just an armed robbery in a bad part of town committed by bad men. But what if it's not?

What if the real perpetrator is someone who no one suspects? Only Jim Monaghan can get to the truth. **But will he be able to escape with his life?**

One-Click The INCIDENT Now!

WANT MORE?

Check out another Jim Monaghan adventure in **The Candidate!**

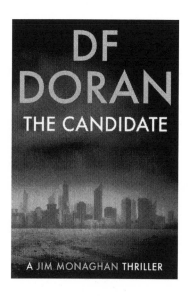

What happens when a story about an Ohio Attorney General's extramarital affair uncovers prostitution and murder?

It's 1964. Kennedy has been assassinated.

Jim Monaghan is broken hearted and in search of a new story. **Then he watches a Gubernatorial candidate slip into a hotel room with a beautiful woman who is not his wife.**

Believing he has an exclusive story of marital infidelity and scandal, Jim fights against the system to find out the truth. Little does he know that he is about to uncover something a lot bigger.

Deception. Abuse. **Prostitution. Murder.** At the highest levels of power.

Will Jim find out the truth and leave with his life? Or will this story be his last?

One-Click The Candidate Now!

SIGN UP for my **newsletter** to find out when I have new books and special giveaways!

Reviews help readers find my books. Please take a few minutes to leave a review on your favorite site. It can be as short as a sentence.

AFTERWORD

This is the first of the Jim Monaghan stories, a fictional series chronicling the trials and tribulations of a newspaper reporter for a midsize newspaper in the 1960s and 1970s.

Jim Monaghan is fictional and bears no relationship to anyone living or dead. All the characters in this novel and following novellas and novels are fictional but there are occasional references to historical figures and events.

There is a Lincoln, Ohio, a small community located near Columbus. My Lincoln, Ohio does not exist.

There is no Reid funeral home in Lincoln, Ohio. It exists only in my imagination and bears no relationship to any funeral home anywhere.

In my research, I never found any instance of a funeral home switching caskets.

There is a Donnellan Funeral Home in Illinois and it has existed for many decades and enjoys an excellent reputation. It is often found in the books of the late Andrew Greeley, one of my favorite authors.

ACKNOWLEDGMENTS

This novel could not have been written without the support and inspiration of my wife, Jan.

My thanks to my son Kevin and his wife Kate, successful authors themselves, for their constant encouragement and editorial support.

A special thanks to Danya, Shannon, and Bryan for their editing, feedback, research and so many other assists.

ABOUT THE AUTHOR

D.F. Doran, when asked what he did for a living, always answers, "Which decade?" Mr. Doran has worked as a staff reporter and an editor for a daily newspaper, served in a senior position in the United States House of Representatives as chief of staff to a member of Congress, and for a Fortune 25 company as a vice-president.

He is married to his wife, Jan, for 49 years. Together, they have four married children and seven grandchildren.

The Dorans live in Highlands Ranch, Colorado

D. F. Doran loves hearing from his readers. Tell him what you think about his books or just drop him a line here: dfdoranauthor@gmail.com

Made in the USA
Middletown, DE
06 September 2018